10/24

THE RUSSIAN'S PRIDE

ALSO BY CAP DANIELS

The Chase Fulton Novels
Book One: *The Opening Chase*
Book Two: *The Broken Chase*
Book Three: *The Stronger Chase*
Book Four: *The Unending Chase*
Book Five: *The Distant Chase*
Book Six: *The Entangled Chase*
Book Seven: *The Devil's Chase*
Book Eight: *The Angel's Chase*
Book Nine: *The Forgotten Chase*
Book Ten: *The Emerald Chase*
Book Eleven: *The Polar Chase*
Book Twelve: *The Burning Chase*
Book Thirteen: *The Poison Chase (2021)*

The Avenging Angel – Seven Deadly Sins Series
Book One: *The Russian's Pride*
Book Two: *The Russian's Greed (2021)*

Stand-Alone Novels
We Were Brave

Novellas
I Am Gypsy
The Chase Is On

THE RUSSIAN'S PRIDE

AVENGING ANGEL
SEVEN DEADLY SINS SERIES
BOOK #1

CAP DANIELS

ANCHOR WATCH
PUBLISHING

** USA **

The Russian's Pride
Avenging Angel
Seven Deadly Sins Book #1
Cap Daniels

Published by:

ANCHOR WATCH
PUBLISHING
** USA **

13 Digit ISBN: 978-1-951021-05-4
Library of Congress Control Number: 2020951923
Copyright © 2020 Cap Daniels – All Rights Reserved

Cover Design: German Creative

Printed in the United States of America

A proud man is always looking down on things and people; and, of course, as long as you are looking down, you cannot see something that is above you.

C.S. Lewis

THE RUSSIAN'S PRIDE

RUSSKAYA GORDOST'

CAP DANIELS

1

ZAKHVAT
(THE CAPTURE)

November 2003

The first man—long, lean, and in his sixties—wore the clothes of a man he had never met. The second man—shorter and thicker—looked over his shoulder as the pair made their way down the darkened, early morning alley of America's oldest city. The ghosts of Saint Augustine drifted above them as if in morbid anticipation of the gruesome episode that lay in the coming moments of the two men's interwoven existence.

Unseen by the pair, but in perfect focus of the Starlight night-vision scope, the predator waited, shrouded by darkness and a lifetime of prowling in the shadows. The predator's veil, woven beneath hammer and sickle and tempered behind the Iron Curtain as the Cold War drew to a close, masked far more than the killer's presence; it encased a skill set second to none within the realm of death's silent delivery.

The watchers, though sworn by impenetrable oath to prevent the coming carnage, made no move and held no thought of upholding their sacred oath.

The two men, unsure of who or what had facilitated their release from the St. Johns County Detention Center, made their way deeper into the coming dawn and ever closer to their imminent rendezvous with what lay beyond the chasm of unthinkable demise before them.

Unknown to both himself and the demons who would receive his soul, the taller of the two men took the final step he would ever tread on the earth. The assassin's blade pierced his navel and met the rounds of his spine, stopping both the man's stride and the killer's plunge. The gasp came in murderous synchrony to the upward draw of the blade. His legs incapable of lifting a foot from the gritty surface beneath him, the man succumbed to the trauma and spilled his life's blood, where he melted to become one with all eternity in the fires of Hell.

The blinding speed with which the killer moved left the second man paralyzed in terror and disbelief. The first blinding slash came just beneath his chin, opening his neck to the pre-dawn air. He threw a wasted right cross well above the assailant's head as the killer's blade pierced the inside of his thigh, exposing and filleting the femoral artery. The man would bleed out beneath a breathless mist of coastal Florida humidity and depart from the realm of the living.

Certain the prey's souls, devoid of Earthly shelter, sank into the bowels of the Earth, the butcher fled into the waiting depths of the city, where legions of spirits of Spaniards, Indians, and slaves drifted on the wind from the Mantanzas River. Like so many times before, the assassin would become the night and dissolve into the wind.

Though hardened by lives spent collecting trophies of men consumed by evil and devoid of humanity, the watchers felt their mouths grow dry and their stomachs heave at the indescribable carnage before them. Duty demanded they not succumb to their weakness, but humanity anchored their feet to the ground. The flooding lights consuming and splitting the darkness drew the watchers from their stupor and drove them forward toward their target. The assassin would fight, lunging with the fury of a cornered beast, but the watchers, superior in number, force, and might, would take the predator alive, regardless of the cost. No other outcome would appease their masters.

The watchers, six-strong —donned in black combat gear from head to toe and protected behind plate carriers bearing steel armor designed to stop the supersonic projectile of a sniper's weapon—stepped into the stage-bright lights as the assassin raised an arm to shield blinded eyes from the piercing white light.

In blind reflective defense, the assassin drew an *avtomaticheskiy pistolet Stechkina*, a fully automatic Russian pistol, from an unseen holster and filled the air of the perimeter with 9x18mm Makarov lead until the magazine fell empty. Two of the six men felt the lead enter their mortal shells but never felt their bodies collide with the ground beneath their feet.

The four men who remained in possession of their souls fired tasers, sending barbed missiles designed to pierce the skin of and render the assailant incapable of continued combat. Two of the missiles found their mark: one in the bicep of the butcher and another in the unprotected thigh.

Reacting without thought, the assassin grasped the two pairs of hair-thin wires connecting the barbs to the pistol-grip launchers and yanked them from flesh before the debilitating weapons could do their masters' bidding. Undaunted by their failure, the watchers unleashed another volley of stunning electrical charges toward their intended victim. The first became hopelessly entangled in the killer's clothing while the second sank deep into the muscle at the base of the assailant's neck.

A punishing surge of electrical current raced through the nearly invisible wires, sending spasms of indescribable agony down the muscular frame of one of the world's deadliest collectors of souls, and sending the fighter collapsing in quivering convulsions of involuntary submission.

The needle of the syringe containing enough sedative to rock a giant to sleep pierced the flesh covering the assailant's thigh and sank into the muscle, bringing undefeatable sleep.

* * *

As the narcotics surrendered their hold on the killer, light filtered through barely parted eyelids, giving the deadly operative the first view of the sterile surroundings: wrists cuffed to a ring welded to the surface of a stainless-steel table, ankles shackled and chained to a second ring bolted to the industrial tile floor, mouth as dry as the Sahara, and a two-way mirror consuming one of the cold, gray walls of the cell.

"Welcome back. Please accept my apology for the accommodations, but we thought it best to make you as uncomfortable as possible, given your history of taking advantage of your surroundings."

Anastasia "Anya" Burinkova, former assassin of the Russian *Sluzhba vneshney razvedki Rossiyskoy Federatsii*, fully opened her eyes, sending daggers through her captor. "What is name?"

"My name isn't important," said the man clad in the cheap off-the-rack suit of the day. "The important thing is who—and what—I represent."

Anya glared up at the man. "You are only representative. Or there are others behind door?"

He glanced across his shoulder at the door behind him. "There are plenty more. I'm far from being alone."

"This means you are weakest of them. You are here only to fail while others watch and listen. It is possible I will kill you while others watch."

The man cracked an arrogant grin. "I don't think you're in much of a position to be making threats. I clearly have the upper hand."

Anya strained against her cuffs. "Is proof you are weakest. You do not identify threat in front of you."

He shot a look at the ceiling-mounted microphones, planted two palms on the table, and leaned in. His whisper would be well beyond the capability of the microphones. "Before this is over, you'll beg me for mercy."

The man looked into her hypnotic blue-gray eyes and puckered up to blow her a kiss but was immediately met with a powerful headbutt that sent his lips against his teeth and blood spraying in all directions. Instead of recoiling backward, he fell victim to Anya's vicelike right arm, her wrist still cuffed to the table.

She tightened the grip with crushing strength until the man's throat collapsed beneath her forearm. His flailing and thrashing lasted only seconds as his body succumbed to the lack of life-giving air into his lungs.

Two men exploded through the door, the first grabbing the man's waist in a vain effort to free him from Anya's grip, and the second prying against her arm, uselessly trying to break her grip on his partner. Realizing their efforts were little more than a wasted expenditure of energy, the second man threw a punishing right cross to Anya's temple. The blow would've been enough to turn the lights out on most men, but Anya Burinkova had conditioned her body, mind, and spirit to withstand attacks under which others would crumble.

She shook off the blow as stars danced around her head and the man locked beneath her right arm fell limp. The second blow from the man was enough to momentarily soften her resolve and ability to maintain the headlock.

In the next breath, the man who'd been Anya's most recent victim collapsed to the floor, foam issuing from the corners of his mouth and his heart barely beating.

As blood dripped from her nose and mouth and her head pounded like thunder, she watched the two men drag the nearly lifeless body of the first man from the room. She wondered who would be the next to walk through the door.

The wait was shorter than she expected. A man in his mid-forties with sleeves rolled to the elbows came through the door. Without a word, he placed a plastic sports bottle with a protruding straw on the table in front of Anya. Beside the bottle he laid a pair of white pills.

She eyed the offering. "What is this?"

"It's water and aspirin. The drugs we used to sedate you in Saint Augustine take a toll on your dehydration, and that one-two-punch you enjoyed probably left a nasty little headache in its wake."

"I do not believe you," she growled. "Is more drugs."

He shrugged, pulled an aspirin bottle from his pocket, and deposited the two pills back into the bottle. Then he gave it a shake, poured two more pills into his palm, and lifted the sports bottle from the table. The man tossed the pills onto his tongue and drank from the straw, sending the pills down his throat.

He shook out two more pills and laid them behind the ring through which she was cuffed. Anya leaned forward, drew the aspirin into her mouth, and sucked a long drink of the warm water from the bottle.

"*Spasibo*," she said, barely above a whisper.

In perfect Russian, the man said, "You're welcome. I'm sorry this has to be so unpleasant for you, but it's the nature of the business I'm in."

"What is business?"

"I'm with the Justice Department, and my name is Ray White."

Anya stared into his eyes. In another time and place—one in which she had not been drugged, kidnapped, and beaten, she might find Ray White attractive. He wore a quiet confidence, unlike the arrogance of the first man who'd threatened her. "Ray White is not real name."

He blinked. "Maybe not, but does it really matter?"

She ignored the question. "Where am I?"

"That also doesn't matter," he said, "but I have a proposition for you."

She waited in wordless anticipation for the next lie to pour from his tongue.

He lifted the bottle from the table and sprayed another mouthful down his throat. "I hate to be the bearer of bad news, but you have a terrible choice in front of you, Anastasia."

"Do not call me this name. Is not for you."

"So, do you prefer Anya or Ana Fulton?"

When she'd defected to the United States, leaving her SVR past behind her, Anya had taken the American first name "Ana" and the last name of

Chase Fulton, the American covert operative who'd flipped her. The American had fallen in love with her, just as her SVR handlers had designed, but the passion and compassion Anya felt for him had not been in their plan.

"Is Anya and no more."

Ray sighed. "Okay, Anya it is. Here are your options. Take a look at this."

He slid a pocket-sized video monitor in front of her and nodded toward the mirror. A grainy night-vision video began to play. The scene unfolded just as it had in the alley in Saint Augustine, of her slaughtering the two men and leaving their bodies in puddles of dark blood.

She mumbled, "They were bad men and should not be alive."

Ray collected the monitor and tossed it toward the door. "I agree, but our opinions don't really matter. I think you did the world a favor, but the Justice Department has a different opinion. You see, to them, you murdered these two men in cold blood, and you have to pay for that. You're going to prison for the rest of your life, Anya."

She stared at the cuffs binding her wrists to the table. "You said there is option."

"Did I?"

"What must I do?"

"We've got a little job for you. If you do this for us, and if you do it well, you can go back to your little make-believe world down in Georgia."

She imagined the simple three-bedroom house with the white picket fence near the University of Georgia campus. The home had once belonged to her father, an American operative turned psychology professor who fell in love with her mother on the gritty streets of Moscow in the bitter days of the Cold War. And she thought of the man, Marvin "Mongo" Malloy, the gentle giant who could rip an oak tree from the earth with his bare hands. His size and strength made the eyes of the world see him as a monster, but beneath his gargantuan exterior lay the gentleness of a lamb and the mind of a philosopher. Anya saw the truth in the depths of the giant, and he saw beyond her physical beauty and deadly skill set to find the humanity within.

"What is job?"

Ray cleared his throat. "We're taking down the *Russkaya mafiya*, and you're going to open the door for us."

She let her eyes meet his. "I do not have keys to Russian mafia."

He slid the bottle closer to her. "You are the key, Anya. Think about that, and I'll be back."

As Ray White pulled the door closed behind himself, Anya felt the clip of the ink pen she'd lifted from the first agent's pocket while he was in her headlock. The broken metal clip was the perfect size to fit inside the keyhole of the cuffs anchoring her to the steel table.

2
CHEREZ ZERKALO
(THROUGH THE LOOKING GLASS)

From behind the two-way mirror, Dr. Andrea Zabaggo watched with the concentration of a hawk in pursuit of a field mouse. "Agent White, why did you do that?"

"Why did I do what? I established trust by drinking her water and taking the pills, I presented options, and I gave her time to consider those options. That's exactly what you profilers want those of us who actually get our hands dirty to do, isn't it?"

Dr. Zabaggo glared at him. "There's no such thing as a profiler, Agent White. I'm a criminal psychologist, and I highly recommend sticking at least two of your *dirty* fingers as far down your throat as possible; otherwise, you and your new pet project in there will be fast asleep in a matter of minutes."

The doctor pointed through the glass where Anya sat covertly thrusting her stolen pen clip into the keyhole of the handcuffs that had been designed and built to be absolutely pick-proof by the Technical Services Branch of the CIA. "By my calculation, you and she will be sound asleep inside of three minutes. Her adrenaline rush will likely keep her awake only slightly longer than you."

Dr. Zabaggo placed her foot against the metal trash can beneath her table and slid it toward White. "Fingers down your throat, Agent."

White slammed his hand on the table. "Was it the water or the pills?"

Zabaggo slid her legal pad and colored pens away from his fists. "Agent White, control yourself. Empty your stomach or find a place to lie down."

He pounded his fist into the table. "Was it the water or the pills?"

The doctor leaned back, shying away from White's intensity. "It was the water, of course."

White spun on a heel, grabbed the trash can, and yanked open the door to the interrogation room. Slamming the can onto the tile floor beside Anya, he ordered, "Empty your stomach, now!"

Anya's eyes darted between the nearly hysterical agent and the open door of the interrogation room. Remembering White's nearly flawless Russian, she said, "*Skazhi mne pochemu.*"

"Because the water is drugged. That's why. Do it now!"

"You also drank water," she hissed.

White shoved two fingers down his throat and emptied the contents of his stomach into the waiting can. Anya narrowed her eyes and stared at her hands securely cuffed to the table. She tried to imagine how she could get a finger down her throat. "What is drug in water?"

Ignoring the question, White ordered, "Open your mouth, and if you bite me, I swear to you I'll cut your head off with that pen clip you stole."

Anya shot another glance toward the door. "Open handcuffs."

White could feel the effects of the tranquilizer racing through his limbs. "I don't have the key. It's your last chance. If you want to stay awake, open your mouth."

Anastasia Burinkova had never suffered from the plague of indecision, knowing there was no greater killer of covert operatives than the inability to decisively take action. She leaned toward the can, looked up into Ray White's eyes, and opened her mouth.

The contents of her stomach soon joined his in the bottom of the battered metal can. He yanked the bottle from the table, tore off the lid, and added the remaining tranquilizer-laced liquid to the can. "I'll be right back."

In Russian, she said, "I'll probably be here when you return."

Ray suppressed a smile, but only barely.

He pulled the plastic bag from the can, tied a knot in the top, and pushed the door closed behind him. Crossing the room in two strides, he deposited the bag of tainted water and stomach contents on top of Dr.

Zabaggo's legal pad. "Drug another of my detainees, and you'll be writing anti-depressant prescriptions for bored, overweight housewives in Dump Truck County, Kentucky. Do you understand me, *Doctor*?"

Zabaggo instinctually slid her chair away from the table and trash bag. "You don't have the authority to threaten me, Agent White. And she is not *your* detainee. She is the property of the United States Department of Justice. Do you understand me?"

White lifted the bag from the table, moved squarely in front of Dr. Zabaggo, and scowled. "Nine fifty Pennsylvania Avenue Northwest, seventh floor. That's where the attorney general's office is. I recommend you knock on his door and ask him who that woman in there belongs to. In the meantime"—he dropped the trash bag onto her lap—"I recommend you take out the garbage you created and leave the real work to those of us who know how to do it."

Zabaggo sprang from her chair, sending the bag sliding across the floor. "I'll have your badge for this!"

White grinned. "Do you want my badge because you don't have one of your own, or because you like to play with shiny things?"

When White returned from the vending machine, Dr. Zabaggo was nowhere to be found. Only a pair of junior agents and a technician remained in the observation room. "Where's the shrink?"

One of the agents said, "She stormed out right after you, sir."

"Good. We don't need her on this. Who has the keys?"

The second agent slid her hand into her pocket. "I've got them, but I don't think it's a very good—"

White snatched the keys from her hand. "You're not here to think, Davis. You're here to learn, and the woman behind that door is about to teach a master class in how to be a badass. You might want to take notes."

He pressed himself through the door as the two other agents remained behind the glass. After three confident strides, he perched on the edge of the table and placed a pair of unopened bottles of water beside Anya's hands. "Choose."

Through weary eyes, obviously the effect of the tranquilizer, Anya said, "Choose for you or for me?"

White shrugged. "It's up to you. I'll drink one, and you'll drink the other. I swear to you, neither has been opened, and there's nothing inside either of those bottles besides water."

"You are trying to gain my trust."

White shook his head. "No, I'm smart enough to know that isn't possible. You're programmed to trust no one except your SVR handlers."

"I am not SVR."

Ray pulled the keys from his palm and opened the handcuffs. "No, not anymore you're not, but you *were*. I know all about your past, Anya."

She rubbed her wrists where the cuffs had pressed indentations into her flesh. "Was not smart to take off handcuffs. You would know this if you really knew all about my past."

"Perhaps not," he said, "but it's going to be tough to drink your water without using your hands. I can put the cuffs back on if you want."

She twisted the blue plastic top from the bottle and heard the seal crack beneath her thumb. "*Spasibo.*"

White nodded. "*Ne upominay eto!*"

She took a long swallow from the bottle. "Your Russian is very good."

"My father was a diplomat in the U.S. ambassador's office. I spent nine years in Moscow as a child."

Anya examined the agent's eyes, the lines of years spent in the weather, and the scars of years spent in places he shouldn't have been. "Your father was CIA, no?"

White shrugged again. "Probably, but I'll never know."

She was supposed to invite him to tell her why he would never know who his father worked for, but her training had taught her never to give a foreign operative an opportunity to lie. She said, "*You* are CIA, no?"

"I told you, I'm with the Justice Department."

"That is not answer," she said before emptying half of the water bottle into her mouth.

"No, Anya, I'm not CIA. I've never been CIA, and I have no interest in becoming CIA. I'm a lawyer with a gun and a badge."

"I am still in America, yes?"

"Yes," he said, "you're still in America."

"What if I demand lawyer? Is my right in America."

He checked his watch. "Yes, once you've been arrested, you have the right to an attorney, but you're not under arrest . . . yet."

She held up her wrists still bearing the marks from the handcuffs. "I was cuffed, shackled, and brought here against my will by federal officers after committing crime. This is definition of arrest, no?"

"I suppose you could look at it that way, but keep in mind"—he took another drink—"if you demand a lawyer, I'll get one for you, but he'll be a criminal defense attorney whose job is to defend you against capital murder charges, not to negotiate a deal."

Anya lifted her chin and stared into the mirror. "Who is behind looking glass? Maybe Alice in Wonderland?"

White shot a look over his shoulder. "Two junior agents and a technician."

"These people are your students, no?"

"The tech isn't. He's recording everything we say or do, but the other agents are still learning."

"Are you also still learning, Special Agent White?"

Ray dismissed the question. "You're a beautiful woman, Anya."

She frowned. "Russian women are most beautiful women on Earth. I think you are probably married to Russian woman, no?"

He held up his left hand, devoid of a ring. "No, I married a girl from Kansas, but it took her less than two years to realize she didn't like being a cop's wife."

"In two years, do you have children with girl from Kansas?"

"No, she had a miscarriage six months after we were married. It broke my heart at the time, but now . . . well, now I think it was probably the best thing for everyone involved."

She laid her hand on his arm with the gentleness of a kitten. "You want to now have Russian wife who understands responsibility of cop, yes?"

He let his eyes wander across her long, delicate fingers, and for just a moment, he let himself imagine those hands caressing his skin and sliding through his hair. Then he pulled away. "You're very good, Anya, but I'm too old to fall into a Russian honey trap."

"Was only question, not proposal for marriage."

"Nonetheless," he said, "you're very good. So, do you want me to formally arrest you so you can demand an attorney now, or do you want to help me take down the Russian mafia?"

"You said you are lawyer with badge and gun. Does this mean you passed bar examination?"

"Yes, I'm a member of the Virginia bar, among others."

"So, this is where I am, Virginia?"

"I'm not practicing law here, Anya. I'm interrogating a killer and offering her an option other than life in prison."

"What if I want for you to be my attorney?"

"That's not how it works, I'm afraid. And as I said, you're very good, but I must insist we stay on track. It's a simple decision. Either I arrest you, and you spend the rest of your life in prison, or you help me dismantle the Russian mafia from the inside. Option one sucks, and option two is likely to get you killed, but the choice is yours. Do you want to go back in the handcuffs or back on the street?"

She smiled, and White immediately agreed that Russians are, indeed, the most beautiful women on Earth. "Murder is not federal crime unless I kill government official . . . like you. What I did is crime against State of Florida, so you do not have *yurisdiktsiya*."

White picked a piece of lint from his sleeve. "Actually, one of the DOJ agents you shot didn't survive, so, technically, I have all the jurisdiction I need."

"In that case, I am now Alice, and you are going to take me to Wonderland. I believe this makes you now Mad Hatter?"

3

PRAVILA
(THE RULES)

Anya focused on the cold, handleless door of the interrogation room. "Is time now for me to meet your students."

Ray White situated himself into the stainless-steel chair across the table from the woman who would likely end his career with Justice. "Not yet. First, we have to talk about the rules."

Anya stared into his soul. "If you know everything of my history as you say, you know I do not have rules."

"Everyone has rules. Even if you claim to have none, that in itself is a rule."

"Is game of words. Rules are only for those who are afraid."

White crossed his legs. "You're right. That's precisely why we chose you for this operation. You're almost fearless . . . almost."

Anya's eyes turned to stone. "You know nothing of me."

"I know you've been to the Black Dolphin Prison and that you never want to go back."

"This is not fear," she demanded. "Is *nenavidet'*."

Ray pulled a pebble from the tread of his shoe and examined the smooth stone. "Now *you're* playing word games. Fear and hatred are almost always interchangeable. You hate the thought of losing your freedom again. While we're on the subject of freedom, let's talk about Chase Fulton."

Anya swallowed hard and pictured the face of the man who'd fallen in love with her; the man who'd risked his life countless times to save hers; the man who'd rescued her from the most notorious prison on Earth; the man who'd given her the ultimate freedom: an American passport.

"I do not know this person Chase Fulton."

Ray rolled the stone between the tips of his fingers. "Don't make this harder than it has to be. I'm not your enemy. I'm just a man doing a job, and right now, that job is to embed you inside the Russian mafia and let you cut your way out."

"I have told you I will do this because I do not want to go back to prison —even soft American prison—but this has nothing to do with person named Chase Fulton."

Ray ran his hands through his hair and believed he could feel the difference between the strong, dark strands and the weak gray ones starting to appear at his temples. "This is the part I most despise, Anya, but you've forced me to prove that we know more about you than you know about yourself."

Anya sat in defiant silence, waiting for Special Agent Ray White to show his hand. He would walk to the door, and one of his minions would hand him a dossier on SVR Captain Anastasia Burinkova prepared by the American CIA. He would put on the reading glasses he so hated, thumb through the folder, and in a vain effort to demonstrate his superiority, divulge tidbits of what the Americans thought they knew. She knew the playbook. She knew every trick Ray White had up his rolled-up sleeve.

To her disbelief, White didn't stand. He didn't walk to the door. And he didn't read from her dossier. Instead, he closed one eye, lifted the smooth, round pebble toward the fluorescent fixture in the ceiling, and peered at the stone. "How old do you think this rock is?"

She gave no answer but found herself focused on the white piece of quartz as the yellow-white light from the bulbs above reflected from its smooth surface.

"We did it," he said. "I knew we could, but I didn't think it would be so easy."

Anya examined his words in search of the trap he'd lain, but no matter how hard she searched, she couldn't see it. "What did we do?"

He laid the stone on the edge of the battered table in front of her. "We focused on the same thing, and all it took was for me to hold it up to the light. Keep that in mind. That's essentially what my job is—holding things up to the light so we can focus on them together."

He is also very good, Anya thought, and she tried but failed to look away from the pebble Agent White had likely planted in the sole of his shoe, specifically for the game he was now playing.

"It was nineteen seventy-six," he began. "The Cold War was still cold, and Leonid Ilyich Brezhnev was the General Secretary of the Communist Party in the Soviet Union. You were an innocent, four-year-old little girl in a cold, dark apartment in the Severnoye Izmaylovo District of Moscow. A senior Communist Party official named Dmitri Alexandrovich Barkov came through the door and cut out Katerina Nikolovna Burinkova's heart, at the kitchen table, in that dank, miserable apartment, and you had to watch your mother die because she was in love with your father, an American CIA operative named Robert Richter."

Anya forced back the tears welling in her eyes. "Stop! Is enough. You do not have to be cruel. I will do for you what you ask."

Ray licked his lips. "I'm sorry, Anya. I told you this is the part I hate the most, but it has to be done. You have to understand the depths to which we've gone to make this operation possible."

"You do not have to speak of my mother for this reason. Is only cruel."

He lowered his foot from across his knee and leaned forward. "No, what I'm doing is not cruel. What I'm doing is holding cruelty up to the light so we can both focus on it. They killed your mother and took you into state custody. What they did to you is unthinkable."

"What you are doing is no better," she said.

He ignored the jab. "You were to become a skater, but you hated the cold so badly you wouldn't stay on the ice."

"I am terrible Russian. I detest cold. This is true, but. . . ."

Ray stared into the corner of the room where one of the dozen microphones rested. "So, they tried to turn you into a gymnast, and you trained with Svetlana Boginskaya, but by the time you were eight years old, you were already too tall and aggressive to be an Olympic gymnast. That's when you caught the eye of a KGB officer named Nicolai Kuznetsov. I'm sure that wasn't really his name."

Anya couldn't stop her mind from returning to the day she met Nicolai Kuznetsov. "His name means *blacksmith*, person who uses fire and hammer to turn iron into tool."

Ray whispered, "Yes, I know. Is that what he did to you?"

She didn't answer, but the agonizing memories poured through her mind like molten lava descending the slopes of a volcano—slow, hot, and unstoppable.

The Academy of Foreign Intelligence is its official name, but when nine-year-old Anastasia Burinkova walked through the gates of the infamous Soviet spy school in Chelebityevo, she had been instructed to consider herself a proud Soviet student of the Yuri Andropov Red Banner Institute, where she would become a weapon of the state. While the other girls on the ice and in the gymnasium would destroy their bodies in pursuit of a gold medal, Anya would hone and develop hers upon the anvil and beneath the hammer of the blacksmith to become a sword for the Kremlin.

White broke her trance. "When did you leave Chelebityevo for Yurlovo?"

She forced the screen in her mind to fall dark. "I do not know. I think I was sixteen or maybe seventeen. You want to know of Sparrow School, no?"

"No, Anya, I don't want you to tell me about Sparrow School."

Just as she'd been taught during hundreds of hours of training in seduction, she tilted her head and focused her blue-gray eyes on an imaginary spot just between his. "Perhaps, then, you would like for me to show you what I learned there."

He felt fire descend his spine and smolder somewhere near its base. The thought of the tall, lean blonde wrapping herself around him temporarily left him willing to surrender his badge to Dr. Zabaggo, or anyone else who wanted to play with it while he played with the seductive beauty chained to the floor only a few feet away from him.

"No, I don't want . . . I mean, I'm not . . ." He shook his head. "I want to focus on Chase Fulton, the American operative you were tasked to seduce and flip. We know who and what he is. What I want to know is exactly what he is to you."

Anya's mischievous smile came. "This is *revnost'*, no?"

"No, this is not jealousy. This is my job. I think we can move on."

Anya watched as tiny beads of sweat formed on White's forehead. She was winning.

"Let's talk about the rules."

"If you wish," she whispered.

He cleared his throat and refocused. "First, you report directly to me. You will think of me as your handler."

Anya let her eyes trace his body from his head to his feet and back again. "Is this really how you want me to think of you?"

He wiped at an invisible irritant on his neck and just above his lips. "Yes. That's exactly how you are to think of me. Second, you are to have absolutely no contact of any kind with anyone from your former life. Not Chase Fulton, Marvin Malloy, or any member of their team. Is that understood?"

"I cannot stop these people from finding me, even if this is what I wish."

He slid his chair closer to the table, close enough for her lethal hands to reach his throat. "Yes, you can. That is one of the things you do best. You will hide from everyone you've ever known, and you will do it inside the Russian mafia."

She leaned toward him. "These are only rules? There are no more?"

"That's it. There are no more."

The smile returned, and she cupped her hand against his face. "This means there is no rule to stop me from—"

He recoiled. "To stop you from doing what? Snapping my neck? Yes, there's a rule—in fact, there's a law—against that."

"You are afraid of me, yes?"

"Anyone who isn't afraid of you is a fool."

"And you are not fool?"

"Not anymore, I'm not. Those days are behind me."

She leaned back in her chair and tugged against her shackles. "If I am to do this for you, I cannot do it with chains on feet."

White bounced the keys in his palm and considered the decision before him. "There's one more thing we have to get straight before I remove your shackles."

"What is this one more thing?"

He let out the deep breath he'd been holding. "If you break the rules, even once, you're going to prison for the rest of your life. That decision is out of my hands. You work for me. I work for the attorney general of the United States. Everybody's got a boss, and mine has a zero-tolerance policy when it comes to operatives breaking the rules."

She watched her reflection in the mirrored glass and imagined the three faces on the other side. "Just rules, or also laws?"

"Laws are flexible," he said. "Rules are not."

4

OPERATSIYA AVENGING ANGEL
(OPERATION AVENGING ANGEL)

"Anya, meet Agents Guinevere Davis and Johnathon McIntyre." Ray White's tone was quite different now.

Anya ignored him and the two agents as she studied her new environment. Unlike the interrogation cell where she'd been chained and cuffed, Special Agent Ray White's office was anything but institutional. A floor-to-ceiling bookcase made up one wall. Ashtrays, paperweights, and a dozen other unnecessary objects rested on shelves in front of hundreds of books, some in Russian. The knickknacks would make excellent weapons should the need arise. A letter opener, stapler, and bronze lamp made to replicate the Washington Monument were even more inviting than the decorations on the shelves. Bulges beneath sport coats and a fourth holster hanging from a hall tree in the corner offered no fewer than a total of seventy-two rounds of 9mm hollow-point in the four Glock 17s. The double-paned window—undoubtedly bullet-resistant—revealed a courtyard with an irrational pattern of maple trees, a few dead leaves still clinging to their branches. Long, eerie shadows, the kind the winter sky in Moscow seemed to cast over every living thing, darkened the northeastern reaches of what had been green grass only weeks before.

"I am in Virginia, yes? Why did you bring me here instead of Atlanta or Tallahassee?"

Ray settled into his chair behind the neatly arranged desk. "Anya, stop looking for weapons, and shake their hands."

Johnathon's gaze was the same as most men's admiring stares. Although the perfect tool for luring men into doing whatever she wanted, Anya's physical appearance rested near the top of the list of things she would change about herself, given the opportunity.

She ignored him and offered her hand to the agent who *wasn't* imagining her disrobed and sweating. "Special Agent Davis."

The young agent took Anya's hand and immediately felt her strength and resolve. "You can call me Gwynn."

Anya's icy expression never faltered. "Which of these men is your King Arthur, Lady Guinevere? And which is Lancelot?"

Davis's expression immediately matched Anya's. "You're a fascinating case, Ms. Burinkova, but I'm neither amused nor intimidated by you."

Anya turned from Davis and faced McIntyre. "How about you, Johnathon? Are you amused or intimidated?"

Before he could respond, she lunged toward the man and gripped his red necktie. He recoiled with disbelief and instantaneous fear in his eyes.

She released the tie and turned back for Davis. The ice had cracked, and Anya smiled. "Then, by Agent White's definition, I have found which of you is fool."

White bit his jaw to disguise his amusement. "Cut it out and sit down. We've got a lot to discuss."

McIntyre drove an index finger toward Anya. "If you ever grab my tie again, I'll break your little Russian arm. Is that clear?"

White shoved a chair toward the agent. "Sit down, Johnny Mac, and if you're smart enough to take any advice, I'd recommend keeping threats like that to yourself."

The young agent eyed Anya with slightly less desire and took the seat.

White pulled a short stack of papers from a sealed file and racked them on the desk. "Now that you've met Gwynn and Johnny Mac, it's time we all learn to act like one big, happy, screwed-up family."

Weary glances filled the following seconds until Anya said, "Families do not force others to do things against their will."

Johnny Mac cackled. "Welcome to America, Sugar Britches. That's exactly what families do."

She ignored the shot, turned to White, and in her native Russian, said, "I will kill him before this is over if you do not control him."

Gwinn giggled, and Johnny Mac stared, waiting for a translation.

Gwynn patted his thigh. "Don't worry, Johnny Mac. She just said she's not sure she'll be able to keep her hands off of you. You're such a catch."

He glowered. "English, or I walk."

"So, that's how we're doing this now, is it? Threats, Agent McIntyre?" White laid the stack of papers in a neat pile between his hands and faced Johnny Mac. "If that's how you want to play, I'm game. So, here's mine. If you make one more threat to anyone—especially me—you'll be a junior bailiff in a godforsaken federal courtroom in North Dakota before the dust settles. Got it?"

Johnny Mac lowered his chin. "I just want it on the record that I don't think—"

"Good," interrupted White. "The record will show that you don't think, and that's exactly how it should be."

Gwynn giggled again, and Anya joined her.

White pulled two sheets from the top of his stack, discarded them, and read silently from the third. When he finished, he let out a long sigh. "This is how things are going to work for the foreseeable future. Anya, we've created a legend for you, including a short stint in a Russian prison. Unfortunately, that part is true. The fictional part is here."

He handed her several sheets of bound paper, and she flipped through them. She frowned at several locations as she read through the fictional history of the character she would become. "It says I am disgraced KGB officer. I have never been KGB, only SVR, and I had for short time FSB credentials."

White nodded. "We know, but there's no such thing as SVR in the minds of the Russian mafia. All intelligence operatives of Mother Russia always were, and always will be, KGB."

Anya held up the papers. "This does not tell me why I am disgraced officer."

"Yes, it does," White said. "Turn to the back page. That's your rap sheet. It's important that you appear to be at least as dangerous as the people you're pursuing. They tend to have trust issues with good citizens."

She flipped to the final page and smiled. "I have issues with authority, and I demonstrate extreme violence when angered. This is not fiction. This is true of me."

White snapped his fingers. "Just one more reason you're our horse. I'd bet on you to win at Belmont, as long as nobody blinds you with a laser from a mile away."

Anya mentally replayed the mission in which she'd lain atop the water tower in Elmont, New York, and blinded Breakers Folly—the horse who was leading the Belmont Stakes—so Dmitri's Barkov's horse, Silent Storm, could become the first Triple Crown winner since Affirmed in 1978. That was the first time American covert operative Chase Fulton had seen her, and also the day both of their lives changed forever.

"I am not same person I was on that day."

Ray considered her sentiment. "None of us are, Anya, but starting today, we have a chance to do something that will make the world a safer place for everyone."

"Not for everyone," she said. "Today, world becomes very dangerous place for *Russkaya mafiya.*"

Gwynn smiled, and Johnny Mac nodded, but Special Agent Ray White only sighed. "Here's the plan—or at least the initial plan. We're going to dangle you in front of the *vory v zakone.*"

Anya couldn't resist the temptation. She turned to Johnny Mac. "That means *thieves-in-law*, Agent McIntyre. This is what Bratva—this means *brotherhood*—call themselves."

McIntyre steamed. "Boss, if she keeps this up. . . ."

White raised a finger. "Do I hear a threat coming next, Potential Bailiff McIntyre?"

The young agent bowed his head. "No, sir."

White continued. "As Anya said, the Bratva, or brotherhood, refer to themselves as thieves-in-law. We're going to entice a man named Zhivot-noye—the Animal—with a morsel he can't resist." He aimed a finger at Anya's chest." That's you. The Animal is a trusted advisor to the piece of crap we really want, a guy named Leo. He likes to think of himself as the king of the jungle. Leo represents one of the greatest threats to the United States since the fall of Communism."

"Communism did not fall," Anya said. "Only Soviet Union fell. Communism is idea, and ideas do not fall. They simply go someplace else to live. If you believe Communism is dead, you are making huge mistake."

"I didn't mean to imply Communism didn't exist. Of course it does, and it's just as dangerous as it ever was, especially in the hands of revolutionaries. But that's not what we're here to combat."

Anya licked her lips. "This is fight for men like Chase Fulton person you talk about, yes?"

White allowed a half smile. "I wouldn't know, but I'll take your word for it."

Anya wondered exactly how much Ray White actually knew about the last six years of her life. How much did *she* really know about those years? "When I am dangled before Zhivotnoye, you want for me to do what?"

White crossed his arms on the desk and leaned forward. "I want you to crawl so deep inside that organization that you'd turn it inside out with a sneeze. The Animal won't trust you, but you'll be too good to ignore. You're going to earn his trust, and he'll deliver you to Leo. That's when the real work begins. It'll take time, and you'll be asked to do some nasty things before they'll let you into the inner circle, but that's where you need to be."

Anya focused on White and ignored the other two agents. "What if Animal wants to keep me for his own and does not offer me to Leo?"

White pushed away from his desk and crossed his legs, just as he'd done in the interrogation room. "I think you misunderstand. I'm not sending you in there as a honey trap. We're offering up the only thing more dangerous than your body. We're offering your skill set."

"I have many skill sets," she said.

"You only have one that will interest the Russian mafia . . . your affection for knives."

Anya's hands curled instinctually around imaginary blades in her palms, and White noticed.

"There may be someone on Earth more deadly with edged weapons than you, but I guarantee Leo's never seen anything like what you can do with a blade."

"You are suggesting I am to kill for Leo and maybe Zhivotnoye. If I do this, I will again be guilty of murder, and you will send me to prison."

White shook his head. "You still don't get it. Working with me is a get-out-of-jail-free card as long as you're not killing cops, feds, or innocents."

Anya beamed. "So, this is license to kill, like James Bond, as long as you approve who is to be killed, no?"

"Something like that."

"This is against laws of United States."

"Let me worry about the laws of the United States," White said. "This operation isn't exactly what you'd call 'public information.'"

"Why would you trust me to do only this?"

"Oh, I don't trust you. I trust the fence I've built around you. Just like a tiger at the zoo, you're free to roam anywhere inside the fence and eat anything I throw in with you. But if you slip through that fence, just like an escaped tiger, you become the hunted." White examined his fingernails. "And

I've proven that I'm a more-than-capable hunter when it comes to catching you."

Anya's capacity to compile, index, and store voluminous amounts of information was but one of her intellectual abilities few others possessed.

"I am now tiger to catch lion inside your fence."

"You're starting to catch on."

"How am I to know where is fence?"

White scoffed. "I think you know quite well where the fence is. And you know it's not stationary. It'll always be at least a hundred miles away from anyone you've known inside the States, prior to meeting me."

"I will do this for you, and you will give to me freedom again when it is done. This is agreement, yes?"

White pulled off his tie, tossed it onto the desk, and unbuttoned the neck of his shirt. "Welcome to Operation Avenging Angel. We've got a lot of work to do."

5

DZHINN V BUTYLKE
(GENIE IN A BOTTLE)

Special Agent Ray White, believing he'd closed the meeting, rose from his seat. "Let's get you a shower, some clean clothes, and something to eat."

Anya's refusal to speak English as properly as she was capable didn't stop her from understanding every word Agent White said . . . and didn't say. "Agent White. Look to my eyes and say to me I am free when mission is finished."

White played with the tie he'd tossed onto the desk. "Look, Anya. I've been a civil servant for nearly twenty years, and in those twenty years, I've never once heard a bureaucrat tell the truth. I'm not a bureaucrat, though. I'm a cop."

Anya interrupted. "You are lawyer with badge."

"Okay, fine. I'm a lawyer with a badge. Let me explain the law to you. I'm allowed to tell you absolutely anything in that interrogation room, and it can all be lies. I can tell a suspect we have two hundred nuns who watched him commit his warped little crime to get a confession out of him, and not a word of it has to be the truth."

He paused, threaded the tie back through his shirt collar, and left it hanging loosely around his neck. "Now, let me tell you how I work. I'll lie my butt off in that room to put bad guys behind bars, but I didn't have to lie to you. I played the tape for you. Not only did we have eyewitnesses—albeit none of them nuns—but we also had the whole thing on video. Even in a room where I'm perfectly within the law to lie to you, I didn't. Every word I told you was the truth as I know it."

He tied the tie in a half-Windsor but left it a few inches from his throat. "My boss authorized me to make the deal I made with you. I won't look you in the eye and swear to you that he won't renege. He's a bureaucrat.

But I believe that if you survive this mission, the Justice Department will pat you on the butt and send you home."

"My home is Georgia in United States. This is home, you mean, yes?"

He snugged the tie. "Yes, Anya. I mean Athens, Georgia, in the good ol' USA."

"I do not trust you, but I believe you, and I believe I have no choice."

White steepled his fingers. "No, you really *don't* have a choice, but if anyone can survive this, it's the woman who survived Russian Intelligence school, Sparrow School, and a stint in the Black Dolphin Prison."

"All of these things do not exist according to bureaucrats in Moscow, but there is one thing you should know . . . When I go to do these things for you, you cannot put genie back inside bottle. I will do things you cannot imagine, and these things cannot be stopped."

"Touché, Ms. Burinkova, and I know full well the havoc you will wreak once I let you out of your bottle. That's exactly what I'm counting on. Now, if you'll go with Agent Davis, she'll get you bathed, clothed, and fed. We have an appointment to make."

Anya turned to the young woman. "It seems, Special Agent Davis, you are now my babysitter."

"I asked you to call me Gwynn, and I'm not your babysitter. I'm now your colleague."

"I will show to you why we are not colleagues, Gwynn." Anya turned to face Johnny Mac. "Special Agent McIntyre, you are good agent, yes?"

He glanced first to his boss and then back to the Russian. "Yeah, I'm a good agent."

"And you did well in training academy in close-quarters battle and hand-to-hand combat, yes?"

He chuckled. "Yeah, you could say that."

Anya lifted a pencil from White's desk. "I can use pencil, yes?"

White nodded. "Yes, but if you hurt one of my agents. . . ."

Anya placed the sharpened end of the pencil in her palm and pointed the eraser at Johnny Mac. "I will hurt nothing more than pride." She waggled the pencil. "Pretend is knife, and do not let me stab in belly, okay?"

The agent dropped his right foot back into a fighting stance and raised his hands. "I can't promise I won't hurt you."

Anya tilted her head and offered a seductive, demure smile to Agent McIntyre. She then held up the pencil and focused on its red eraser. Johnny Mac followed her eyes to the harmless rubber tip. She tossed the pencil into the air above her head, and the agent's eyes followed. As he watched the pencil reach its apex near the ceiling and reverse course back toward the floor, Anya stepped into him with blinding speed, drew his Glock 17 pistol from its shoulder holster, field stripped the slide and magazine from the weapon, and caught the pencil on its descent.

Johnny Mac's attention shot from the falling pencil to the dismantled pistol in Anya's left hand, just as she buried the eraser beneath the front plate of his body armor protecting his chest and abdomen.

Anya laid the pieces of the pistol on White's desk. "*If* Russian Intelligence school exists, each of its graduates could do that. If I have colleagues, they can also do."

White was barely able to contain his laughter. "Put your pistol back together, Johnny Mac. We'll learn to play pickpocket another day."

He gathered the parts, reassembled, and holstered the Glock without so much as a glance toward Anya.

Gwynn pulled the pencil from Anya's hand and rolled it across the desk. "Come on, let's go. But you're teaching me how to do that before the day is over."

"We will have girl time and maybe get pedicure, yes?"

As Anya and Gwynn left the office through a side door, Johnny Mac turned to White. "Why did you let her do that?"

White grinned. "She didn't steal my gun. You're the one who let her take your sidearm. Why didn't *you* stop her?"

"Look, boss, I'm sorry I don't speak Russian. I thought Arabic, German, and Spanish would be enough."

White pulled on his jacket. "Don't be sorry, Johnny Mac. Be better."

* * *

Gwynn motioned toward a doorway. "You can use that bathroom. It's ladies only, so you don't have to worry about the boys sneaking in. There are toiletries on the counter beside the sink—a toothbrush, hairbrush, razor, and a few hair ties. I recommend a ponytail. I'll have some clothes for you when you finish. You can leave what you're wearing on the floor."

Anya said, "I am size four American."

Gwynn laughed. "Yeah, I know. Me, too."

With the door closed, Anya stood in front of the mirror staring into the face of a woman she barely recognized. Her thoughts still came in Russian, as did her self-expectations.

How has my life come to this? Will I ever truly know freedom? Will I ever see my friends, my American family, again?

She brushed her teeth, pulled the razor from the package, and stepped into the shower. As the warm water ran over her face and down her body, she remembered the feeling of the tropical sun on her skin as she lay on the deck of a boat in the Caribbean, the summer breeze blowing through her hair, and the brave young American, who so adored her, at the helm.

With her body clean but her mind still entrenched in the mire of her past, she stepped from the shower and wrapped herself in a soft towel. Her long, blonde hair dried quickly beneath a second towel and a few minutes with a blow-dryer. As the brush pulled through her hair, she remembered sitting between his knees as he stroked and brushed her hair, just as her mother had done when she was a child in the Soviet Union.

A black elastic band held her ponytail halfway up the back of her head, and the woman in the mirror began to look familiar. She'd never worn makeup. Her natural Eastern European beauty required no supplement. A pair of Levi's blue jeans hung from a hook beside the shower, and a T-shirt and hoodie rested, neatly folded, on the lid of the toilet. Underclothes sat beside the sink, and a pair of size 8 1/2 hiking boots rested by the door. The clothes fit but didn't feel like her own, and she wondered if she'd ever feel anything that was uniquely hers again.

She rolled the towels, washcloth, and bathmat into a tight bundle beside the clothes she'd worn for at least two days, maybe longer, and left them on the floor as she'd been instructed. One more look in the mirror revealed only one thing missing—the tiny plastic American flag she'd carried in her left front pocket since her defection and the belated Fourth of July party at Bonaventure Plantation in Saint Marys, Georgia. That was when she was accepted as a member of an elite team of American covert operatives who made her feel more like part of a family than merely a teammate.

I'll see my team, my family, again, no matter what the tiger hunter on the other side of that door says. I'm an American now . . . even without my tiny flag.

The tiger hunter wasn't waiting outside the door; instead, it was Agent Gwynn Davis. "Oh, good. The clothes fit. Did you enjoy your shower?"

Anya pulled at the sweatshirt. "Is a little bit too big, but shower was nice. Thank you."

"Do you want a hat?"

"Can I have one that says FBI?"

Gwynn laughed out loud. "I don't think you'd want one of those where we're going, but I can probably find a baseball cap. You know how guys like to see girls with ponytails hanging through the back of them."

Flashbacks of her first baseball game at the University of Georgia, when she sat ten rows up and directly behind home plate with Chase, ran through her mind. She'd worn a UGA cap and ponytail that day, and she'd also dropped her first chili dog onto her shirt. Baseball and chili dogs weren't in her immediate future.

"Is okay. I have hood on sweatshirt if I am cold."

Gwynn shrugged. "Suit yourself."

"Is your job to make me feel comfortable, no?"

Gwynn stopped in her tracks. "You're a killer. I wasn't there, but I saw the video. You're a serious, honest-to-God assassin, but you're still a woman. It's my job to do the things the men will never understand. While we're on the subject of men, it wouldn't hurt if you laid off of Johnny Mac. He's not such a bad guy. He's just got a little ego, and he doesn't speak Russian yet."

"Yet?"

Gwynn raised her eyebrows. "Yes, yet. He speaks a bunch of other languages, and he's crazy smart, so I'm sure he'll have the headset on tonight with a Russian language CD blaring. He'll pick it up. Just wait and see."

"I can see he is smart, but he is *reaktivnyy*."

Gwynn's smile was always sincere but also expressive. She couldn't hide her agreement. "Yes, he's definitely reactive instead of proactive sometimes, but he'll learn. By the way, are you going to teach me that thing with the pencil and the gun?"

"Yes, I will teach to you, but it takes many hours of practice with many kinds of guns. Pencil part is easy. Works even better with knife."

"Speaking of knives," she said, "we've got a little field trip planned for this afternoon."

"What is field trip? I do not know this phrase."

"You know . . . it's like when we used to take trips from school to go to a museum or a play. A field trip, like that."

"This is American thing, this field trip. In Russia, we do not have this. School is for learning only and not for museums or plays."

Gwynn's smile never faltered. "Well then, this'll be your first. You know what they say. ... you never forget your first."

An elevator ride to the ground floor led the pair into a bland lobby—clearly governmental—where Ray White waited beside a potted tree. "Well, don't you look like the all-American girl in your jeans and hoodie?"

Anya reached for White's necktie. "I am American girl, and you are terrible at tying necktie." She undid the knot and replaced it with a full-Windsor, leaving each side of the knot a mirror image of the other.

White checked his look in the reflection of a pane of glass behind Anya. "Nice. I like it. You'll have to teach me to tie that one."

"Is going to be very busy for me to teach Gwynn to strip pistol and to teach you to tie proper necktie knot. I may not have time to save world from Russian mafia."

"You're funny," he said. "Let's go. Johnny's waiting outside with the truck."

They left the building and climbed into the heavy, covertly hardened Chevrolet Suburban. Gwynn rode in the front passenger's seat while Anya and White climbed into the back.

Thirty seconds into the ride, Anya said, "I was right. I am in Virginia."

"Yeah, but not for long," Johnny Mac said from behind the wheel. "We'll be in D.C. in a matter of minutes."

In Russian-accented Arabic, Anya said, "I am sorry for earlier. I was rude to you."

After thirty minutes in the Suburban, they pulled up in front of a building that could've been a thousand things other than what it really was. White's keycard granted them access through a side door and into a stainless-steel elevator. When the doors opened, the four stepped into the bright fluorescent glow of Anya's ultimate toy store.

Ray White laid his hand on her shoulder. "Welcome to the CIA's Office of Technical Services, formerly known in the Cold War era as the Technical Services Division. You're likely the first former KGB officer who's ever seen this place."

6

MAGAZIN IGRUSHEK
(THE TOY STORE)

A short, bulbous man in Coke-bottle glasses, who had a ring of white hair surrounding the polished dome of his perfectly round head, shuffled through a doorway. Without a word, he silently examined White, Johnny Mac, and Gwynn, lingering on Anya at least twice as long as the DOJ agents.

After nearly two minutes of awkward silence, the man reached up, took Anya by the hand, and tugged her toward a corridor. "Come, come. I've waited for this day for half a century."

Unsure if she should let the little man lead her away, Anya turned to Agent White.

"It's okay. Go with Bernard. He has a goody basket for you."

White motioned down the corridor. "Go with them, Gwynn. Otherwise, we'll never get her back."

Agent Davis obeyed and followed the garden gnome and his new favorite assassin as they disappeared down the hallway.

Bernard slid a keycard through a reader, and a pair of sliding doors opened to reveal a collection of Cold War spy paraphernalia like no other assembly on Earth.

Anya shot a look over her shoulder. "You were correct, Gwynn. This is field trip to museum."

Bernard handed Anya piece after one-of-a-kind piece of gadgetry with an explanation of exactly how everything worked. The room contained more Soviet toys than American, some of which Anya had never seen.

She admired the vast assortment. "This is fascinating collection, but why am I here?"

"Oh, that, yes. Why are you here, indeed?" Bernard squirmed like an excited puppy, and Gwynn thought the troll of a man might actually pee on the floor. "You are here because the Justice Department tasked me—well, us . . . not just me—to build fighting knives, throwing knives, concealable knives, covert knives, and any other kind of knife you want especially for your magnificent hands."

He held Anya's hands in each of his and turned them every direction. "Oh my, these are perfect hands for knives. I . . . well, again, I meant *we* will build for you such magnificent knives. You cannot imagine what I can put in these hands. Oh, this is the best day. Simply the best day."

Anya caught Gwynn's attention and mouthed, "Help me!"

Agent Davis sprang into action. "Dr. Claiborne, I hate to interrupt your . . ."

As Gwynn spoke, he leapt repeatedly as if he were on a springboard. "Oh, dear, it's just Bernard. Only Bernard. *Doctor* sounds so formal, and I have in my hands the hand of a Soviet-trained Russian spy."

"I am not spy," Anya said. "I am assassin. And now I am American."

"Oh, dear me. Of course you're not a spy. That's exactly what a spy would say. What else may I show you of my collection? Well, I suppose it isn't really mine, but it is under my care, so perhaps that makes it mine. Don't you think so?"

Anya squeezed Dr. Bernard Claiborne's hands in hers. "It is magnificent. I have never seen its equal, and every piece cries out that it belongs to you."

"Oh, you are such a delight. Those Soviets are so good at creating spies, but you, you are an astonishing example. You are perfect from top to bottom, I say. Simply flawless."

Anya smiled at the wasted flattery. "I am not perfect, doctor. I do not have knives."

Bernard pulled his glasses from his face and wiped them furiously on his untucked shirttail. "Oh, yes, I almost forgot your knives. I have them, I do."

Refusing to release her hand, Bernard led Anya back through the door and into another secure area requiring two more swipes of the keycard. They finally stopped in a workshop with black rubber mats on the floor and unidentifiable machinery in every direction.

Anya took it all in. "What is this place?"

"This is the edged weapons lab. This is where the perfect knife for your perfect hand will be built. Look, look . . . See what I have."

Anya stared into a blue plastic container holding an array of knives of her choice: four throwing knives, two Bowie-type fighting knives resembling the American Ka-Bar favored by the Marines, and two curved-blade close-quarters battle knives designed to pierce flesh and hook internal organs with the intention of making them external organs.

Anya reached toward the container, but Bernard slapped her hand. "No, no, not those. You don't want those."

"Yes, I do. These are my knives."

"Yes, yes, of course they are, but I'm making better ones for you." He offered her a flat handle attached to a cluster of wires that led into a black box the size of a loaf of bread. "Here, hold this as if it were a throwing knife."

Anya took the metallic handle and cradled it between her thumb and index finger. Numbers and symbols rapidly began scrolling across a computer monitor above the black box, and a machine whirred to life somewhere behind Bernard.

"Okay, okay, fabulous. This is so good." He then offered her a rounded shank of metal with the same wires running from the hilt. "Now, hold *this* as if it were your fighting knife."

Anya took the stalk of metal into her palm and carefully wrapped her fingers around the object until it felt like a fighting knife should feel.

Bernard stroked the keys of a computer. "Now, do it again with your left hand."

She did as he instructed, and again, another machine whirred into action.

The whole process was repeated with a smaller shank, obviously meant to represent the handle of the hooked gutting knives.

By the time she finished demonstrating her preferred grips on each weapon, the first machine fell silent, and Bernard slid back a plastic shielding hatch. He reached inside and pulled out a throwing knife that looked nearly identical to the four in the blue plastic container. He wiped it clean and placed it gently into Anya's palm.

She inspected the blade and found the balance to be impeccable. Bernard motioned for her to follow, and they rounded a corner into an indoor range with corkboard targets placed at various distances.

"Go ahead," he said. "Give it a throw."

She stuck it into the center of a board at three, seven, and twelve yards. As she pulled the blade from the twelve-yard target, she examined it. "I would like one thousand of these, please."

Bernard beamed. "I knew it. I knew you'd love it. We machined the blanks roughly oversized from the set the DOJ acquired from you recently. Then, the modeling module crafted the perfect design based on your grip. Before you leave, you will have one dozen of these, but I can make a budget request for nine thousand nine hundred eighty-eight more if you wish."

Gwynn stepped in. "No, twelve throwing knives are quite enough."

Bernard provided a ballistics gel dummy for Anya to stab, slice, and otherwise maul with the fighting knife and hooked blade. Each knife performed like the precision-crafted custom tool it was. Anya approved each, and Bernard provided four fighting knives and six hooked-blade knives.

"Now it's time for your pistol. Come, come."

Gwynn and Anya followed as Bernard led them to the opposite side of the lab, where the process was repeated with pistol grips until two customized Makarov 9x18mm pistols were molded to perfectly fit each of her hands.

"Now for some unexpected blades," he said as he opened a cabinet containing items that looked nothing like blades of any kind. He held up a credit card with Anya's name embossed across the bottom.

"I do not need credit card," she said.

He held up a finger. "You need this one, princess. Not only is it a no-limit card drawn against the covert operations budget of the Justice Department, but it's the ultimate cutting-edge card."

"What does this mean?"

He lifted it from her palm, squeezed two opposing corners, and slid half of the card away, revealing a razor-sharp edge on each half. "Never leave home without it."

Anya pulled the two blades from his hands and slid them back together. She marveled at the craftsmanship. "This is astonishing."

"Yes, yes, I know."

Back at the entrance to the facility, Bernard wrapped himself around Anya as if she were his favorite daughter headed off to college. Anya returned the hug with a pair of leather duffels hanging from her shoulders. The bags contained the tools of the trade Bernard had created just for her. She leaned down, kissed him on the cheek, and whispered something that left every inch of skin on his face, neck, and head glowing bright red.

On the elevator ride back to the surface, Gwynn leaned against Anya and whispered, "I have to know what you told him before we left."

Anya chuckled. "I said to him there is nothing a girl loves more than a sexy man who gives her everything her heart desires. And maybe I accidentally let my tongue trace his ear."

Gwynn belly-laughed. "I want to be just like you when I grow up."

* * *

Instead of returning to Agent White's office, Johnny Mac pulled up in front of a brownstone in Georgetown.

White opened the door. "Come on, Anya. This is where we get off. You'll sleep here tonight."

"What is this place?" she asked.

White looked up the stone façade. "This is where I get to spend a couple dozen nights every year . . . and where I get my mail."

She slid from the seat and stepped onto the sidewalk. "It is beautiful. I am sorry you do not get to spend more time at your home."

"Home is where you make it," he said. "And besides, if I had a nine-to-five, I'd never meet Russian spies turned lion killers."

7

NOVAYA PARA KRYL'YEV
(NEW PAIR OF WINGS)

Anya stood in the foyer of the brownstone and took in the surroundings. "Do you often bring prisoners to your house, Agent White?"

White surveyed the home he hadn't seen in over two weeks. "No, Anya, I rarely bring anyone here, but this assignment—and you—are anything but typical, so, as they say, desperate times call for desperate measures."

Anya felt the words pound in her head. "Who says this thing about desperate times?"

White chuckled. "I don't know. *They* do. Whoever *they* are."

"In my experience, *they* are correct about this. Most of my life has been desperate time."

White removed his coat and hung it from a hall tree. "You can pull off your hoodie if you want. You won't be here long, but you might as well make yourself comfortable."

She slithered from the sweatshirt and placed it beside White's coat. "How long is long?"

He motioned with his head toward the living room. "Have a seat, and we'll talk about that. Would you like some tea?"

"I will help with tea. Is not for you to serve me. I am your prisoner."

White emptied the contents of his pockets onto the table beside the door. "You're not my prisoner. You're a confidential cooperating participant in a DOJ operation."

Anya considered the phrase as she followed him into the kitchen, where the environment made a dramatic change. She studied the contents and arrangement of the room: a Viking commercial gas range, a two-door commercial refrigerator, a wrought-iron pot rack with a massive collection of Calphalon cookware, and a marble-top center island. "You are chef, yes?"

White washed his hands and filled a stainless-steel teapot with filtered water. The blue flame from the stove danced beneath the pot, spreading its burning tentacles across the waiting metal.

Anya stared into the flames. "Is how I feel."

White allowed himself to become lost in one of the few, and by far the most beautiful of the women who'd been inside his home. "What is how you feel? The flame?"

She shook her head. "No, I am not flame. I am teapot. I cannot move to protect myself from fire. I must remain where you place me, and I must endure flame no matter how hot or how much I boil inside."

White withdrew a wooden box of tea bags from the cupboard and slid it across the counter. "I'm sorry, Anya. I don't like doing this to you, but I don't have any choice."

She fingered through the tea bags and chose a rich black tea from the back of the box. "No, Agent White, you are only person inside kitchen who does have choice. You can stop job and become lawyer without gun."

He placed a pair of mugs on the counter beside the stove and studied the delicate features of Anya's face. She wore the beauty and grace of a ballerina, perhaps from the Bolshoi, but her deep, mysterious eyes held the wisdom of agony and scars of imprisonment. "How many people have you killed?"

She showed no reaction. "I do not know this number, but I have for you same question."

White disappeared inside his own mind as he relived the night that would never leave his torturous dreams. "One too many."

The kettle whistled its shrill announcement, and White jerked himself from the scene pouring through his head. Anya didn't flinch; instead, she lifted the pot from the burner and poured the steaming water into the waiting mugs.

She replaced the pot on the stove, stepped toward Ray, and placed her palm on the center of his chest. Her touch felt like ice wrestling fire, and his heart raced against her fingertips. She leaned closer, and he could feel her warm, inviting breath against his skin. Resistance was but a fleeting thought, dismissed without consideration, and he closed his eyes. He knew she would destroy him, but just like the kettle, he, too, was powerless to move away from the flame.

She reached above his shoulder, opened the cupboard, and pulled down a small ceramic pot of honey. "I am not going to seduce you, Special Agent Ray White. You are exactly kind of man who will give away soul for night in arms of devil like me."

"You're no devil, Anya. Quite the opposite, in fact. You're the Avenging Angel who's going to swing her sword through the Russian lion."

She spooned the honey into her mug and stirred until she felt the viscous sugar melt into the dark, steaming tea. "Angel is not opposite of devil, Agent White. You have Bible on table in other room. Inside your book, Devil is angel and takes other angels with him when he is cast from Heaven. To say I am angel is not to say I am good. Is only to say I am powerful."

White replaced the honey pot in the cupboard. "Then, I'm right. You are an angel. It simply remains to be seen whose side you're on . . . the sweet or the bitter."

He sank into a well-worn recliner and placed his mug beside the Bible Anya had so conveniently mentioned.

She curled onto the corner of the sofa, pulled a crocheted afghan across her knees, and cradled her mug between her cupped hands. "What is next?"

He stared into the barely visible white foam floating on the surface of his tea. "Tonight, we sleep . . . maybe. And tomorrow, we buy you a new pair of wings."

They silently drank their tea, each considering what lay ahead. Anya knew well the world into which she would be slipping. It was a world of lies, betrayal, hatred, greed, and misery—a world not so different from the one in which Special Agent Ray White lived every day. His world, though, was run by men in ties and suits who'd spent millions of dollars of other people's money to win elections to positions that paid little more than White earned every year. Anya believed she was the honey that would dissolve into the darkness of a world run by angry men who'd fled—or been cast out of—Mother Russia, and sliced and clawed their way to the top of a pyramid of evil, destruction, and violence; a pyramid she feared may become her tomb.

The sleepless night gave way to a morning that hardly qualified as anything less than an extension of the night. Gray, ominous clouds hung near the treetops and spat out stinging flakes of snow that felt like thousands of tiny razors biting at Anya's face.

The jeans, boots, flannel overshirt, and hooded Columbia jacket Gwynn had delivered just after dawn did little to ward off the cold.

"When I am to be dangled as bait, surely you are not cruel enough to make me stay here in city for this."

White turned up his collar against the wind. "No, my little snow bunny, you won't be staying here. Where you're going, there won't be any need for that jacket."

She turned to Agent Davis. "In this case, you may keep. Is very nice coat, and you will look pretty."

Gwynn tried not to smile as Anya let their hands brush lightly together as they made their way to the waiting SUV. Johnny Mac held the door for Gwynn and Anya while White climbed into the front passenger's seat.

Back behind the wheel and without his gloves, he turned to White. "Where to, boss?"

"Nine thirty-five Pennsylvania Avenue Northwest."

D.C. traffic was lighter than usual. Perhaps it was the threat of half a foot of snow before noon, or maybe even the traffic gods wanted to hasten Anya's departure from the frozen capital.

When they pulled into the parking garage off Pennsylvania Avenue, Anya noted the position of every surveillance camera, guard dog, barricade, and potential area of cover or concealment. "Why would you bring me to FBI building?"

White glanced into the mirror on his visor. "I told you. We're buying you a new pair of wings."

"What does this mean, new pair of wings?"

Gwynn leaned close and whispered, "Don't worry. I've got you. Just think of it as a shopping trip with your favorite uncle's credit card."

"I do not have favorite uncle because I do not have uncle."

"Sure, you do," Gwynn scoffed. "You've got Uncle Sam, and his credit card never gets declined."

Ten minutes later, Anya found herself standing on an elevated, carpeted box, while two women and a man stared at her as if they were planning to cook her for dinner.

The three FBI tailors turned up the heat, at least as far as White and Jonny Mac were concerned, but they didn't toss her into a pot. Instead, they fitted her with a wardrobe consisting of everything from yoga pants and sports bras to elegant gowns, and then took her on a foray through the high-priced call-girl department.

Anya held up a pair of five-inch red heels and a skintight black dress. "This is your idea of wings, Special Agent White?"

He shrugged. "Something tells me you're going to look absolutely angelic in those."

"In this, I will look like *shlyukha* on corner of street."

White gave her a wink. "What's the use in dangling bait if the bait isn't something the fish want to bite?"

"You are making me to prostitute."

"No, Anya, the Kremlin did that to you. I'm simply making you everything our boy Leo can't resist."

After two hours in the basement of the FBI building, Anya tried on twenty-four complete outfits, sixteen pairs of shoes, and accessories of every imaginable variety, from watches to earrings and trinkets to be worn on parts of her body Anya never considered decorating.

They left the building with two relatively small bags and left the remainder of the clothes behind.

One of the tailors made copious notes inside a leather-bound pad and then looked up. "Don't worry. We'll have everything in the apartment when she arrives."

The parking garage gave no indication of the severity of the winter storm approaching from the northwest, but as they pulled onto the street, two inches of snow covered everything in sight. Anya shivered at the sight of the blizzard, and Gwynn cocked her head. "What? Growing up in Moscow, you should be used to this."

Anya turned from the window to avoid the sight of the snow. "I told you, I am terrible Russian. I hate caviar, I do not drink vodka, and I detest cold."

Agent White pulled his cellphone from the pocket of his overcoat and then mumbled something beneath his breath. "Hey, Dad. What's going on?"

He listened for several seconds, then said, "Dad, I've told you this before. You have to call the police. There's nothing I can do." The conversation continued with White growing more impatient with every word. "Okay, I'll call you tonight, but listen to me. Call the cops. They'll take care of it. There's nothing I can do."

Johnny Mac eyed his boss. "Still those thugs?"

White rolled his eyes. "He thinks I can take care of some vandalism in New Smyrna Beach. He won't listen."

Johnny Mac tapped the wheel. "I could make some calls down there and see what I can find out."

"No," White demanded. "Just drop it. We've got more to worry about than some out-of-control kids breaking into a second-hand bookstore in Florida. We've got to get those two on an airplane."

Johnny Mac leaned forward, peering into the ever-darkening sky. "In this?"

"Yeah, in this, before it gets any worse."

Anya turned to Gwynn. "You are coming with me?"

The young agent nodded. "Yes, I'm coming, but only because I look less like a fed than either of those guys. We can't risk you being spotted with anyone who screams 'Hey, look at me, I'm a cop.'"

The four-wheel-drive SUV made navigating the snow-encrusted streets relatively easy, but the accumulation was continuing to amass, and Johnny Mac couldn't stop looking at the sky. "There's no way anything's taking off in this."

White sighed. "Yeah, you're probably right. I'll get the National Weather Service on the phone, and we'll find someplace with a runway that isn't socked in."

After five minutes on the phone with the weather guessers, White hung up. "Looks like we're going to Richmond. It's a little over a hundred miles, and in this weather, that's going to take three hours."

Johnny Mac shook his head. "Some things never change. Davis gets to fly to South Beach with the Russian goddess back there, and I'm stuck driving you around in a blizzard."

At the sound of South Beach, Anya suddenly forgot all about the twenty-knot freezing wind and deluge of snow outside her tinted window.

8

MAL'CHIK NA POBEGUSHKAKH
(ERRAND BOY)

The Pratt & Whitney turbine whistled to life in the nose of the Pilatus PC-12 turboprop only seconds after Anya and Special Agent Gwynn Davis buckled their seatbelts. Minutes later, they pierced the low overcast as they climbed southward toward the penance she would have to pay for the sins she'd committed.

In stark contrast to the cutting wind and blowing snow that lay behind them, Miami boasted afternoon temperatures in the low eighties. Anya stepped from the plane and reveled in the feel of the sunshine on her face and the gentle sea breeze in her long hair.

Gwynn left the bottom step of the airstairs and let the warm, salt air fill her lungs. "Ah, this is more like it."

Anya sighed. "You would also be terrible Russian."

Gwynn accepted her rolling bag from the pilot. "I like the cold and snow on my terms, but my terms are typically on the ski slope."

Anya slung her bag across her shoulder. "Perhaps we can sometime ski together when all of this is. . . ."

Gwynn grinned and met her gaze. "I think I'd like that, and this *will* be over. It's not forever."

"It is forever if someone finds out who I really am and kills me."

Gwynn motioned toward Anya's shoulder. "I've seen what you can do with the contents of that bag. You're not exactly easy to kill. Come on. Your car is waiting."

"My car?"

"Yes, your car."

They made their way through the terminal and into the parking lot, where a pair of young men who looked exactly like they belonged on the beach stood beside the perfect South Beach ride.

Anya looked between Gwynn and the car. "*That* is mine?"

Gwynn smirked. "It looks like it."

The younger of the two men made a show of dropping a key onto the front seat before turning with his partner and vanishing into the jungle of parked cars.

With bags stowed, Anya and Gwynn pulled their hair into high ponytails and watched the convertible top fold itself away. Top down, hair in the wind, they—and their Porsche 911—joined the throngs of perfect bodies, priceless cars, and endless hedonism that was Ocean Boulevard.

The relentless Cuban beat and bodies begging to be adored decorated and punctuated the scene.

Gwynn shook out her hair. "Ever been to South Beach before?"

"Yes, and I have wound to prove it. I will show you."

The agent eyed the spy. "You're going to show me your wound . . . now?"

"No, I will show you where wound happened."

The slow progress northward on Ocean Drive proved more of the same scenery regardless of the block. Reaching Fourteenth, Anya spun the wheel beneath a red light and raced through the intersection to the protest of horns and shouts of their blowers. The turbo three feet behind the women made their time in the intersection almost negligible, but that didn't quiet the horns.

Three more red lights ignored, Anya slid the car to a stop in front of a two-story monstrosity that qualified as a South Beach mansion. "This is where I was shot."

"Shot?"

"Yes, once in back, above shoulder blade. It was nine millimeter, and I fell from stairs maybe three meters."

Gwynn grimaced in sympathetic pain. "How did you survive that?"

"A man carried me from house and into car. I was taken from hospital by people like you."

Gwynn sighed. "Like me, huh?"

"American CIA."

"This man who took you to the hospital . . . Was his name Chase?"

Anya sent the accelerator to the floor and dropped the clutch; more horns, more ignored traffic lights, and no answers.

Seven blocks from Ocean Drive, only minutes after the sun had fallen behind the mainland, a black van braked hard, and Anya swerved to avoid wedging the nose of her Porsche beneath the bumper of the stopping van. A row of parked cars forced her foot onto the brake even harder. Gwynn braced for impact, but the collision didn't come. Instead, Anya brought the car to a sliding stop inches from a parked delivery truck, and the rearview mirror filled with the grill of a battered Monte Carlo.

Anya's gaze shot to the side mirrors as her hand flew to her waistline. Before she could open the door lever, a well-tanned left hand landed on top of her door, and the muzzle of a pistol landed beneath her left ear.

A glance to the right showed Gwynn's right hand hidden low, no doubt her Glock resting in her expert grip.

Anya didn't look up. "What do you want?"

"Your car, for starters, and maybe some of—"

"You are making terrible mistake. If you walk away now, I promise I will not make you bleed on my car."

The jacker laughed. "I don't think I'm going to be the one bleeding. Now, get out of the car and leave it running. Do as I say, and you don't have to get hurt."

The van pulled away, providing an escape if she chose to take it, but the opportunity at hand was too much to resist.

Anya finally looked up and met the stare of the man who'd likely jacked more cars in Miami than he could remember. If he survived this one, though, it would be one he'd never forget. "If you bleed on my car, I will kill you in street and play in your blood. I am not person who surrenders."

The man thumb-cocked the pistol now pointing just beneath Anya's chin, and the two women sprang into action simultaneously. Gwynn raised her Glock, sighting on the man's face as Anya thrust her first short-bladed knife into his bicep. With her left hand, she caught the barrel of the pistol, twisted it from the man's grip, and sent a crashing hammer blow to his left hand still resting on the door.

In the same instant, she shoved the door to its stop, sending the man careening backward into the street with blood pulsing from his arm. As her feet hit the pavement, a second knife appeared in her palm, and the man scampered backward like a wounded crab.

Gwynn, believing Anya had the first man well under control, leapt from the car and turned for the Monte Carlo. Smoke boiled from its rear tires as the driver reversed in a desperate attempt to escape the scene. By the time she rounded the back of the car, Gwynn was too late to stop Anya from fulfilling her threat to the would-be carjacker. The man lay on his back with his head driven against the curb on the opposite side of the street. Anya's left knee was planted solidly in his groin, and the blade of her second knife protruded from his right thigh, blood pooling beneath him.

Anya glowered over the man, a perfect smile on her flawless face, and her shoulders and neck muscles relaxed. Gwynn had never seen anyone so tranquil during a fight.

From Anya's perspective, though, there was no fight. She'd defeated the man long before he ever cocked his pistol. The speed, ease, and agility with which she moved was like nothing Gwynn had ever imagined possible, and certainly unlike anything she'd ever seen. She lowered her pistol as she approached, hoping against hope the man was still alive and she could do something, anything, to stop the Russian.

Anya's smile turned glacial as she pressed the razor tip of her blade to the man's chin. "You will tell me who you work for, or I will gut you like pig."

"I don't work for nobody, you crazy bitch! Get off of me."

Gwynn moved to the sidewalk, certain she could do nothing short of putting a bullet through Anya's head to stop what lay ahead.

Anya moved to within inches of the trembling man's face and whispered, "I am Anya. Say my name."

The man froze in terrified disbelief. "What?"

"Say my name, you weak little child."

"Anya. Your name is Anya."

Without a word, she withdrew the knife from the man's chin, leaving a thin line of crimson, and in one stroke, sliced from his neck to his crotch in a motion far too fast for the human eye. His shirt fell open, revealing tattoos, scars, and a single gold chain, but no blood. She hadn't even scratched the skin of the man's torso.

"This correct. I am Anya, and I will let you live, for now, but you will not forget my name, and you will tell to man you work for, yes?"

"Yeah, yeah, whatever."

"Good," she hissed. "I will take shirt to clean blood from car, you filthy pig."

Another blindingly swift pass of the blade, and Anya held half of the man's grungy shirt in her hand. The droplets of blood that had fallen to the top edge of her door were gone with one pass of the cloth.

The pair pulled into the traffic lane and back toward the beach, where the sinister element lay a little further from the surface, but the ferocity of sinners ran far deeper.

After five blocks and no more ignored traffic signals, Gwynn let out a long sigh punctuated by a schoolgirl giggle. "That was amazing. Believe it or not, that was the first time I've ever pulled my gun on duty."

Anya's expression never wavered. "Was for me also first time."

Gwynn furrowed her brow. "First time for what?"

"For letting person live when I say I will kill him."

Special Agent Gwynn Davis's excitement turned to stone as the realization of her new existence found purchase inside the innocence of her mind. "Were you really going to kill him?"

"When I stepped from car, it was plan to gut him like pig and leave in street."

"Why didn't you do it?"

Anya pointed to her left collarbone. "Tattoo."

"What tattoo?"

"On neck. This means he is errand boy for Bratva."

"Oh, that's perfect. That means we've dangled our first bait."

"He will tell boss, but is one problem."

"What's the problem?" Gwynn asked. "That's exactly what we want him to do, right?"

Anya nodded. "Yes, but he will not only tell boss about crazy bitch with knife. He will tell also story about other one with gun."

Gwynn swallowed the lump in her throat. "Oh, that *is* a problem. They were never supposed to see me."

"Is too late for this now. We must change plan. You are now part of plan, yes?"

"I don't know," Gwynn whispered. "That's not up to me. I was just supposed to get you settled into your apartment. I was never supposed to be part of the operation. Maybe you *should've* killed him."

Anya hit the brakes, spun the wheel, and accelerated hard, turning the car around in little more than its own length.

Gwynn grabbed the seat. "What are you doing?"

"I am taking you back."

"Back where?"

Anya grinned. "Back to kill errand boy. I will give to you knife, and I will watch."

* * *

Relieved both that Anya did not make her kill the errand boy and that the Russian actually had a sense of humor, Gwynn led Anya from the elevator to the door of her apartment and handed her a set of keys. "You do the honors. After all, it's your new home."

Anya took the keys, released both locks, and pressed her way through the door. The apartment was elegantly furnished but not extravagant.

She pulled back the blinds to reveal a massive window overlooking Ocean Boulevard and throngs of perfect bodies in every direction on the seemingly endless beach. "Is beautiful here."

Gwynn joined her at the window. "Yeah, it really is. Too bad it's not a vacation. Maybe they'll let you keep this place when it's all over."

Anya placed her finger lightly against the glass and drew an imaginary line across the horizon. "Do not be naïve. This will never be finished. I will do for you what Agent White asks, but when I am finished, he, or maybe Agent McIntyre, will kill me."

Gwynn took Anya's hand. "No, that's not how any of this works. No one is going to kill you. We're the good guys."

Anya pressed her lips into a thin, horizontal line. "You have much to learn, Gwynn. I will teach you, but is possible you will have to do it."

Gwynn frowned. "It's possible I'll have to do what?"

"Is possible you will be one who must kill me."

9

NOVYYE DEVUSHKI V GORODE
(NEW GIRLS IN TOWN)

A sharp knock arrested the spiral of conversation, and Gwynn reached for her Glock.

Anya stopped her before she could draw the pistol for the second time in her career. "Is only man from building. I am sure. You do not need to kill him, but I promise time will come for you."

Anya pulled open the door without checking the peephole, and a bald, muscular man with a black sport coat over a black T-shirt stood in the corridor. He let his eyes explore her body, but not in the way most men do. Anya thought he was sizing her up for a weapon instead of putting together a pickup line.

"Good evening, ma'am. I'm Michael. I manage the door and any concerns our guests and residents may have." He pulled a card from his pocket and held it toward her. "You can reach the man on the door anytime at this number, and my personal cell is on the back. If you need anything at all, at any hour, don't hesitate to call."

Without looking away, Anya took the card from the man's hand. His shoulders, chest, and arms were well developed, but not from manual labor. His hands were devoid of callouses, and his tan extended beneath the line of his shirt, meaning he likely spent a lot of time in the gym and on the beach with as few clothes as possible.

"Thank you, Michael. I am Anya, and is very nice to have big strong man like you"—she gave his bicep a squeeze—"to manage door and my concerns. Perhaps *you* might be my concern, but unfortunately"—she cast a self-conscious glance across her shoulder—"my girlfriend is inside and very jealous of big strong men."

The man leaned slightly to his left to risk a glimpse inside the apartment and at her girlfriend. "Well, I'm sure she has *almost* nothing to worry about, so if there's anything I can do, you have my number." He offered an almost imperceptible bow and turned for the elevator.

Anya watched him go and closed the door. "See, was only man from building. He is pretty man and wanted me to be impressed by him, but I was not."

Gwynn pressed her Glock back into its holster. "He *was* pretty, and *you* called me your girlfriend."

"Michael would be trouble if he thinks we are interested in becoming his lover. I take this trouble away if he thinks we do not like men."

Gwynn chuckled. "In my experience, that only makes men try harder."

"Is sometimes true, but I have plan for new friend Michael. He will break rules for us, and we will need this soon."

Gwynn shook her head. "How long did it take for you to learn all this?"

Anya let her gaze fall to the floor. "Thirty years—all of life. And I am still learning. When learning stops, living also stops."

"I guess I've still got a lot to learn."

"I will teach you, and you will make sure I do not stop learning, yes?"

"Absolutely, but I want to ask you a question. What's it like to kill someone?"

Anya let the question hang in the air as she stepped through the doorway into the small kitchen. "I think I will have tea. Do you want?"

Gwynn followed her through the door. "That's one of the things the advanced team was supposed to take care of. We thought you'd want tea."

Anya filled the kettle with water and slid it onto the stove. "You have been watching me very long time, yes?"

"Well, it's not like we've been sticking our noses that far up your skirt. It's, actually, not that hard to guess that a Russian native probably wants her hot tea."

Anya pulled open the cupboard and pointed to the bottle on the shelf. "You guessed also that I want vodka, but this is wrong. I told you, I am terrible Russian."

Gwynn pulled a pair of mugs from the shelf. "Maybe, but something tells me you're making a pretty great American."

Anya subconsciously reached for her right front pocket and felt an instant sadness.

Gwynn held up one finger. "Just a minute."

Anya watched the agent leave the kitchen and return seconds later with a tiny, plastic American flag between her fingers. "Looking for this?"

She took the souvenir from Gwynn and twirled it between her thumb and index finger. "I have always with me until . . ."

"I know. That's why I brought it. But it may not be a great idea to carry it while you're undercover."

"Am I now federal agent undercover?"

"Not exactly, but close enough. Speaking of which, we need to check in."

As she dialed the phone, the tea kettle whistled, and steam rose from the spout.

"Agent White, it's Davis. We're in the apartment, and everything appears to be in place. We did, however, run into a little trouble on the way."

While Anya poured the tea, Gwynn laid out the details of the attempted carjacking and the encounter with Michael, the building's doorman.

"Put her on the phone," White demanded.

Anya handed Gwynn a steaming mug and took the phone. "I told you genie cannot go back inside bottle, and you rubbed bottle."

White let a chuckle leave his lips. "You did warn me, but now you've dragged Davis out of the bottle with you. That wasn't part of the plan."

Anya beamed. "This means plan is finished and I can now go home, yes?"

"No, not hardly, genie. You're not getting off that easy. Tell me how you knew the carjacker was an errand boy for the Bratva."

"He had tattoo of *serp* on left side of chest near neck. This means he is only person to do menial labor. If also has *molotok*, he will dictate labor for others. *Serp* is *sickle* and *molotok* means *hammer*."

"Yeah, you may remember I speak a little Russian, and I've been studying the mafia for almost ten years now. What's the guy's name you assaulted?"

"I did not assault. Was only self-defense."

"Okay, Xena, according to your sidekick Gabriel, it was a little more than self-defense. She said you threatened to cut him and play in his blood."

Anya wrinkled her brow. "Who is Xena person?"

"Get Davis to explain it to you. I've got too much work to do trying to clean up the mess you made by dragging her into your little production down there. Just lie low for the night, and I'll have a plan for tomorrow. Do you need anything?"

"Special Agent White, genie is out of bottle, and genies do not lie low. I will dangle bait, and you will catch fish. This is why I am here."

White cleared his throat. "Anya, listen to me. This is my operation, and you will—"

"No, Ray. This *was* your operation. Is now *my* operation. You said this yourself. I will tell you when is time to set hook, but I must now go and have tea with girlfriend. We are new girls in town and have big plans tonight."

Anya handed the phone back to Gwynn, and the agent stared at the screen in disbelief. "Did you just hang up on Agent White?"

Anya shrugged. "I was finished with conversation."

Gwynn raised her mug. "You really are out of control, aren't you? I guess, here's to the new girls in town."

The Russian clinked her mug to Gwynn's. "To *novyye devushki v gorode*."

They drank, each pondering what the coming days would bring. Anya was confident she could get inside, but what she didn't know was exactly how she'd get back out. Would she have to cut her way back to the surface, or would Agent White come riding in on his trusty steed, slapping handcuffs on everyone in sight? Handcuffs would do no good. The Bratva wasn't afraid of prison. They understood only one rule: stay alive to fight another day.

Gwynn thought back to her days as a promising young law student at Columbia. She thought she'd graduate, pass the bar, and go to work as a junior associate at some big-city law firm, where she'd claw her way to the top until her name was on the letterhead and above the door, but fate dealt another hand.

Anya swallowed a warm mouthful of the aromatic tea. "I will answer your question about how it feels to kill someone, but first, I want to know why you became police officer."

Gwynn laughed. "I was just thinking about that very question. I went to law school at Columbia. My mother was a paralegal, and my dad was a schoolteacher. Mom would come home and tell us stories about the cases she was working on, and I thought being a lawyer who had paralegals just like my mom would be the greatest thing ever, so I set my sights on that."

She paused for a drink, and Anya sat carefully taking in every word.

"About halfway through my third year in law school, a bunch of recruiters came to meet the next wave of legal eagles Columbia Law would spit out. There were tax attorneys, criminal defense guys, high-priced corporate lawyers with five-thousand-dollar suits, and then there were the G-men."

Anya frowned. "G-men?"

"Yeah, government agents. Instead of carrying briefcases and wearing Armani, they wore cheap suits and had bulges under their left arms and shiny handcuffs dangling from the backs of their belts. I liked the idea of wearing designers like the corporate guys, but there was something about the feds, and I knew instantly what I wanted to be when I grew up. I thought I'd be an FBI agent, but I ended up at Justice, working for Agent White instead. And now I'm really glad."

"This makes you and me very different."

Gwynn cocked her head. "What do you mean?"

Anya took another sip. "You were given many choices, and you became what you want. I did not have these choices. Someone else made them for me, and this is still happening."

Gwynn sat in silence, wishing she could come up with something to say that could make the Russian understand she still had options and that the mission would come to an end.

Anya rescued Gwynn from her dilemma. "Do you know how to fight?"

Gwynn shook her head. "I told you all of that, and you're first question is 'Do you know how to fight?'"

"You passed bar examination, yes?"

"Yeah, sure. I passed it on my first attempt."

"So, now you have license to practice law, but this will do no good for us. We are going after man who thinks he is lion. Lions do not care about license to practice law. They care only about eating, killing, and finding female lion, and I think you know what they do with female. If you cannot fight, you will be eaten, killed, or you will be treated like female lion. You do not want any of those things to happen to you."

She scowled. "No, of course not. And yeah, I can fight. I did pretty well at the Academy."

"In Academy, no one tried to kill you. Fighting on street is very different than inside gymnasium on mat."

Anya swallowed what remained of her tea and stood. "We will put couch against wall, and you will show to me what you learned at Academy."

Gwynn helped with the couch and then stood three feet in front of Anya with her fists raised. Anya drew a concealed throwing knife from her belt and lunged toward Gwynn with the blade at neck height.

Gwynn reacted instinctually by taking two shuffling steps backward, drawing her pistol, and leveling it between Anya's eyes. "Drop the knife, or I'll drop you."

Anya leaned down, placed the knife on the ground a few feet in front of Gwynn's feet, and the agent relaxed. As Anya rose from placing the knife on the ground, she spun with blinding speed, ripped the Glock from Davis's hand, and landed a thundering sidekick to her chest. The kick sent Gwynn reeling backward until she collided with the wall of the apartment.

Gwynn gasped for breath and stood in amazement at Anya, who was standing only a few feet in front of her and holding the Glock that had been in her grip only seconds before. "How did you do that?"

"I took advantage of you when you thought fight was over. Knife was only distraction. Now I have gun, and you have no weapon. I think they did not teach you this at Academy."

The following hours were spent with Anya explaining the psychology of fighting and survival, and Gwynn was an excellent student. The explanations were rarely verbal, and Gwynn would soon have the bruises as reminders that survival on the street is not academic, it's physical.

Winded, sweaty, and enlightened, Gwynn listened as Anya said, "If person is willing to take your life, you must decide if you will give to him *your* life, or take from him his. Is always better if you are alive. Is very different when you kill someone with bullet than with hands, but is always terrible."

"I knew when I took this job I'd have to pull the trigger sooner or later, but I never thought about killing anyone with my bare hands or even with a knife."

Anya retrieved a pair of water bottles from the kitchen and sat on the floor beside Gwynn. "When time comes to fight, you will be afraid, and brain will be difficult to control, but you must always stay alive. I will teach you, and you will learn every day. You will become good fighter, but is now time for shower and night on town."

10

PROGLOTIT' NAZHIVKU
(TAKING THE BAIT)

Michael, the doorman, watched the two women step from the elevator and couldn't believe his eyes. There was no shortage of beautiful people on South Beach, but the leggy blonde Russian and her girl-next-door brunette friend would stand out in any crowd.

He held open the door but couldn't remove his sight from the pair. "Good evening, ladies. You two look astonishing."

Anya touched his cheek. "Hello, Michael. You will get for us car and driver, yes? We want to go dancing."

"I have a car on the street just for you."

Michael opened the door of the waiting Town Car as the pair slid inside. Anya gave the doorman a glimpse he hadn't expected as she rearranged her skintight dress across her thighs. He winked, and she offered a flirtatious smile.

The driver shot a glance into the mirror, then couldn't resist turning around to get a look at the two beauties in his back seat. "Well, hello. Where are we headed tonight, girls?"

Anya glanced at Gwynn and then back to the driver. In an even heavier accent than usual, she said, "We will go to dancing club where vodka is from Russia and men are strong. You will take us to place like this, yes?"

The man checked the traffic and pulled onto the street. "I know just the place, but I don't know if you really want to go in there. It's not exactly the environment for a pair of unescorted ladies."

Anya laced her arm through Gwynn's. "We are strong Russian girls, and we are not afraid. Take us to this place."

He shrugged. "Whatever you say, Red Sonja."

They pulled up in front of the club with a pair of shaved heads atop fire hydrant bodies guarding the door, and Anya slipped the driver a pair of bills. "Thank you for ride. You will come for us at midnight, yes?"

The driver looked down at the cash. "You bet I will. I'll be right here when the clock strikes twelve. Have fun in there, but be careful, okay?"

Anya smirked. "Perhaps others inside should be careful of us."

One of the bouncers opened the car door, and Gwynn stepped from inside. Seconds later, Anya let her long, toned legs glide from the back seat, and the bouncer let out a low whistle. "*Krasivyye kotyata.*"

In harsh Russian, Anya growled, "We are not kittens. We are tigers."

The second bouncer held open the door of the club as Anya and Gwynn slinked through the opening and into the darkness and felt the pounding beat of the music inside.

Anya pulled Gwynn tightly against her side. "Is time to find Zhivotnoye, the Animal. You will know him if you see him, yes?"

Gwynn scanned the darkness as her eyes adjusted. "He'll be easy to find. I've never seen him in person, but in every picture, he has a huge, unlit cigar hanging from the corner of his mouth, and his shirt is always unbuttoned halfway down his chest."

Anya whispered, "Dance with me, and we will make the Animal come to us."

"I don't think it works that way. It's far more likely that he'll send for us, but I'll play along."

"You do not speak Russian?"

"A little," Gwynn said, "but definitely not conversational."

"Is okay if you do not understand. Just have same reaction as me. I will not let anyone hurt you."

Gwynn squeezed Anya's arm. "I'm a special agent with the DOJ. I'm not afraid."

"This night, you are not. This night, you are sexy girl in short dress dancing in Russian club with other sexy girl in even shorter dress. Russian men are not like Americans. Remember, *no* means same thing in both languages, but sometimes in Russian, *no* must also come with slap."

"Oh, I can definitely handle that. Now, let's get some attention, shall we?"

Anya stepped onto the dance floor with Gwynn's hand held tightly in hers. "We shall."

Gwynn didn't recognize the Russian techno music, but the beat was enough to drive her inner party girl into a sweaty, gyrating performance against her girlfriend's body as the strobe lights and lasers painted the bodies of the other dancers around them.

Anya never stopped scanning the room except for the two-second intervals during which she watched Gwynn twist and grind in front of her. "You are very good at this."

Gwynn pulled her hair back and looked up at her. "I love to dance. This is so hot."

The track ended, and another even harder song began. A few dancers left the floor and were replaced by others who apparently liked the faster beat. A man of perhaps forty stepped between Anya and Gwynn. His thinning hair was slicked back, and his open-collar black shirt stuck to his sweaty skin.

Anya pressed her body against his and pulled Gwynn against both of them. The three moved in time with the music, pushing the man further into a frenzy with every movement of their hips. His hands took the women's movement as an invitation, and he roamed about their bodies as if he had some license to do whatever he wanted. Anya let him explore without resistance until one of his hands found its way past her thigh and up the inside of her dress.

She caught the man's wrist, pulled it from its target, and clamped his hand in a vicelike grip. He let out a sharp protest, and Anya twisted his hand until the soft tissue of the wrist began to tear and the man crumbled to his knees.

He howled, and she sent a palm strike to his nose, sending him onto his back, blood pouring from his face. She placed a spiked heel against his throat and hissed, "Do not touch without asking permission."

Gwynn didn't understand Anya's Russian, but the tone left little doubt that it was a warning. Before she could add her heel to the threat, the pair of bouncers from the front door parted the crowd and yanked the man to his feet. One of them twisted his arm behind his back and frog-marched him toward the door.

Anya reached for Gwynn and continued dancing as if nothing had happened.

Gwynn looked up. "That was crazy."

"Yes, but was also nice show for the Animal. Do not look now, but he is in corner of room behind you."

They continued dancing until they'd turned a hundred eighty degrees, giving Gwynn a view of the man Anya believed to be their target. Before she realized it had happened, she felt her eyes lock with his, and she offered a timid smile.

The man raised one finger in a come-hither motion and then held up two fingers.

Gwynn whispered, "That's him, and he's motioning us over."

Anya spun to face the man and pulled Gwynn tightly against her body, giving him a show he couldn't buy—not even in the back room where hundred dollar bills and Colombian cocaine were, no doubt, the only currency allowed.

Zhivotnoye, the Animal, leaned toward a young, well-dressed man across from him. "Have you ever seen those two before?"

The younger man focused on Anya and Gwynn as they continued their performance. "No, sir, but it looks like they enjoy being watched."

"That's good," he said, "because I'm enjoying watching them."

The younger man joined his boss as they took in the show. "Shall I bring them over?"

"No, I think they'll come over when they believe they've adequately gotten our attention."

Gwynn leaned against Anya's ear. "Are we going over there?"

"Yes, but we will make them wait a little longer."

She draped her arms across the agent's shoulders and continued showing off for the growing audience.

The music, if it could be called such, ended, and Anya led Gwynn from the dance floor and toward Zhivotnoye.

As they approached, the man with the unlit cigar pushed a dark-haired woman from beside him as if she were nothing more than a fly.

Anya reached down and lifted the glass of clear liquid from in front of the man and poured it down her throat. Ignoring the hatred she held for distilled potatoes, she licked her lip and set the glass back on the table. "*Privet*, you called for us?"

The man patted the empty seat beside him. "*Da, da, privet*. Sit down, join us. I am Zhivotnoye, and this is my friend, Alexi."

Anya took the seat and motioned for Gwynn to sit with the other man across the table.

"That was quite a show you put on for us out there."

Anya glanced back at the dance floor. "You liked watching us dance?"

Zhivotnoye motioned toward his glass and waved his finger in a circular motion across the table. "Another round for us and our new friends."

A cocktail waitress lifted the empty glasses from the table and glared at Anya with an air of distrust, and perhaps even disapproval. She returned seconds later with four glasses and a bottle of Stolichnaya Elit. Zhivotnoye snatched the bottle from her hand and waved for the glasses. The waitress deposited them on the table and vanished.

He removed the top and tossed it into the crowd as he poured the clear liquid into each glass. "This is best vodka in world. Do you know who invented vodka?"

Gwynn winked at the man. "Was it you?"

He roared with laughter. "Ah, I love this one already, but no it was the monks at the Chudov Monastery in the Kremlin in the fourteen hundreds. I could never be a monk. I am a man of hedonism, not humility." He pushed the glasses toward Anya and Gwynn and raised his high into the air. "To the humble monks of the Kremlin!"

The two women and Alexi raised their glasses. "*Monakham, zdorov'ye!*"

Railing against her desire to spit the vodka back into the glass, Anya swallowed the spirit as if it were the best she'd ever tried. "You have very good taste in vodka, but why do you call yourself the Animal?"

Zhivotnoye emptied his glass and poured another. "I do not call myself this name. This is what others call me because I am dangerous man who fears nothing."

Anya hissed, "You fear nothing? Not even me?"

He roared with laughter again. "Why would I fear you? You are only woman."

"You saw what I did to man on dance floor."

His laughter continued. "Man was drunk and foolish. I am neither. I have no reason to fear you."

Anya leaned toward the Animal, withdrew a pair of throwing knives from beneath her dress, and drove the first behind the man's gaudy cufflink at his right wrist, pinning his arm to the table. The other she buried between the man's thumb and index finger, barely missing the flesh.

Alexi drew a Makarov pistol from his waistband, but Gwynn caught the slide of the weapon as he raised it to fire. She shoved the slide to the rear and thumbed the magazine eject. The chambered round flew out of the ejection port and through the air as the magazine fell to the floor between Alexi's feet.

Anya lifted her glass from the table and poured the remaining vodka and ice onto the floor. "You do not summon us. We are not servants. I am Anya, and even animals are smart enough to fear predator."

She stood, took Gwynn's hand, and led her back to the dance floor as the pounding beat of the music continued.

As they danced, Gwynn couldn't resist shooting looks back at the two men at the table. "That was amazing, but why did you threaten him?"

Anya motioned toward the table with her chin. "I did not threaten him. I only introduced myself and left impression he cannot forget. He is telling his boss, the Lion, about us right now."

Gwynn looked to see the man pressing a cell phone against his face and yelling into his cupped hand. "I think you're right. Your plan is working."

"Is not my plan. Is Agent White's. I am merely bait, and fish he wants to catch is taking bait."

11

YA NE MEDSESTRA (I AM NOT NURSE)

To the delight of every man in the club, Anya and Gwynn continued dancing to the never-ending beat as the night wore on. Would-be suitors came, danced, and departed until Alexi, the Animal's young friend, stepped between the two.

He moved in time with Anya and leaned close, his two-day growth of beard brushing against her skin. "Zhivotnoye asked me to tell you he is very sorry for disrespecting you earlier, and he would like to invite you back to the table for another drink."

Anya ran her fingers through Alexi's black hair. "Tell your boss we are thirsty because we have been dancing for him, and we drink first water and then only champagne . . . good champagne."

"Zhivotnoye is my friend, not my boss."

Anya traced the lobe of the man's ear with the tip of her tongue. "We both know this is lie, and you do not have to lie to me. My friend and I like you. Do not make us dislike you with lie, okay?"

Alexi felt his body react to her tongue against his skin. "Okay, I sometimes work for him, but he is still my friend."

Anya pressed her teeth into the flesh of his earlobe. "This is now lie you tell yourself, and is more dangerous than lie to others."

Alexi pulled away. "Fine, I'll tell him. But what about your friend?"

Anya reached around Alexi and pulled Gwynn, still dancing, in front of her. "Where one of us goes, we both go. Is rule we have together."

Alexi nodded. "I like that rule." He pushed his way through the horde of dancers and back to the table with the Animal . . . his boss.

Gwynn nudged Anya. "What was that all about?"

"Zhivotnoye sent his manservant to apologize and ask us to come back."

"Oh, really? And what did you tell him?"

"I told him we only drink water and champagne if we come back."

Gwynn chuckled. "You really are a terrible Russian, aren't you?"

Anya patted her hips and thighs. "I do not have pocket for little American flag."

Gwynn slid her hands down Anya's hips. "You didn't seem to have any trouble finding a spot for your knives."

"Knives are part of body for me."

Gwynn scanned the room. "Judging by the looks you're getting, every guy in the club would love to be one of your knives."

They danced for several more minutes before Anya took Gwynn's hand and led her toward Zhivotnoye's table. When they arrived, the Animal threw his hands into the air. "Ah, I see you've accepted my apology and come back to me."

Anya leaned across the table. "You did not give to us apology."

"Sure, I did. I sent Alexi to tell you I was sorry for disrespecting you."

Anya glanced to Alexi and back at Zhivotnoye. "And this is apology when you send it by someone else?"

"Yes, sure it is."

Anya planted her knee in the seat beside him, allowing her dress to slide up her sweaty thigh. "You are very handsome man. I would like to give to you long, passionate kiss. This is okay with you?"

He licked his lips. "I think you should do exactly what you want."

Anya stood erect, slid around the table, and sat on Alexi's lap, facing the young man. She ran her fingers through his hair for the second time and pulled his lips against hers as she ground her body against him. The kiss lasted nearly a minute before she pulled away, let out a long sigh, and stood. "Now give to Zhivotnoye my kiss because this is how he likes to have things delivered . . . through you, Alexi."

Alexi's eyes darted between Anya and his boss as he sat trying to regain his composure.

Anya drove her fist into the table. "Give to him kiss!"

Zhivotnoye took Anya's hand in his. "Your point is taken. Apologies, like kisses, should be delivered in person, so I am sorry for disrespecting you and your friend earlier. You will accept my apology, yes?"

Anya slid onto the seat beside him and reached for the glass in front of her. "This is only water, yes?"

"Yes, Alexi told me that is what you wanted first before good champagne."

She set the glass in front of him. "You drink first. I am new girl in town, and everyone tell me to be careful, especially in club like this."

He slowly nodded. "I like that. You're a cautious girl."

Anya slid the glass closer to the man. "I am woman. Girl would try drink without challenge."

"Indeed," he said as he lifted the glass to his lips and swallowed at least a fourth of its contents. "Satisfied now, cautious woman?"

She drank the remaining water and slid the second glass toward Gwynn, who did the same.

Small talk ensued, sometimes in Russian, but Anya nudged the conversation back to English to keep her "girlfriend" in the know.

Zhivotnoye pushed a strand of hair out of Anya's face and laced it behind her ear. When he did, his gold Rolex Presidential caught the light, the twelve diamonds glistening as he moved.

Anya took his wrist in her hand. "Is beautiful watch. You are important man, no?"

He shrugged. "Some might say that, but I'm just an immigrant doing my best to get by."

Anya fingered the bezel of the Rolex. "I think you are getting by very well. What do you think, my dear?" She moved his wrist so Gwynn could see the watch.

Gwynn ran her finger across the crown and turned to Alexi. "Where is yours?"

Alexi shot his cuffs, exposing a stainless-steel Rolex Submariner. "I have one, too, but I'm not as flashy as some."

Gwynn unclasped the watch, then slid it from his wrist and onto hers. "And maybe not as rich?"

Alexi watched her fasten the clasp on her thin wrist as the oversized watch slid down to cover the back of Gwynn's hand. "It looks sexy on you. You keep it. I have plenty more."

Zhivotnoye pulled the watch from his wrist and slid it across the table to Alexi. "Take mine. Is gift for friendship."

Alexi slid the twenty-thousand-dollar watch across his hand and glared at Anya. "Friendship, indeed."

Anya leaned down to inspect the watch. "Is *poddelka*."

Zhivotnoye pounded the table, sending glasses in every direction. "How dare you accuse me of wearing a fake Rolex?"

Anya calmly returned the glasses upright. "I wasn't talking about Rolex."

If Alexi's stare had been a dagger, Anya's blood would be pooling at her feet.

She returned the stare with a mocking smile. "Is almost twelve o'clock, and we turn to pumpkin at midnight, so we must go."

"Nonsense," roared Zhivotnoye. "We're just getting started. Stay, stay."

Anya brushed the back of her hand lightly against his clean-shaven face. "I am sorry, we cannot. But we will see you again, yes?" She stood and indicated Gwynn should do the same.

Instead, the agent leaned toward Alexi, parted his lips with the tip of her thumb, and pressed her mouth to his. The two kissed for a long moment before she pulled away and hissed, "Thank you for the watch, friend Alexi."

They left the club without looking back, but the two men couldn't look away as the new girls in town made their exit.

Just as promised, the black Town Car was waiting on the curb. The driver was leaning against the trunk, smoking a cigarette and people-watching. He checked his watch and saw Anya and Gwynn leaving the club, then held the door for them, noticing the sweat on their skin and hair.

He closed the door and slid behind the wheel. "It looks like you ladies had quite a night."

Gwynn let out a long sigh. "It was amazing. We danced for hours."

The driver shot a look into the mirror. "Just danced, huh? It looks like you two ran a marathon. There's some bottled water in the bar back there. Help yourselves."

Anya swallowed the contents of a bottle and turned to look out the rear window. "Do not take us back to apartment. Turn right and then left at every intersection."

The driver shrugged. "Whatever you say. Are you expecting a tail?"

Anya said, "No, I am *hoping* for tail."

The driver made alternating turns as she'd instructed, and Anya watched cars continue through the intersections while a dark sedan followed them through every turn.

"Take us to darkest corner in city."

The driver checked the mirror again. "Okay, but if you get us jacked, you're paying for the car."

"Tell me when turn is coming at darkest corner."

"Okay, lady. Here it comes."

Anya leaned against Gwynn and whispered instructions just before the driver made the turn. As the Town Car rounded the corner, Anya kicked off her shoes, pulled the handle, and shoved open the door. Seconds later, she was rolling across the dark pavement.

Gwynn yanked the door closed and leaned across the front seat. "Get us around the block as fast as this thing will go, and stop as soon as we get back to that corner. Got it?"

The driver sent the accelerator to the floor, and the heavy car picked up speed. The driver of the sedan giving chase followed suit and kept pace with them. Tires barked their protests as they rounded three more corners, ignoring stop signs and traffic lights. Back at the corner where Anya had rolled from the car, the driver slammed the brakes, and the driver of the following sedan had to swerve to avoid the collision.

The driver of the sedan leapt from his car, pistol in hand, and headed for the Town Car. As he approached, he raised the pistol, aiming at the driver's head. "What is game you are playing? Get out of car!"

Out of the darkness, Anya's blade sank into the back of the gunman's hand, sending the pistol skidding across the asphalt. He yelled in agony and yanked the blade from his hand. Turning to find the source of the flying knife, he stepped into Anya's knee-shot to his crotch and melted to the ground. Before his body had come to rest on the pavement, Anya landed on his back with one knee at the base of his skull and a second knife pressed against his side. The man writhed beneath her in a wasted effort to escape.

She pressed the blade deeper against his side. "If you move again, you will bleed to death in street."

The man froze. "What do you want?"

"Why are you following us?" she demanded.

He grunted. "Get off of me. You do not know who you are messing with."

She lifted the knife she'd thrown from the pavement and pressed it against the inside of the man's upper thigh. "I am messing with you, and you will be dead soon if you do not tell me why you are following me."

Detecting her accent, the man switched to Russian. "You know exactly why I'm following you, and even if you kill me, somebody else will take my place."

She pressed her chin to his shoulder, and with her lips an inch from the man's ear, she said, "My name is Anya. Say it!"

"Your name is Anya."

"That is correct. And I am worst nightmare for weak man like you."

She sent her foot down the man's leg, kicking his shoe from his foot. In one swift motion, she leapt from his back and drove her knife through the bottom of his foot until the glistening tip protruded through the top, leaving blood pouring from wounds.

The man howled like a dying animal, and Anya rolled him onto his back. "You have choice to make. No one is going to help you. You will tie tourniquet around ankle to stop bleeding, or you will die. If you stand, you will bleed more and die faster. Choice is yours, but before you die, you will tell your boss my name. Do you understand?"

"I don't know how," the man groaned.

"You do not know how to do what?"

"I don't know how to tie a tourniquet. Do it for me, please."

Anya growled. "I am not nurse. I am Avenging Angel. You will do it, or you will die."

As she walked away, leaving the bleeding man writhing in the street, she saw Gwynn standing beside the Town Car and staring at the man who was only minutes away from passing out and never seeing the sun again. "You can't leave him like that. He'll bleed to death."

"I told him to tie tourniquet."

"He's in shock, Anya. Is that really what we're doing? Killing people in the street because they're following us on orders from the people we're really after?"

Anya turned back to her victim, retrieved the pistol he'd dropped when her blade sank into the back of his hand, and knelt near his punctured foot. She fieldstripped the pistol, removing the barrel, and yanked the laces from his remaining shoe. With two quick wraps, she encircled his ankle, tied a knot, and slid the barrel of the pistol behind the knot. "This is beginning of tourniquet. Make tighter every five minutes by turning gun barrel one half turn . . . or you can die alone in darkness."

12

ZHELANIYE SMERTI
(DEATH WISH)

Back in the Town Car, Anya retrieved her shoes and leaned forward to lay her head on the top of the front seat. "What did you see?"

The driver raised his head and turned to meet Anya's gaze. "I saw you try to save a man's life who was bleeding to death in the street."

Anya let her hand fall across the driver's shoulder. "This is exactly what you saw, and now man's blood is on your jacket. This means you must also have helped me save his life, or maybe you cut him, and only I saved life. Is up to you, but is better if we do not tell any story, yes?"

The man cleared his throat. "Like I said, ma'am, I didn't see a thing. The two beautiful women I picked up at the club and dropped at their building looked like they had a great night out, and the ride was quiet and uneventful."

She planted a kiss on the driver's cheek and deposited a nice tip onto the seat beside him.

When they stepped from the car, both women were disappointed to see that Michael wasn't on the door, but an equally impressive physical specimen held the door for them.

"Good evening, ladies. I hope you had an enjoyable night on the town. Are you in for the evening, or will you be needing another car?"

Gwynn let her hand fall on top of his on the ornate handle of the door. "We're in for the night, and you're not Michael."

"No, ma'am. I'm Nick, the midnight-to-six man."

"It's nice to meet you, midnight-to-six man. Enjoy your shift."

As the elevator doors closed, Anya cast a disapproving look. "What was game with new doorman?"

"Oh, I was just having some fun. My job is the epitome of boring most of the time, but since you showed up, all of that's changed, and I'm loving every minute of it. Well, almost every minute. I'm not sure I'll ever get used to you sticking knives in people."

"If person is trying to kill us, he is no longer person. He is target. This must be how you think when you are on street."

Gwynn slid her key into the door, and Anya grabbed her forearm. "Wait!"

Gwynn froze, and Anya ran her hand along the line where the top edge of the door met the casing. She plucked a barely visible hair from the crease and held it up for the young agent to see. "Is good. No one opened door while we were gone."

"That's brilliant. Where did you learn that little trick?"

"Is basic tradecraft. Remember, I was once Russian spy."

With skintight dresses exchanged for T-shirts and yoga pants, Anya delivered a piping-hot mug of chamomile tea. "This will help you fall asleep after exciting night."

Gwynn took the mug in both hands. "Thank you. Hey, can I ask you something?"

Anya nestled onto the opposite end of the couch. "My English is not perfect, but I think you already did ask me something by asking if you could ask."

Gwynn blew across the surface of the tea and took a tentative sip. "I guess you're right, but what's going to happen next?"

"Next, we are drinking tea and going to bed."

"You know what I mean."

"Yes, I know," Anya said. "Next, we wait for word on street to get back to Zhivotnoye about Russian woman with knives. When this happens, he will have no choice. He will have to tell his boss, Leo, about me . . . and probably about us."

Gwynn let the upcoming sequence of events play out in her imagination. "What do you think will happen when you, or we, meet Leo?"

Anya let the hot tea melt down her throat and enjoyed the sensation. "Russian mafia is dangerous animal. Men like Leo use everyone around them to get what they want, and that is always one of three things."

Gwynn raised her mug. "Women, money, and dead enemies."

"You are not as naïve as you pretend to be."

Gwynn raised an eyebrow. "Thank you, I think."

"Is compliment. When we are *taken* to Leo—and this is how it will happen, we will be taken to him—he will first think maybe we are just women. For men like him, women are throwaway things, like diapers. He uses them and throws them in trash. We will not be this for him."

Gwynn took a long sip. "If he thinks we're just women, what do we do to keep from being that?"

"We will kill someone for him. This is only way to prove to him we are valuable for more than pretty face."

"Yeah, but we are pretty."

"Yes, we are very pretty, but pretty girls are in every direction here." She drew the smallest of her throwing knives, stirred her tea with the tip, then licked the blade clean. "I can give to Leo something he cannot so easily get. Assassin."

Gwynn finished her tea and turned to Anya. "What about me? What do I have to offer him?"

"This I do not know yet, but I think you have admirer."

"An admirer?"

"Yes, I think Alexi likes kiss with you better than me."

Gwynn blushed. "I don't know about that. He seemed to enjoy having you in his lap and your tongue down his throat. By the way, that was some point you made that apologies should come from the source. Nicely done."

"This was spur-of-moment idea. Is very dangerous to do. Is always best to have plan and only do plan."

Gwynn bit the edge of her bottom lip. "I kind of hate to bring this up, but I think it might be a good idea for us to work on your use of English articles."

Anya swirled the remains of her tea. "Yes, we should do this. When I was taught English in state school—*the* state school—this was difficult for me, but I know rules of language. Is habit."

"If you want, I'll remind you. It seems like a fair trade, right? You teach me to kill people, and I teach you when to say *the*, *a*, and *an*."

"Is fair. I am now going to the bed. Have good night."

Gwynn chuckled. "Actually, there was no *the* needed before bed in that sentence, but I don't know the rule for that one. Good night, Anya, and thanks for *accidentally* dragging me into this operation."

* * *

Special Agent Gwynn Davis watched the sun break the eastern horizon as she wrestled with the endless fear, doubt, questions, and excitement playing through her mind. South Beach was still asleep, with the exception of early morning fitness buffs jogging, biking, or skating their way north and south beneath the window. A few delivery trucks were parked haphazardly, while their drivers carted kegs of beer and cases of liquor to the clubs and restaurants lining the western sidewalk of Ocean Drive.

Her watch said ten past seven. Agent Ray White would be having his third, or likely, his fourth cup of black acid he called coffee. She dialed the number.

"White."

"Good morning. It's Agent Davis."

"Ah, Davis. I heard you had quite the night on the town. Let's hear your version."

Gwynn cleared her throat and glanced down the short hallway, ensuring Anya's door was still closed. "We met Zhivotnoye and a guy named Alexi. Anya is amazing. You should've seen her."

"I have no doubt. I didn't expect you to make contact this quickly, but I can't really say I'm surprised. Tell me about the excitement with the tail after the club."

Gwynn frowned. "How did you know about that?"

"Just tell me what happened, Davis."

She laid out the details of the late-night encounter, and he listened intently.

When Gwynn finished, White asked, "So, do you think she was going to let the guy bleed out in the street?"

"I think she has a philosophy."

White sighed. "Oh? I can't wait to hear this."

"I think she believes in preserving life until someone threatens to kill her or someone she cares about. After that, there are no rules."

White leaned forward in his chair as if his subordinate were sitting across the desk from him. "You listen to me, Davis, and you listen good. That woman isn't capable of compassion or caring for anybody. She doesn't have it in her. She's not like the rest of us. She's a killer, and she'll use everything and everyone in her environment to do exactly what she wants to do. Don't fall into her trap. She doesn't give a . . ."

"Oh, good morning, Anya. We were just talking about you."

Anya stretched, offered Gwynn a brief smile, and headed for the kitchen.

Davis turned back to her phone. "I know she's dangerous, Agent White, but I think she might be more human than you're giving her credit for."

"Davis, listen to me. That woman stopped being human when she was six years old. The Soviets cut her open, yanked out her soul, and turned an innocent little girl into a killing machine for the Rodina. She's trained to seduce everyone who crosses her path, including you, and there may be no one on Earth better at it than she is. I'm warning you. If I get the slightest feeling she's sucking you in, I'll yank you out of there faster than you can say *proshchay*."

"Okay, I hear you, boss. I'll be careful. But I do have a request."

"What is it?"

"I need some clothes. I wasn't supposed to be in on this thing. I was just supposed to get her settled and head back to Virginia. I have three sets of clothes. If I'm staying, I need to go shopping, or you'll have to send me something to wear."

White chewed on the inside of his jaw. "I'm still not sold on the idea of you staying inside this one, but it would be tough for Anya to come up with answers when the Bratva starts asking about the American brunette. I'll have the Miami Field Office deliver a package this morning. Don't leave the apartment until they arrive. Got it?"

"I'll stay right here. Thanks, boss."

"Don't thank me, Davis. Just keep your eyes open, and don't be gullible."

Anya emerged from the kitchen with a mug of tea and her hair pulled back into a loose ponytail. "That was Agent White, yes?"

"Yes, it was Agent White. He's my boss, and I have to check in regularly."

Anya yawned and took a cautious sip. "He told you I am dangerous, and you cannot trust me, yes?"

Gwynn pocketed the phone. "Yeah, that's exactly what he said, but he said something else that bothers me a little."

"What is it?"

Gwynn sat on an overstuffed chair near the window. "He knew about the encounter with the guy last night. The one you stabbed in the street."

"Of course he did. Driver is FBI."

Gwynn sat up. "What? How do you know that?"

"Is driving technique taught to American FBI and CIA. He might be now retired, but he was once agent."

"He was once *an* agent," Gwynn said.

Anya parted the blinds to look out over the beach. "Is too early for English lesson. I will have tea, and we will go for *a* run, yes?"

"Nicely done," Gwynn said, "but I don't have running clothes. In fact, I don't have any clothes. Agent White is having someone from the Miami Field Office bring me something this morning. We're supposed to stay inside the apartment until they come."

"We or you?"

Gwynn cocked her head. "What?"

"You said *we* are supposed to stay inside apartment. Did you mean both of us?"

"Yes, that's what Agent White said."

Anya emptied her mug and headed for her bedroom. "I will be back to apartment after my run."

* * *

When Anya returned, she found Davis pushing the couch against the wall. "What are you doing?"

Gwynn looked up. "I'm getting ready for today's lesson. You've been running for an hour, so maybe I'll have a chance."

"Did FBI man come with clothes?"

Gwynn stopped and stood erect. "Just say *the*. Just say it. It's not that hard. Did *the* FBI agent come with *the* clothes?"

Anya smiled. "Maybe I am tired from running, but you are tired inside brain . . . inside *your* brain. This means I have already won."

Gwynn dropped her head. "I'm sorry. I know it's not really that important, but—"

Anya stepped between Gwynn's feet, hooked her left ankle with her heel, and sent the agent thudding to the floor, flat on her back. Using the shock of the instant, Anya continued the assault, rolling Gwynn facedown and pinning her to the floor with one knee between her shoulders and another on the back of her right thigh. "You were preparing room for fighting, and yet you were not prepared to fight. This must change. Fight will come when you look down or when you relax."

With her face pressed against the floor, Gwynn groaned. "You meant *a* fight. You left out the *a*, but that isn't all you forgot."

Anya smiled and pressed her student harder into the floor. "What do you think I forgot?"

Gwynn's reply came through clenched teeth. "You forgot to control my gun hand."

Anya stared down into the barrel of a Glock 19, and its nine-millimeter muzzle stared back from beside Gwynn's hip with her thumb resting precariously against the trigger.

The Russian eased the pressure and allowed Gwynn to roll onto her back, but the muzzle of the pistol never left its potential target.

Pleased with her student, Anya helped her to her feet and grabbed the Glock's slide, shoving it backward a quarter inch as she demanded, "Pull trigger!"

"No! What's wrong with you? Have you got some sort of death wish or something?"

"Pull the trigger. I use English article, so do it. Pull the trigger."

Gwynn struggled to pull the pistol from Anya's grip. "I am not going to shoot you."

"This is right. You will not shoot me. Now, pull the trigger. I will step to side—*the* side—so you cannot shoot me. Now, pull the trigger."

Anya cleared the centerline and held the Glock's slide still barely out of battery, and Gwynn met her frozen glare. "You really want me to pull the trigger, *and* you'll pay for the damage to the apartment?"

"Yes, I will pay for all damage and will pay you ten times amount to repair apartment."

Gwynn squinted, turned her head in preparation for the convulsive shot, and squeezed. The familiar break of the trigger mechanism came, and the sound of the spring launching the firing pin came, but what didn't come was the explosion of the primer and powder and the exodus of the hollow-point projectile from the brass casing.

Muscle memory and hundreds of hours of range time sent Special Agent Gwynn Davis's hands into action. Slap. Rack. Reengage. She yanked the Glock from Anya's grip and slapped the palm of her left hand into the bottom of the magazine, ensuring it was well-seated in the weapon. A split-second later, she racked the slide, ejecting the round that should've fired when she pulled the trigger, and sent the next round from the magazine into battery in the pistol's chamber. Before she could reengage and pull the trigger again, Anya drove the weapon to the left with unimaginable speed. The sweeping motion ripped the pistol from Gwynn's single-handed grip. Anya let her momentum carry her through a three-hundred-sixty-degree pirouette that ended with the sights of the pistol centered on Davis's nose.

Gwynn froze in disbelief, still astonished her weapon hadn't fired when she pulled the trigger. After countless thousands of rounds through the pistol, the Glock had never failed to fire . . . until Anastasia Burinkova put her hands on it.

"Do not look at the weapon. It cannot hurt you. It is only a machine. I am the killer. Look at me."

Mesmerized, Gwynn locked her eyes on the Russian's, awaiting the coming lesson.

"Do exactly as I tell you," Anya insisted. "Step with right foot, and plant foot beneath my right elbow."

Gwynn did so, and suddenly, the weapon was pointing across her right shoulder. Even if Anya pulled the trigger, she wouldn't be hit. The sound of the explosion would be deafening, but she wouldn't bleed.

"Now, reach up with right hand, grab slide of pistol firmly, and push backward toward my hand."

She followed the instruction to the letter and felt the slide move backward, perhaps a quarter inch, separating the slide from the chambered round. The instant the slide moved ever so slightly to the rear, Anya pulled the trigger, and the weapon clicked but didn't fire.

Gwynn's jaw dropped in amazement, and Anya released her grip on the pistol, surrendering it back to its rightful owner.

"I do not have death wish. I have wish to never die, and have same wish for you."

13

SROCHNAYA DOSTAVKA
(SPECIAL DELIVERY)

With the couch back in its place and a new addition to Agent Gwynn Davis's skill set fresh in her head, the doorbell rang.

Gwynn leapt to her feet. "That must be my special delivery."

Anya watched her as she reached the door and peered through the peephole. "Who is it?"

The man on the other side of the door held up his FBI credentials to the peephole. "Do you really want me to identify myself right here in the hallway of your apartment?"

Gwynn unlocked the door and swung it inward.

The man held out a small white envelope. "I assume you're Davis."

Gwynn took the envelope. "I am, thank you."

The man peered across Gwynn's shoulder and into the apartment. "Where's your roommate?"

"What roommate?"

He said, "You're what, maybe twenty-seven?"

Gwynn put her hands on her hips. "Twenty-eight, and why do you ask?"

"It's just that you're too inexperienced to be on assignment without adult supervision, so I figured you must have a babysitter in there somewhere."

Gwynn opened the envelope and pulled an American Express card from inside. "How old are you, Agent Amex?"

"As if it's any of your business, I'm forty-one."

"Hmm, imagine that," Gwynn said. "A forty-four-year-old FBI agent reduced to delivery boy. Maybe I'm not the one who needs the babysitter after all."

The man huffed. "I said I was forty-one."

Gwynn winked. "Yeah, I know that's what you said, but it was a lie. It's two thousand and three, and your class ring says nineteen seventy-nine, so unless you were some kind of boy genius who graduated from college at fourteen, you're at least forty-four." She swung the door toward the jamb. "Goodbye, Agent Pinocchio. Don't let me close your nose in the door."

Gwynn pocketed the Amex and headed back for the living room.

Anya looked up. "What was all of that?"

"Oh, I was just having some fun with an FBI agent. Those guys are so predictable. He called me inexperienced and said I needed a babysitter."

"He is right."

Gwynn scowled. "What?"

"I said he is right. You are inexperienced, and I am your babysitter."

"Yeah, but he couldn't have known that just by looking at me."

Anya motioned toward the door. "He knew you were inexperienced be-cause you looked through hole in door to see who was on other side. I mean, who was on *the* other side."

"What do you mean? That's what peepholes are for."

Anya stood. "Come with me, and I will show you."

Gwynn followed her to the door. "Stand in hall and look at hole in door. This is named peephole, yes?"

"Yes, it's a peephole," she said as she stepped into the hallway.

With the door almost closed, Anya said, "Do you see light through peephole?"

"*The* peephole. And yes, I see light."

Anya placed her cheek against the door and peered through the tiny window. "Do you now see light through *the* peephole?"

"No, it went dark."

"This means I am looking through and blocking light. This means you know where to put bullet if you want to send it into my brain."

Gwynn sighed. "I'll never look through another peephole as long as I live."

Anya pulled the door open. "You are learning tradecraft, and I will maybe have my wish that you will not die."

"Why don't they teach us this stuff at the Academy?"

"I think maybe your country has too many kinds of police. In Russia, even the local police know these things. Everyone is trained to be always aware of danger around them."

"It's *your* country now, too," Gwynn said.

Anya pulled the plastic flag from her pocket. "Yes, is my country, too."

Gwynn held up the Amex. "I don't know about you, girlfriend, but I'm going shopping."

Michael arranged for the same Town Car and driver.

"Good morning, ladies. It's good to see you two outside in the daylight. I was beginning to believe you might be vampires who only come out at night."

"How lucky we are to have same driver again. What are chances of this?"

The man nodded. "*Htoby vsyo byla harashoh.*"

Anya turned to Gwynn. "This mean 'so everything goes well' in Russian. It also means our driver is CIA and not FBI."

The driver threw up his hands. "I don't know what you're talking about. I'm just the son of immigrants, lady. Now, where would you like to go this morning? It's a little too early for clubbing, if you ask me."

"We would like to go shopping," Anya said. "We have our favorite uncle's credit card, but first, we would like to know your name since it feels as if you will be here as long as we are."

He touched the brim of his cap. "Here's to favorite uncles and their credit cards. And you can call me Claude."

Two hours and four thousand dollars later, Anya fidgeted in a poorly padded chair outside a boutique dressing room.

Gwynn emerged in a dress that would be impossible for any man to ignore. "What do you think?"

"Is nice. Looks good on you."

Gwynn ignored the mirror. "What's wrong? It's almost like you don't enjoy a girl's shopping trip."

"Is first time for me."

"What do you mean it's your first time? Surely you've been shopping with girlfriends."

"I do not have girlfriends."

Gwynn smoothed the dress. "You mean a real girlfriend, not like friends who are girls, right?"

Anya lifted the price tag from beneath Gwynn's arm. "I do not have friends who are girls, and also, I do not have girlfriend."

Gwynn glanced down at the tag and saw the four-figure price. "Oh! I've got to get out of this thing. There's no way Uncle Sam will foot the bill for one dress that's almost two grand."

Anya took Gwynn's hand. "I will buy for you. You are my friend who is girl, yes?"

"No, I can't let you do that. It's too much."

Anya squeezed her hand. "I want to buy it for you. I have enough money for this. My father left for me money when he died, and also, I have money from doing job."

"But it's eighteen hundred dollars."

Anya playfully pushed Gwynn toward the dressing room. "Take off dress. I will buy. If you do not wear, I will. It will look better on me anyway."

Gwynn returned with the dress hanging across her arm. "Are you sure about this? I mean, it's really a lot of money, but I do love it."

Anya pulled the dress from her arm. "I will hold so you cannot change your mind."

Uncle Sam's card covered the stack of reasonable items Gwynn could justify on her expense report, but Anya's black Mastercard drawn against her Cayman Island account did the job as the most beautiful dress Gwynn had ever seen found its way into a designer hanging bag.

The clerk asked, "Will you be taking the dress with you, or would you prefer to have it delivered?"

Claude answered for them as he stepped through the front door of the shop. "We'll be taking it with us, but we'd prefer to take it out the back if that's all right with you."

Anya's mind turned from girlfriend to assassin in an instant as she scanned the street. Gwynn did the same and reached for her Glock.

"What is problem on street?"

Claude checked across his shoulder. "No problem. Just somebody you probably don't want checking up on you. I'll take your bags and meet you behind the shop. Don't open the door until I knock."

The driver nonchalantly returned to the Town Car with an armload of bags, pretending to ignore the man on the opposite sidewalk. Meanwhile, the clerk led Anya and Gwynn through the back of the shop.

Gwynn said, "I'm sorry for the trouble, but thanks for helping us out. There's a guy—"

The clerk cut her off. "No worries. I know exactly how it is. I've got a crazy ex-boyfriend, too. You're lucky to have that driver guy to look out for you, though. I wasn't so lucky."

She turned and pulled up her shirt, revealing two dozen round scars on her back. "Cigarette burns because he thought I was cheating on him. I wasn't, but I couldn't make him believe that."

Claude's knock came at the oversized door, and Gwynn pushed it open. "Let's go. We don't have much time."

Gwynn followed Claude's order, but Anya took the clerk by the hands. "Boyfriend who did this to you . . . he is gone now, yes?"

The clerk stared at her feet. "Not really. He still comes around sometimes. It was probably at least some of my fault. I mean, I didn't . . ."

"Give to me pen."

Anya took the pen from the clerk and hurriedly scribbled on a scrap of paper by the door. "Next time boyfriend tries to hurt you, call me, and I will make him go away forever. I am very good at this."

She shoved the paper into the clerk's hand and joined Gwynn in the back of the car.

"Who was in front of store?" Anya asked.

Claude checked the mirrors and accelerated from the alley. "It was Alexi Pendropov. I think you met him in the club with Zhivotnoye. He's a low-level enforcer who's trying to move up in the organization. He's rumored to have pulled off a couple of hits in the last twelve months, but nobody's been able to pin anything on him other than some misdemeanor stuff."

Anya scanned the street behind them. "Was he following us?"

"No, I think it was just an unlucky crossing of paths. He was in the cigar bar across the street when we pulled up. I didn't notice him, but he picked you two out of the crowd. You are hard to miss, but I think it was all a coincidence."

Anya settled back into her seat. "Maybe next time coincidence happens, you will let us *accidentally* bump into him. We can use this happy accident to get closer to Zhivotnoye."

Claude checked the mirror. "Yeah, I thought the same thing, but you probably don't want him knowing where you live, right?"

"This is true for now, but time will come when this is unavoidable."

Claude continued scanning the mirrors. "I don't see a tail, so I don't think he's following us."

Gwynn took her turn peering through the back glass. "Just in case, why don't we cross the causeway and pull an SDR?"

Claude hit the blinker. "Whatever you say. I'm just the driver."

Anya grinned. "Surveillance detection route is good tradecraft. Good thinking. I am proud of you."

Gwynn shrugged. "I may not make a habit of sticking knives into people, but I know a little."

Twenty-five minutes into the SDR, Claude pulled to a stop inside a multi-level parking garage. "Are you satisfied there's no tail?"

Anya nodded. "Yes, but you pulled into garage where we are cornered. This is terrible plan."

"Actually," Claude said, "there are four exits from this particular garage. Like your friend there, I may not be in the habit of sticking knives into folks on the street, but *Ya znayu, nemnogo.*"

Anya laid her hand across Claude's shoulder. "I have feeling you know more than a little."

"So, is it back to the apartment for you ladies?"

Gwynn shot a look toward Anya. "Yes, please take us home, Claude. We have another exciting night to get ready for."

14

POLUCHENIYE VNIMANIYA
(GETTING ATTENTION)

Michael met the Town Car at the curb with a rolling cart and hauled the day's trophies up to the apartment. "It looks like you had quite a shopping trip."

Gwynn stuffed a folded bill in his hand. "I'm new to the climate in South Beach. My sweaters and boots don't exactly fit in down here."

Michael pocketed the tip without inspecting it. "From what I've seen, you make everything look amazing. Let me know if there's anything else I can do for you." He vanished as quickly as he'd appeared.

Anya stuck her head into Gwynn's room. "I think he likes you."

Gwynn rolled her eyes. "I think he likes anything in a skirt. What time are we going out?"

Anya checked her watch. "Maybe around nine. Is this good for you?"

* * *

Just after nine, Gwynn emerged and turned the short hallway of the apartment into a Paris runway. Anya did her best catcall, but apparently, Russian cats call a little differently.

Gwynn screwed up her face. "Thanks . . . I think."

Anya grinned. "That was terrible, I know, but you look amazing. No one will notice me tonight at club. At *the* club."

Gwynn curtsied. "Thank you, but you know that isn't true. You're hotter in sweatpants and a ratty old T-shirt than most women after a day at the salon. I'd kill to look like you."

"You are beautiful woman, Gwynn. I have only different look here in South Beach. In Eastern Europe, I am like everyone else with blonde hair and fair skin, but you have dark eyes and hair with this skin. Your parents are maybe from Cuba or South America, no?"

"My mother is from Spain, and my dad is Greek, so I'm kind of a Mediterranean mutt."

"Is perfect look for South Beach. Let's go have some fun."

Gwynn picked up the phone. "I'll call down and have Michael get Claude."

"No, not tonight. We will take Porsche."

* * *

They pulled up in front of the club and stepped out of the sports car to the lustful stares of men and the ire of women standing in line. The valet took the keys, and one of the bouncers on the door motioned for Anya and Gwynn to ignore the line. Despite the groans and scowls, they took advantage of the bouncer's insistence.

The club looked the same as the night before, but the behavior of the bouncers was unquestionably different.

One of them took Anya's arm and spoke in Georgian-accented Russian. "Zhivotnoye instructed me to bring you to his table when you arrive, so please, come with me."

Anya pressed a thumb into the man's throat and pulled her arm free of his grasp. "I will not be delivered to any man, and you will never again touch me. You understand this, yes?"

The man took a step closer to her. "I can deliver you to Zhivotnoye, or I can throw you and your friend into the street. It is up to you."

Anya reached for Gwynn's hand and raised her arm above her head. The bruises from their hand-to-hand training were obvious beneath Gwynn's bicep. "If you put hands on me again, Zhivotnoye will know that you made these bruises on my friend. We now have understanding, no?"

"I never touched her," the man demanded.

"Is word of you against word of me. Take your chances. We are going to dance, and you are going to tell Zhivotnoye we will come to his table when we see water and good champagne, but not before."

Anya led Gwynn beneath the pulsating lights and into the rhythmic beat of the dance floor, and the pair began their performance.

A fifty-something man with an extra forty pounds protruding over his belt took Gwynn's hand and leaned in. "Nice dress. I think it would look even nicer on the floor of my hotel room."

Before Gwynn could react, the man collapsed to the floor, and Alexi Pendropov stood in his place with the man's hand pressed beneath his Italian loafers. "I apologize for this man's rudeness. He will not bother you again."

Gwynn eyed the man on the floor and then looked up at Alexi. "Thank you. That's sweet of you. Would you like to join us?"

Alexi looked between Anya and Gwynn. "Thank you, no, but Zhivotnoye would like for you to know that ice water and Dom Pérignon will be waiting for you when you would like refreshments."

Gwynn planted a delicate kiss on his cheek and whispered, "Thank you again for taking care of"—she shot a look to the floor—"him. My girlfriend would've probably killed him."

Alexi stared at Anya. "Your girlfriend sounds like a dangerous woman. Maybe I should be afraid."

"Maybe you should," Gwynn breathed, and turned back to rejoin Anya.

Twenty minutes later, Gwynn tugged at Anya's arm. "I have to go to the ladies' room. Come with me."

Anya followed Gwynn from the dance floor and leaned in. "I will meet you at bar when you are finished."

Gwynn's eyes widened. "Are you sure it's safe for us to separate?"

"I can see bathroom door from here. I will watch for you."

"Whatever you say. I'll be right back."

Gwynn disappeared into the ladies' room while Anya ordered water at the bar.

Gwynn could hear the sounds of the club even inside the bathroom stall. Another woman stood at the sink, washing her hands and checking her makeup. Through the crack in the stall door, she watched two men in dark suits, with tattoos protruding from their cuffs, push their way through the door. One of the men grabbed the lady from the sink and forced her back through the door and into the club. Gwynn watched as the man turned the deadbolt lock behind him.

Get in here, Anya. I need you.

She instantly regretted not insisting that Anya come with her. She was cornered—trapped inside a tiny room with no weapon and no way to escape.

Don't get distracted. Focus on the fight. Find a weapon. Where the hell is Anya?

Never taking her eyes off the suited men outside the door for more than a few seconds at a time, Gwynn scanned the interior of the stall for anything she could use as a weapon. Realizing there was nothing in the stall she could use, she pulled the paper from the roll and mentally prepared for whatever was about to happen.

As the paper came off the roll, the tell-tale sound of metal against metal came in repetitious clicks. She pulled the roll from the brackets and discovered a stainless-steel shaft about the diameter of a pencil. Both ends were blunt, but it was better than nothing. She slid the roll over one of the brackets and palmed the steel shank.

Anya watched the two men enter the ladies' room, and seconds later, saw the woman being forced through the door. She reached beneath her dress and withdrew a throwing knife small enough to conceal in her palm and behind her wrist. She slipped from the bar and made her way through the darkness to the hallway leading to the bathrooms.

The lady who'd been thrown out grabbed at Anya's arm. "You don't want to go in there right now."

Anya eyed the woman. "Are you hurt?"

"No, I'm okay, but there's a couple of guys in there and a woman in one of the stalls. You should really stay out."

"Is okay. I will tell them I really have to go."

She pressed against the door and felt the resistance of the deadbolt. The heavy door refused to move. Anya glanced back down the hallway toward the club. No one was approaching, so she wedged her knife into the jamb and pried at the bolt. The wood splintered in shards as she pried, but the bolt held fast.

Inside the bathroom, Gwynn stood, swallowed the lump in her throat, and pushed open the stall door. The two men stepped to within inches as she stood in the doorway. "We do not want to hurt you. We only want to take you to someone who wants to talk with you."

Gwynn gritted her teeth. "I'm warning you. Don't put your hands on me. I'm walking out of here, and you're going to step aside while I do."

The closer of the two men reached for her wrist. She let him take it and then raised her hand high into the air, exposing the man's ribs. With a rapid underarm swing, she drove the stainless-steel shaft into his armpit, sending the man staggering backward with blood pouring down his side.

With the fight now one-on-one, Gwynn liked the improved odds. The second man shot the briefest of glances toward his partner, and Anya's lesson about distractions during a fight came pouring back. Gwynn lunged forward with her weapon high and aimed for the man's eye. He caught her approach and sent a forearm racing through the air to deflect the coming blow. The steel shank flew from Gwynn's grip and rattled to a stop inside the porcelain sink. The block sent Gwynn spinning to her right. Just as she'd practiced dozens of times inside the apartment, she used the momentum of the spin to throw an elbow strike.

The man stumbled backward, crashing into a metal trash can, and Gwynn took advantage of the opening to rush the door. Her thumb and index finger grasped the deadbolt at the same instant the bleeding man's tactical baton struck the base of her neck. Her eyes didn't close, but she crashed to the ground, though not before the deadbolt receded into its base beneath her grasp.

Anya felt the door give way from the other side, and she drove her shoulder into the heavy barricade. The crushing collision shoved Gwynn's semi-conscious body deeper into the room and left Anya face-to-face with the raised baton. She thrust the throwing knife skyward in a desperate attempt to slow the falling strike. The blade grazed the inside of the man's arm and sent the baton sliding down Anya's left side.

Gwynn watched through the haze of her condition as the fight continued.

Anya shoved a forearm into the man's throat and drove him backward until he was pinned in the corner where the wall met the partition of the stall. The second man rejoined the fight as he gathered his wits and charged Anya, but she sent a mule kick to his gut, doubling him over.

She withdrew a second knife from beneath her dress and slid it across the floor toward Gwynn. "Kill him if he gets up!"

Gwynn retrieved the knife and shook the cobwebs from her head. Her knees lacked the stability to support her weight, so she slid across the floor with the blade extended in front of her. The man groaned and tried to scamper to his feet.

"Kill him!" Anya demanded, and Gwynn dug her heel into the ceramic tile floor, desperately trying to find purchase to launch her attack. She found the brace she needed as her heel met the edge of the door that was still ajar. She bent her knee, pressed hard, and lunged for the man who was crouched like a frog in front of her.

An instant before the blade found its mark, the porcelain sink exploded after the hiss of a suppressed pistol sounded from the doorway.

Before anyone could react to the gunshot, Gwynn's blade entered the man's abdomen just above his navel. As the blood began to pool on the cold tile floor, Anya and Gwynn turned to see Alexi Pendropov standing in the doorway with smoke rising from the muzzle of his suppressed Makarov.

"Enough!" he demanded. "Put down the knife, and let him go." His tone was calm but firm, the voice of a man who knew he was in command of the environment and possessed the tools and skill to retain that command.

Anya let her knife fall to the floor, and she stepped back, allowing her prisoner to pull himself from the corner. Gwynn turned, still without the strength to stand, and stared up at Alexi, her hand dripping with her victim's blood.

Anya glared at him. "Why did you make us do this?"

Alexi turned the gun on the Russian. "Pull your dress above your waist. Do it now!"

Anya sighed and lifted the hem of her dress to reveal two more throwing knives strapped to her upper thigh.

Alexi motioned toward the blades with his muzzle. "Take those from her."

The man who'd been pinned into the corner tentatively reached for the knives and slid them from their elastic band.

Alexi waved the pistol at Gwynn. "Get her on her feet, and let's go."

The man hefted Gwynn to her feet and shoved her toward the door. Her knees had regained the strength to carry her, but everything inside screamed for her to fight rather than submit to Alexi's demands.

Anya laced her arm through Gwynn's. "Just do as he says. I think we finally have their attention."

The back door of the club burst open, and a pair of men who could've been the front-door bouncers' twins stood flanking the opening.

Alexi directed Gwynn and Anya through the door, his pistol still in hand. "Do not make this harder than it has to be. We only want to talk."

Anya growled. "Men in ladies' room did not want to talk. They wanted to die. We gave to one of them his wish. Maybe you will be next."

One of the bouncers opened the back door of an obscenely gaudy, long white car. "Get in."

Anya followed Gwynn into the back seat, and someone closed the door behind them. A darkened window separated the front seat from the back.

Gwynn turned to Anya. "What's happening right now?"

"I think they want to talk. Are you okay?"

"I don't know. I think I just killed a man with your knife."

"He is not dead yet. It takes a very long time to die from stomach wound. He is in worst pain of life, though."

Gwynn almost smirked. "Good."

The window hummed and slowly lowered three inches, still giving no view of the front seat. A slow, measured cadence in an accent Anya recognized as Ukrainian flowed through the opening in the glass. "You are making quite the mess of my city, leaving blood in the streets and whispering your name—if it is really your name—to the men you leave in pools of their own blood. Why are you doing this on *my* streets in *my* city?"

Anya narrowed her eyes. "If this is *your* city, this means those men are also *your* men, and if this is true, then you sent them to threaten me. I have rule, and rule is same in all cities . . . even yours."

She paused, awaiting the man's response, and she wasn't disappointed when it came.

"I do not care about your rule. I only care to know why you are in Miami."

"I am here to enjoy sun and beach and sometimes dancing in club, but every day in city you believe is yours, a new person attacks me, and I am forced to hurt him. This city that is yours is not so nice."

The voice from the front was suddenly directed to someone else. "I like her."

Zhivotnoye said, "I knew you would."

The window continued its motion until it disappeared into the seatback, revealing the front-seat occupants. Zhivotnoye sat behind the wheel, and a second man neither woman had ever seen in person was in the passenger's seat pressing a toothpick against his lips. "Do you know who I am?"

Anya offered a seated bow. "Everyone knows you are king of city."

The man turned and locked eyes with the Russian. "That is right. I am king of this city, and this city is a jungle. That makes me the king of the jungle."

Anya glanced at Gwynn. "Then I was wrong. I am not here to enjoy sun and beach. I am here to see the king."

"Welcome to the king's court, my lady. I am Leo, and if you are not lying, you are Anya."

Anya offered a slight bow but didn't answer.

Leo let his eyes play across the two women for a long moment before settling on Gwynn. "I know your friend's name—or at least what she wants me to believe her name is—but I'm afraid I don't know yours."

Gwynn matched his stare, praying the man couldn't see the fear raging behind her eyes. "Do you like the theater, King Leo?"

"You mean, like Bolshoi Theater?"

"Sure, that one will do. Do you like the Bolshoi?"

Leo gave Zhivotnoye a backhanded slap to the shoulder. "What is she talking about? What is all this talk of the Bolshoi?"

Zhivotnoye shrugged. "You'll have to ask them. I told you I can't figure them out."

"Okay," Leo said, "I will play silly game with you. Yes, I love the Bolshoi. Now, what does that have to do with two women running around my city with knives and leaving bloody trail behind?"

Gwynn shot a brief look toward Anya. "Well, since you're a fan of the theater, you'll understand what I mean when I tell you I'm simply Anya's understudy."

Another slap to Zhivotnoye's shoulder, and Leo belly-laughed. "Did you hear that? She's an understudy. So, you are like Xena and Gabrielle, warrior princess and sidekick. Is that what this is, a make-believe television show?"

Anya didn't laugh. She leaned forward to stare directly into Leo's soul. "You are second person to call us those names. Yes, this is exactly what we are, make-believe. Just ask men we left bleeding in street and in bathroom. We are not real."

Leo's laughter ground to a silent, determined gaze. "What do you want?"

Anya didn't hesitate and motioned toward Gwynn. "I first want you to pay for dress. Is beautiful and brand-new. Your man in bathroom ruin it with his blood."

Leo waved a dismissive hand toward Zhivotnoye. "Get out. Get out of car. I will discuss business privately."

Zhivotnoye shot a look into the mirror before following Leo's order. When the door closed, Leo raised a finger. "You do not come to my city and make demands."

"Is not demand," Anya protested. "Is answer to your question. You asked what I want. I paid for dress, and is now ruined. This is your fault because your men are sloppy and unable to win fight with two women in bathroom in club."

Gwynn's mind reeled in disbelief. After only two days in Miami, she was face-to-face with the man she'd spent months studying, researching, and learning to loathe. Now, he was only feet away. If she had her Glock, she could end the Lion's reign of terror in a heartbeat, but Anya could rip the life from his body with her bare hands. She'd never stared into the face of pure evil before that moment, but she knew it was a moment that would never leave her mind.

Leo held up two hands as if cupping a pair of bowling balls. "I'll say this for you. You've got some real cojones. Men—big, strong, angry men—they tremble in my presence. But not you. You come into my city, into my club, and now even into my limousine, and you say to me you want me to pay for dress. I will tell you something. I know who you are, and I know *what* you are."

Gwynn swallowed hard. If Leo truly knew who and what they were, they'd never see the outside of the limo. Suddenly, the blowing snow back in D.C. didn't seem so threatening.

"This is not true," Anya said. "You do not know who and what I am. Because if you do, you would not sit alone in car with me."

Leo inspected his fingernails. "I suppose this is maybe true. You are dangerous woman. You are killer, but you are not here to kill me. I know this because I am still alive. I am not bad man. I am businessman. This is all. Look at this car. Do you know what this car is?"

"Is waste of money. Is too big, too slow, and too flashy."

Leo raised his eyebrows. "Oh, too flashy, like convertible Porsche, no?"

"My car is not unique in this city. Your car is maybe only one like it in all of world."

Leo snapped his fingers and pointed to Anya's chin. "That is exactly right . . . just like me. Is only one in all of world. Is nineteen sixty-one Rolls-

Royce Bentley touring limousine. Is most comfortable car in history. You are comfortable, yes?"

Anya pressed her fingers into the leather of the seat and examined the interior of the car. "There is icepick inside bar. With this, I could turn your brain into pin cushion. There is glass also inside bar. With these, I can break and make knife to cut out your heart. There is—"

Leo held up a hand. "Yes, I get it. You are killer, and you are turning also Gabrielle into killer. Believe me, I am sufficiently afraid of you. And this is something I have never said to any man, but I say it to you. I know you were inside Black Dolphin, and I also know you are only person who ever escaped from this prison. How is this possible?"

Anya ignored the reference to the Black Dolphin, Russia's most notorious maximum-security prison; a prison that until her had only housed men . . . the worst of men. "If this is true, then you know I cannot go back to Russia." She held up her palms. "Why would I want to go back to Russia when here in United States, I can sit in back seat of most comfortable car in history and dance inside beautiful club owned by king of city?"

Leo slowly began nodding. "You know something? I think I am really starting to like you. How much was dress at Kmart?"

Anya glared at the man, and his raucous laughter returned.

"I am only talking jokes with you. Is beautiful dress. I apologize for blood. If man is still alive, I will take from him money for new dress."

He paused, turned, and opened the glove compartment. Gwynn's breath caught in her throat at the thought of a pistol emerging from the dash, but instead, Leo pulled a banded stack of one-hundred-dollar bills from inside and tossed it onto the luxurious back seat. Buy for yourselves new dresses, and I will pick you up at eight o'clock tomorrow night in front of your building. We will have party and nice dinner, and we will discuss business."

Anya pulled twenty bills from the stack. "I have rich uncle who buys for me dresses, but not for Gabrielle, so I will take only money for new dress for her. This is good business."

She pulled the latch and stepped from the limousine with Gwynn trailing in her wake. Standing beside the car, they saw Zhivotnoye, Alexi, and the pair of bouncers.

Anya stepped in front of Zhivotnoye, pulled the cigarette from his lips, and placed it between her own. After a long pull, she removed the cigarette and exhaled a long plume of white smoke. "Your king is still alive. Thank you for introduction. Now, give to me my knives."

He nodded toward one of the bouncers. "Give her the knives."

The man pulled four knives from a bag beside the door, the blood of the man from the bathroom still gleaming on one of them. He tossed the knives at Anya's feet. She knelt in her dress, lifted them from the pavement, and sent one racing through the air toward the bouncer. It sailed between his thighs and buried its tip deep in the wooden door behind him. Anya closed the distance between herself and the bouncer in two strides, pinning him to the wall with her right hand shoved into his throat. "Is not nice to throw knives onto ground. This is reason you are only bouncer and not real man. I will buy for you book of manners."

Gwynn watched in admiration as Anya's left hand relieved the man of his pistol. She retrieved the knife from between his legs, fieldstripped the pistol, and dropped the disassembled weapon on the ground at the man's feet.

16

ZHIZN' UBIYTSY
(LIFE OF AN ASSASSIN)

With the top down and the wind in their hair, Gwynn and Anya raced through Leo's jungle.

"That was intense," Gwynn said. "I've gotta tell you, I was scared out of my mind in the back of that car."

"I like what you did with theater reference. I have never had understudy before you."

Gwynn shook out her hair and breathed in the salty night air. "Is it always like this?"

"I do not understand question."

Gwynn threw up her hands, letting the wind blow through her fingertips. "I mean, I feel like I'm flying. Sitting in the back seat of that car was terrifying, but I've never felt more alive. This must be what it's like to do cocaine."

The MacArthur Causeway became the Dolphin Expressway when they crossed Interstate 95. Ten minutes later, they were on the Tamiami Trail, one of the longest, straightest stretches of road in South Florida. The trail pierced the Everglades and gave both Anya and the Porsche 911 the freedom to unwind.

They accelerated through 150 miles per hour with ease and roared through the river of grass. Gwynn screamed like an excited schoolgirl, and Anya negotiated the few curves they encountered like a seasoned racecar driver.

Gwynn yelled over the roar of the wind and turbo-charged engine behind them. "Where did you learn to drive like this?"

Anya ignored the question as the lights of Naples came into view on the western horizon, flooding the previously star-spangled sky with artificial light. With masterful clutch and brake work, she slid the 911 onto the entrance road to Collier-Seminole State Park and executed a flawless one-eighty, bringing the car to a stop on the sand-covered asphalt.

She turned to Gwynn. "Your turn."

Anya covered the seventy-five-mile stretch of Everglade darkness in just over thirty minutes. It took Gwynn a little longer to reach the outskirts of Miami. Eighty miles per hour on the interstate felt like a snail's pace after the rocket ship ride they'd experienced on the trail.

As Gwynn pulled into the parking garage back at the apartment, Anya laid a hand across her wrist. "Now you have something more exciting than back seat of limousine with Leo."

"Is *that* what this was all about?"

Anya nodded. "Yes, I remember first time for me. I could not sleep for many nights."

"So, do you really think I killed that guy in the bathroom?"

Anya took Gwynn's hand and placed it against her stomach. "Show me where you stabbed him."

Gwynn wrapped her fingers around an imaginary knife and replayed the scene, pressing her fist against Anya's stomach just above her navel and drawing upward several inches.

"This is how you made wound?"

Gwynn nodded. "Yeah, exactly like that."

Anya covered Gwynn's hand with hers. "Welcome to life of assassin."

Anya quickly fell asleep after tea and a shower. Gwynn did not. She lay in the darkness, reliving the events of the night. She'd taken the life of another human with nothing more than a blade of steel.

Has my life truly been hanging in the balance? Would the man have killed me, or maybe Anya if I hadn't buried the steel in his gut?

She'd never know the answers to those questions, but she would never again be able to stand in front of the mirror and look into the eyes of innocence. She was suddenly, somehow, both more and so much less than she'd been the day before. She'd willingly stepped into a bottomless pit from which there could be no escape. She'd taken life, and that could never be undone. There had to be answers to the endless questions pouring through her head, and those answers had to reside inside the mind of one of the world's deadliest assassins sleeping just down the hall.

Gwynn slipped from her bed and into the hallway on bare feet, moving in silence toward Anya's door.

Surely, she's awake. It couldn't be possible for anyone to sleep after a night like we experienced.

She pressed a palm against the door and felt it glide silently on its hinges, casting a dim swath of light across the room beyond. The rhythmic refrain of slumbering breath was the only sound coming from within the room.

Anya opened one eye barely enough to make out Gwynn's silhouette slipping through the doorway. She consciously continued the deep breathing of restful sleep. Gwynn was no threat. She was coming for comfort, for reassurance, just like Anya did on the night of her seventeenth birthday . . .

She'd been driven to the Hotel Savoy at the corner of Puschechnaya Ulitsa and Ulitsa Rozhdestvenka, less than two blocks from Lubyanka, the old KGB Headquarters. The mighty Soviet Union was still two years from crumbling, and the Iron Curtain still stood strong. Her target, Yevgeny Nikolaevich Demidov, a Communist Party official turned British informant, sat by the marble fireplace in the Hermitage Bar on an eighteenth-century Italian sofa that seemed to struggle supporting his bulk. The man carried at least an extra hundred pounds on his five-foot-eight-inch frame. His decades inside Red Square had left him soft, weathered beyond his sixty years, and wealthy by socialist standards.

Her assignment had been simple: approach Yevgeny under the guise of being the prostitute he'd ordered from the stable of Eastern European beauties kept in waiting for important Party officials like him. She would swoon at his wealth and power, drawing the man deeper into her web as the night wore on. She had approached the man and offered her hand as submissively as she could manage, not daring to look him in the eye. "I am Irina, and tonight I am yours."

The bulbous man had devoured her body with his lecherous eyes. "You will do. Sit down and have drink with me."

The introduction worked flawlessly, and the plan seemed to be playing out exactly as designed by her KGB masters.

"I would like vodka if you will permit me."

The disgrace to the hammer and sickle laid his meaty hand on her thigh as if she were nothing more than a morsel for his consumption. "Tonight, my pet, the world is yours. You may have anything you like."

"I would like most of all having you, sir."

The script she'd rehearsed ad nauseam and believed was ridiculous was actually working, and the man let himself believe every word of her act.

He'd ordered the finest vodka the hotel owned and insisted on drinking straight from the bottle as Anya sipped at her crystal glass. The time came for the line she knew would set off warning bells inside Yevgeny's head, but she had no choice. She had to deliver the ludicrous line as if it were a compliment of the highest order.

"You are great man. I think you could drink vodka like huge Russian bear, and no one would know you are not drinking water from spring."

She delivered the line and waited for the backhand she not only would receive, but also deserve after such an obviously rehearsed line.

The slap never came; instead, Yevgeny called to the barman. "Another bottle, immediately!"

Between bottles two and three, the old communist forced himself from the sofa, the experience requiring more than a little effort. "I will return in minutes, and if you so much as look at another man while I am gone, you will not see tomorrow sunrise. This is clear?"

"I'd never consider looking at another man when I'm with greatest of them all."

The line wasn't scripted, nor had it been rehearsed, but Anya delivered it as if from the depths of her heart.

In his absence, she pulled the vial from her clutch and emptied its deadly contents into the waiting bottle. When Yevgeny returned from the men's room, he'd devour the bottle just as he'd done with the first two, leaving himself fully unconscious in seconds and dead only minutes after that.

Anya remembered how her young hand trembled, sending the empty vial tumbling to the floor just as her target returned, stumbling with every stride. She'd rolled the vial beneath the sofa only seconds before Yevgeny would've noticed it lying on the marble floor, and then she patted the seat beside her. "I missed you, my big Russian bear."

Her first mission was seconds away from ending in glorious success, and she could return to the state school with her head held high. But it wasn't to be . . .

Instead of planting his three hundred pounds back on the elegant, cushioned sofa, he grabbed Anya's wrist and yanked her from the seat. "Enough vodka in front of fire. Now, we eat!"

Anya stared at the lethal bottle still resting on the table. The poison she poured into the bottle was enough to kill everyone in the bar, and the bottle was still full.

"I must get my purse." Another unscripted line, but it worked and gave her the window of opportunity she needed to retrieve the bottle. "We must not leave such an expensive bottle of vodka behind."

Yevgeny yanked the bottle from her grasp and roared, "Nonsense! I can afford every bottle of vodka in Moscow. One bottle means nothing." He turned and threw the bottle into the fireplace, sending liquid flames across the hearth.

The Restaurant Savoy, with its mirrored, ornate ceiling above the marble fountain, was like nothing Anya had ever seen. Such opulence was unimaginable after having slept in dormitories with hundreds of other trainees and eaten alongside those same boys and girls in cold, decaying kitchens for over a decade.

Yevgeny leaned against a marble statue. "You like the fountain? I will buy it for you."

"It's the most beautiful thing I've ever seen."

The script was a thing of ancient history, and the rest of the night would be up to Anya to not only survive, but to complete the mission she'd failed in the bar.

Appetizers of Russian pancakes and premium sturgeon caviar with Vologda oil, served with green onions, eggs, and sour cream came first. The pop of the caviar between her teeth and the rancid taste that followed left seventeen-year-old Anya barely able to swallow the delicacy that Yevgeny shoveled into his mouth like a starving animal.

Wild elk dumplings with wild lingonberries came as the hot appetizer, and after the caviar, she discovered the dumplings to be magnificent.

The meat course was next, and Yevgeny ordered for them both. He demanded the lamb loin on the bone with Dijon sauce rare for himself, and grilled marble entrecôte for her. When the dish arrived, she was delighted that it was marbled beefsteak with green salad and barbeque sauce, but the element of the meal she most treasured was the bone-handled, razor-sharp steak knife the waiter placed between her plate and wine glass. With the poison aflame in the bar fireplace, the only remaining option was to get Yevgeny Nikolaevich Demidov alone and dispatch him with the one weapon she understood.

A fish course arrived, followed by a dessert of fried mushroom, veal, and cabbage pies in a dough so flakey it was impossible to catch the falling crumbs. Port wine accompanied dessert, and Anya discovered that even her young palate savored the rich Portuguese wine. While Yevgeny reached for the last of the pies, she slipped the knife she'd palmed, between the meat and fish courses, into her purse.

"You will take me to your house now, and we will make love until morning, yes?"

The old communist pounded the table, rattling the dishes. "Never! My wife would slaughter me in my sleep if I brought you to my house. I have the finest suite in the hotel just for you, my darling."

"Even better. I will do things for you that your wife would never dare."

He stumbled to his feet, bracing against the table. "That's exactly what I wanted to hear. Let's go, my love."

His hands groped her young, toned body as the elevator carried them to the top of the hotel and deposited them in front of the Grand Suite, a luxurious three-room suite, the likes of which Anya had never dreamed of seeing.

Having endured his paws in the elevator, Anya believed she could stomach almost nothing more of the man she'd grown to despise more for his absolute absence of humanity than for his betrayal of the Rodina. Regardless of the reasons, his death would come in grand fashion.

"Stand for me beside bed, and I will undress you. It will be my pleasure and for me a dessert more intoxicating than the port."

Yevgeny did as she asked and savored her hands sliding across his flesh as she removed first his jacket and shirt, then finally his trousers and boxers.

By the time she'd pushed him onto his back and allowed him to watch her seductively peel her dress from her body, he was poised and ready for everything she could offer.

He reached for her hand and demanded, "Lie down, and I will devour you like no man you've ever known."

She pressed her hand against his pudding-like chest and whispered, "No, my love. Tonight, I will do for you what no other woman has ever done." She situated her body on top of him in such a position that she could still access her thin purse on the bedside table, then she leaned down and kissed beneath his ear. "Close your eyes, and I will take you to another world."

He moaned in ecstasy for the last time, and then clawed at his throat as his life's blood poured from the gaping wound.

"You are traitor to your country, and now you will spend eternity in Hell for your betrayal."

Although Gwynn's first time tearing the life from another human had been far less dramatic, Anya knew the emotions she was experiencing carried the same anxiety.

Gwynn stepped silently across the room, pulled back the cover, and slid into the bed beside Anya. She whispered softly as their bodies touched, "I hope I didn't wake you, but I . . ."

Anya turned and pressed her finger to Gwynn's lips. "Is okay. I remember how it feels. Now sleep, and I will hold you. I wish someone had done this for me when I first learned I was assassin."

17

KOROLEVSKIY DVOR
(THE KING'S COURT)

At precisely 8:00 p.m., Michael rang the apartment's doorbell, and Gwynn, wearing her new bloodless red dress, stepped into the foyer but did not press her eye to the peephole. "Who is it?"

"It's Michael, from the door, ma'am. Your limo has arrived. When should I tell him you'll be down?"

Gwynn turned to Anya and whispered, "Should we make them wait?"

The Russian checked her watch. "Tell him we will be down in five minutes."

When the pair stepped from the elevator, every eye in the lobby turned immediately and admiringly toward the stunning duo. The olive-skinned brunette with the red dress like second skin and the Eastern European blonde in all black left the audience unable to look away.

As they passed Michael holding the door, Gwynn pressed a finger against the bottom of his chin. "Close your mouth, Michael, and act like you've seen a pretty girl before."

He blushed, closed his mouth, and enjoyed watching them go at least as much as he'd enjoyed their approach.

An unmistakably Russian man in his late twenties held open the rear door of the Rolls-Royce limousine. "*Dobryy vecher, damy.*"

Anya followed Gwynn into the car. "Good evening to you, too. Where are you taking us?"

The driver ignored the question, closed the door, and made his way behind the wheel. He lowered the partition and laid an arm across the back of the seat. "Um, forgive. English no good."

In her native tongue, Anya set the young man's mind at ease. "Russian is just fine."

The relieved driver smiled. "If you would care for a cocktail, the bar is available, but it is only a short ride. Maybe ten minutes for the car."

Gwynn caught *cocktail*, *ten minutes*, and *car*. Everything else was a blur.

Anya declined the drink and gave Gwynn a reassuring nod.

Nine minutes later, the driver pulled the Rolls off Alton beside the Murano Grande and tapped the horn. A velvet-jacket-clad young man leapt from behind the valet stand and hurriedly tossed three orange traffic cones onto the curb. The driver expertly positioned the limo in the spots and held the door while Anya and Gwynn stepped from the car.

Gwynn shot a look into the garage and then up the exterior wall. "Leo lives here?"

Anya gave a shrug, and the driver seemed to understand the confusion. He stammered for English, and Anya reminded him, "*Russkiy khoroshiy.*"

He continued in the only language he knew well. "Do not worry. I know this seems odd, but your next ride is just up above."

Gwynn understood none of what the driver said, but the look on Anya's face told her something wasn't what she expected.

The driver led them to an elevator and stepped inside. As the doors closed, Gwynn gave a quizzical look, and Anya squeezed her hand in reassurance.

The squeeze gave the agent at least some degree of comfort, but the four hours she'd spent earlier in the day with the couch pushed against the wall, learning the basics of knife-fighting, was the thing that gave her the most confidence that evening. The cold steel of the two knives pressing tightly against the inside of her upper thigh wasn't as good as the Glock, but it was better than nothing.

The elevator opened to a swimming pool and tennis court four floors above the street. The area was an oasis for guests of the Murano Grande, but the black Sikorsky S-76 helicopter resting on the tennis court was unmistakably the property of the king of the jungle.

The driver opened the rear door of the helicopter and helped them in-side. The plush, leather interior made the back of the chopper look more like an elaborate home theater than a flying machine. They settled into their seats, and the limo driver closed the door behind them.

Gwynn took in the surroundings. "Where do you think they're taking us?"

Anya shrugged. "I do not know, but Leo wants us to be impressed. Are you impressed?"

Gwynn twisted her bracelet. "A little."

The turbines whistled to life, and the blades rotated overhead. Seconds later, they were climbing out over Biscayne Bay. Anya watched the city of Miami pass off the right side as they continued south toward the Florida Keys.

Gwynn leaned toward the window. "Any ideas where we're headed yet?"

Anya pointed to the water. "I once sank a sailboat and killed five people down there."

Gwynn shook her head. "You know, Anya, that's just weird. My other girlfriends are like, 'Oh, look, that's where Bryan kissed me for the first time.' But not you. You're all like, 'I sank a boat and killed some people right there.' Please tell me you realize that's weird."

Anya cocked her head. "Who is Bryan?"

For the first time in thirty-six hours, Gwynn laughed. "We're in some guy's helicopter, flying over the water, going to God knows where, and you're not nervous. That's weird, too."

"Is strange for me, too. I am not nervous for me, but for you. I would feel better if I were doing this alone, but I have to also keep you alive."

Gwynn rolled her eyes. "Well, that's reassuring."

Anya continued watching the islands of the Florida Keys pass beneath them. "I think we are going to house in Key West."

Gwynn joined her in counting islands. "Do you really think this is just dinner and a party, or are they going to try and kill us tonight?"

"I think is only dinner and party. Leo knows I am killer, and he has terrible enemies. He will try to buy from me the death of his enemies."

The flight continued for twenty more minutes, and the pilot began a descent toward the water.

Gwynn craned to see what was beneath them. "Uh, I think your Key West theory is a bust. I don't know where we are, but I don't think there's anything dry down there."

Anya leaned back in her seat as if nothing was out of the ordinary. "I was wrong. We are not going to Key West. We are going to boat."

Seconds later, the landing gear deployed and touched down on the stern deck of a motor yacht. The door came open, and Leo stood, arms wide, on the deck beside the helicopter. "Welcome aboard *L'vinaya Gordost'* – *The Lion's Pride!*"

He held out his hands to help them from the helicopter, and they took in the gargantuan yacht for the first time. Leo kissed their cheeks and waved his hands toward the bow. "I must show you the boat. Isn't she beautiful? Almost as gorgeous as the two of you."

They followed Leo as he gave the grand tour. "She is eighty-six meters. This is two hundred eighty feet. She was a gift from my dear friend. You will meet him now. Come with me."

The sound of the helicopter departing caught Anya's attention, and she shot a glance toward the stern.

Leo laid a hand against her shoulder. "Do not worry. He will come back for you whenever you'd like. You are my guests. Enjoy the yacht."

A pair of electric sliding-glass doors opened into a lounge, where a tall Latino man rose from a captain's chair with a tumbler in one hand and a long dark cigar in the other.

"Here he is," Leo declared. "Tony, meet Anya and her understudy, Gabrielle."

Tony placed his glass and cigar on the table and took Gwynn's hands in his, kissing the back of each in turn. "My friend Leo told me that two beautiful women would be joining us for dinner and drinks tonight, but he didn't tell me you were goddesses from the stars above."

The four took their seats, and a uniformed steward materialized.

Leo raised a hand. "Our guests drink only water and the finest champagne." He turned to Anya. "I have this correct, yes?"

She rewarded him with a brilliant smile, her dimple and deep blue-gray eyes leaving him mesmerized.

When Leo was finally able to look away, he motioned toward the ceiling. "Oh, and open the top on your way out."

The steward bowed, turned, and made his exit. Seconds later, the glass ceiling of the magnificent yacht parted, revealing the starlit sky above.

Gwynn gasped. "That's incredible. I've never seen anything like it."

Leo reveled in her admiration and raised his glass toward Tony. "The rewards of friendship."

Tony took a long draw from his cigar and raised his glass to meet Leo's. "To friendship . . . Especially *new* friendship."

The steward returned with champagne flutes, tiny bubbles climbing through golden wine inside. As if rehearsed, Anya and Gwynn raised their glasses and locked eyes with their hosts, the Russian staring into Leo's soul, and Gwynn drinking in Tony's chiseled features and jet-black hair. Glasses touched again with the unmistakable *tink* of fine crystal, and the four drank.

Small talk ensued until the steward returned and announced dinner. To their surprise, the stern deck where the helicopter had landed had been transformed into a luxurious and intimate outdoor dining room. Anya sat across from Leo while Gwynn allowed Tony to hold her chair as she seductively took the seat.

As the meal progressed, conversation turned from meaningless to investigative.

Leo wiped the corner of his mouth with a linen napkin. "I would like for you to look at this situation from my perspective. This deadly assassin, trained by the KGB, who was imprisoned inside the Black Dolphin—and escaped, I might add—she suddenly appears in my city like an angel sent from God to me." He frowned and tilted his head from side to side. "For men like Tony and me, these things sometimes concern us, and we don't like to be concerned. I'm sure you can understand that."

Gwynn felt the lump growing in her throat, but she forced it down with another mouthful of the three-hundred-dollar-per-bottle champagne.

Anya smiled and stood, twisting her arm behind her back. She took two strides to the side of the table, pulled the zipper of her dress down her back, and let the garment fall to the deck. Her matching black lace bra and panties were the only items of clothing beneath the dress, except, of course, the black elastic garter holding a pair of glistening throwing knives inside her left thigh. "You are afraid we are undercover government spies, no? You think we wear recording devices or transmitters. This is why you bring us all the way into ocean on boat. As you can see, there is no microphone."

She knelt, pulled her dress back into its proper place, and returned the zipper. Leo and Tony ignored Anya as she redressed and turned their attention to Gwynn.

Following Anya's lead, she stood and approached Tony. "I cannot reach my zipper. You'll have to do it for me."

Without standing, he looked up at Special Agent Guinevere Davis and ran his fingertips between her breasts and across her flat stomach. He paused as his fingers detected the same garter Anya had displayed with the pair of knives.

His brilliantly white teeth shone as his smile came. "I'd love to help you with your zipper, but perhaps later. For now, I trust that you are not wearing a wire. I do have one question, though."

Gwynn brushed his hand from her thigh. "And what is your question?"

"If you are Anya's understudy, what is she teaching you?"

She leaned down and whispered into his ear, "She's teaching me to cut the hearts out of men who put their hands on me without asking."

"Touché."

Gwynn reclaimed her seat, giving Tony's ankle a brush with her foot.

Anya slid her champagne flute to the edge of the table, ensuring Leo noticed the empty two-hundred-dollar glass. "If we are spies for government, you will have us killed before morning, and there is nothing we can do to stop you from this. But it would be a terrible shame to waste something so valuable when it is right in palm of hand."

She slowly lifted a knife from the table and placed the blade against the base of the glass. With the slowest, most obvious gesture, she slid the glass toward the edge of the table until it fell toward the deck.

Without taking his eyes from her, Leo caught the glass only milliseconds before it shattered against the teak. "I'm not in the habit of wasting valuable things."

Anya licked the blade of the knife and replaced it on the table. "Good, then we can finally stop playing silly game and talk about why you brought us here."

Tony was the first to get down to business. "Do you remember Pablo Escobar?"

Gwynn chuckled. "Everybody remembers Pablo Escobar, but he's been dead for ten years."

Leo and Tony shared a knowing glance, and Leo said, "Pablo was the greatest gangster who ever lived. Thirty-billion-dollar net worth. Nobody can touch that."

Anya tried to look bored. "Money doesn't matter when you are dead. Thirty dollars or thirty billion is all the same to him now."

Tony leaned forward and drove his finger into the table. "That's where you are wrong, chica. Pablo is not dead. He is reincarnated, and I am the new Pablo Escobar."

Anya raised an eyebrow. "You?"

"That's right, me. How do you think I can afford to give gifts like this yacht to my friends if I am not the new Pablo Escobar?"

Anya ignored the question and reached for Gwynn's hand. "We have money of our own, so we are not impressed."

The two men scoffed, and Leo said, "An ex-KGB assassin on the run from everyone. How much money can you have? Do you have a yacht like mine?"

Anya took in the lavish surroundings. "Yacht like this is very big target, and big target is easy to hit. Something like this means you want everyone to know how much money you have. You are full of foolish pride, and this will bring you to your death."

"Who's going to kill the Lion, huh? You? Your little understudy? Is that why you're here? To kill the Lion?"

Anya motioned toward her empty flute. "I thought I was here to drink good champagne, but on this expensive yacht, my glass is always empty."

As if summoned by an invisible force, the steward appeared with an ice bucket and uncorked a bottle of Dom.

Anya waved the man away and poured her own glass. "I do not need servants, and I do not need boat to impress anyone with how much money I have. I am disgraced KGB officer and killer. I have only one reason now to be alive, and this is to do the thing I love. And that is gutting men like pigs and making them pay for hurting my friends. You and Tony are now my friends, no?"

Tony and Leo shared a look of two men who'd just struck gold, and glasses went into the air.

"We are definitely your friends!" Leo said. "But what about her?"

All eyes fell on Gwynn, and Anya wasted no time. "She is always with me unless is too dangerous."

Tony took a sip of his cocktail. "So, how much does this friendship cost every time a pig is gutted?"

Anya stared through her champagne flute. "With only this glass, I could kill everyone on boat. Maybe not her, she is very strong, but everyone else on boat, I could kill. This, for me, would be exciting, and excitement is what makes heart beat inside my chest."

Leo lowered his gaze to Anya's heart. "Are you saying to us that you do not wish to be paid?"

"I am paid because of friendship of beautiful men with beautiful boat and helicopter. I do not *need* these things, but we sometimes need place to enjoy sunshine and good company. This is acceptable to you?"

Tony licked his lips and studied the two women. "I think you are full of shit."

Silence consumed the table, and Anya smiled. She poured the champagne from her flute into the ice bucket and snapped the stem from the glass. Then she rolled the glass in her napkin and struck it with the heel of her hand, crushing the crystal into long, razor-like shards. Unrolling the napkin, she lifted three of the shards and held them between her thumb and forefinger before looking up at Leo. "Call for steward to bring dessert."

Leo touched the barely visible controls beneath his foot, and the steward appeared with four plates of key lime pie on a tray above his head. Anya launched the three shards of glass in quick succession, and the waiter never noticed.

When the dessert was served, three shards of crystal protruded from Tony's pie, and Anya leaned forward. "Skin of human neck is same texture as pie. Do you still think I am full of shit?"

Tony pulled the shards from his dessert and laid them beside the plate. "I wasn't questioning your ability. I was questioning your motive. Nobody kills for free."

Anya licked a tiny trickle of blood from her index finger. "Nothing is free, friend Tony, but it is not money that I want. Is only pleasure. Do not take from me my pleasure."

Leo watched the exchange and then leaned his glass toward Anya. "You're terrifying, and I'm pretty sure I love you. If you want to prove you're not full of shit as my friend suggests, I have a pig in mind who is in particular need of gutting. And if you pull this one off, you can consider my boat your personal sunbathing spot."

Anya leaned back in her chair. "I am listening."

"His name is DEA Special Agent Jerry Carmichael."

Gwynn's heart stopped, but she fought through the terror and kept her composure by focusing on her champagne and pretending to be bored.

"Do you have picture of Jerry Carmichael?"

Leo scoffed. "No, I don't have a picture. In my business, people aren't fond of having their pictures taken, but he's a fed. If you are as good as you think you are, how hard can it be to find a fed named Jerry Carmichael?"

Anya slid her fingertip across the edge of the table and watched the crease in the linen tablecloth surrender to her touch. "What did this person do to hurt my friends?"

Leo turned to Tony. "Do you want this one?"

Tony flashed his million-dollar smile. "Yes, I'll take this one. This bastard Carmichael stole one hundred thousand dollars from me."

Anya continued her manipulation of the tablecloth. "How does a federal government agent steal that much money from the new Pablo Escobar?"

"He was on the payroll," Tony began, "then he decided to go off the reservation. When I put a hundred grand in a pocket, I expect that pocket to have some loyalty. Now that piece of shit has vanished off the face of the Earth with *my* hundred grand."

"This is problem. Do you want money back, or just his head on silver platter like dessert?"

Tony pulled a cigar from a pocket humidor, toasted the end, and slid it into the corner of his mouth. "I don't care about the money. I want his thumbs on Popsicle sticks for my dog to chew on."

Anya's smile broadened as her eyes searched the stars.

Leo looked into the heavens with her. "What do you see up there that makes you smile like this?"

"It isn't the stars," she said. "Is first time to kill drug enforcement agent, and I love first times. You will call helicopter pilot now for us."

Tony waved his cigar. "Not a chance. You're staying the night. We'll drop you off in Key West tomorrow or maybe the next day. Let's have some fun."

Anya frowned. "For me, fun is finding and killing Jerry Carmichael. When job is finished, we will play with boys on boats."

Leo lit a cigar of his own. "I told you, these girls are the real thing. I told you you'd like them."

"You were wrong," Tony belted. He pointed his cigar toward Anya. "This one I like." Then he pointed toward Gwynn. "And this one I love."

Gwynn ran her bare foot up Tony's leg. "Don't worry. We'll be seeing a lot of each other real soon, and I'm going to take you up on that unzipping you still owe me."

As promised, Leo called the pilot, and the Sikorsky landed on the deck twenty minutes later. Tony and Leo installed their new friends into the helicopter with more than a little groping, and the chopper took to the northeastern sky.

The two men watched the lights of the Sikorsky grow dim and finally disappear into the night sky, and Tony shook his head. "What was that? Are you kidding me with these girls? Are they really going after that rat-bastard Carmichael?"

Leo sent a white cloud of cigar smoke into the night sky. "What can I say? God loves us, and He just dumped a gold mine right in our laps."

Tony inspected his cigar. "I'll take a gold mine like that in my lap any day."

Aboard the helicopter, Anya and Gwynn sat on the left side, facing each other so they could both watch the Upper Keys pass out the window.

Assuming the helicopter was bugged, Anya glanced toward the ceiling. "I like our new friends."

Gwynn caught the warning. "I do too, and we're going to have some fun with them."

"We are first going to have fun with Carmichael and his thumbs."

Gwynn laughed for an uncomfortable moment as she thought about actually killing an American federal agent. Surely, that's not *really* what Anya had in mind.

Back at the Murano Grande, the driver met them beside the pool. His English had not improved, but he did seem to enjoy returning the tennis net back to its rightful place after the helicopter departed.

In Russian, he said, "Helicopter is nice, yes?"

"It's extremely nice," Anya said. "I thought maybe you were the pilot."

He blushed. "No. I am only the driver, but maybe someday I will learn."

The limo ride back to their apartment was made in utter silence, but once inside the elevator, Gwynn couldn't hold back any longer. "Oh, my God. Can you believe what we just did? And did you get a load of that Tony? He is gorgeous."

Anya tried not to smile. "He is very handsome man, but I think he is terrible man and also dangerous."

"Dangerous to us? You don't think he'll hurt us, do you?"

"I do not think so, but he is suspicious. It will take some time to make him trust us. Leo is clay in potter's hand, though, and I am potter."

"What were you thinking dropping your dress like that? I mean, it got their attention and all, but I can't believe you let them see your knives."

Anya straightened the dress across her stomach. "Is only body. Everyone has a body, and surely they knew I would have knife."

Gwynn looked Anya up and down. "Yeah, but not everybody has a body like that one."

The door opened on their floor, and Anya whispered, "I think you are jealous I showed body to men."

"Maybe a little," Gwynn admitted as she pulled the key from beside her set of knives tucked behind the garter.

As she lifted the key to the lock, Anya caught her wrist and pointed toward the top of the doorjamb. Gwynn looked up and froze.

"The hair is missing. Somebody's been inside."

19

NARUSHITEL'
(THE INTRUDER)

Anya withdrew the pair of knives from her garter and motioned toward the deadbolt. "Open as quietly as possible."

Gwynn slid the key into the slot as slowly as she could move. Before turning the key, she whispered, "Maybe it was just Michael."

Anya slowly shook her head. "Maybe it is Alexi waiting on other side with pistol."

Gwynn silently vowed to never leave the apartment without her gun again. "Are you ready?"

Anya nodded, and Gwynn turned the key. The deadbolt receded into the housing, and Anya crept inside with Gwynn following closely behind. The light from the stove cast an eerie shadow across the kitchen but was the only source of light in the apartment. Gwynn sidestepped into the kitchen as Anya continued toward the living room with its floor-to-ceiling window overlooking the street below. Even with the shades drawn, a human would be silhouetted against the dim light filtering in from outside.

The blinds offered no indication of an intruder, and Gwynn was pleased to find her Glock exactly where she'd left it. She took up a position near the entrance to the hallway as Anya stepped into the living room. Believing the apartment was clear, Anya flipped the pair of light switches to illuminate the living room and hallway.

The room was empty but not undisturbed. Pressed against the lampshade was a yellow scrap of paper with a single blonde hair taped across the top. Beneath the hair, the note read:

Meet me on deck tomorrow at noon where you turned around last night . . . and don't bring a tail.

P.S. Reload your pistol, Davis

R. White

Gwynn yanked the note from the lampshade and pulled back the slide on her pistol. The chamber was empty, and the orange follower visible at the top of the inserted magazine told her the mag was just as dry as the chamber.

"This is why I prefer knives," Anya said. "No bullets required."

"He can be such a pain sometimes. What is he doing in Miami? I've been checking in every day."

"Maybe he wants to have picnic at park tomorrow."

Gwynn rolled her eyes. "Yeah, I'm sure that's it. By the way, I'm driving."

"We will see about that," Anya teased. "It is good that Agent White wants to see us now that we have target."

Gwynn waggled a finger. "Now that we have *a* target."

Anya ignored the correction. "With his help, maybe we will not have to really kill Carmichael."

Gwynn's hand flew to her heart. "Were you seriously going to kill him?"

"If he is on payroll for new Pablo Escobar, he is on the wrong side and should not be alive."

"That's a little harsh, don't you think? Just because he's on the take doesn't necessarily mean he deserves to die. Yeah, I think he should go to prison, but I mean, here in America, we don't just kill dirty cops just because they're dirty."

Anya shrugged. "This is very different in Russia."

"I can't argue with that logic. We'll see what Agent White has to say at our picnic tomorrow. I think I'm actually going to be able to sleep tonight without crawling in bed with my favorite assassin."

Anya chuckled. "You did not have to kill anyone today. It was a better day. I think maybe you will dream of Tony, and I'm sure he is dreaming of you."

"Stop it. I'm not the one who took her dress off in the middle of dinner."

"Good night, Special Agent Davis."

"Good night, comrade Anya."

* * *

Anya conceded. "You can drive, but police will stop you if you go too slow."

Gwynn yanked the keys from Anya's hand. "I'll show you slow. Just get in and hold on."

The Tamiami Trail wasn't the deserted stretch of road it had been in the wee hours of the morning. Tourists anxious for an airboat ride and the chance to spot a gator made the stretch of asphalt across Florida's wetland wilderness anything but a speedway. Gwynn occasionally saw triple digits on the speedometer, but not for more than a few seconds at a time. It took slightly more than an hour to make their way to Seminole-Collier State Park, southeast of Naples.

Gwynn pulled the Porsche into a spot and thumbed the button to bring the convertible top back into position. "What do you think he meant by 'Meet me on deck'?"

Anya pointed toward a brown-and-white sign that read "Wildlife Observation Deck." She said, "Maybe that is what he meant."

Gwynn turned off the key. "Some fed I am, huh?"

Anya stood from the car and cast a glance across the top at Special Agent Davis. "You are only fed I have ever liked."

Gwynn closed her door. "Um . . . what did you say?"

Anya smiled. "Only that I think you are very good fed."

Gwynn checked her watch. "We've got ten minutes to find Agent White. He has this thing about people being on time."

Anya stared down the boardwalk leading into the mangroves. "Is one half mile to platform. I can do this in less than two minutes. Can you?"

She never heard Gwynn's answer, just her footfalls on the boardwalk as she sprinted toward the meeting. Anya's two-inch height advantage gave her a slight edge, but it was her endless routine of keeping her body in the best physical condition possible that put Gwynn twenty seconds behind when they reached the platform where Supervisory Special Agent Ray White stood tossing pebbles into the marsh.

Anya caught her breath while Gwynn was making excuses. "I didn't have time to stretch."

The Russian sighed. "You are right. It was unfair. I am certain your enemies will give time to stretch before chasing."

"You've got an answer for everything, don't you?"

"That's enough," White said. "We've got a development that may change everything about this mission."

Anya spread her feet and massaged her thigh. "We have also unexpected development."

White surveyed the boardwalk and found no one within earshot. "Let's hear yours first."

Gwynn bent at the waist with her hands on her knees, still catching her breath. "They want us to kill a DEA agent named Jerry Carmichael. This guy, Tony, who thinks he's the reincarnation of Pablo Escobar, says Carmichael was on the payroll and bolted with a hundred grand of his money."

White turned to Anya. "Is that how you understand the story?"

Anya nodded. "Yes, this is exactly what Tony said."

White scratched his chin. "A DEA agent on the take, who ran off with a hundred G's of cartel money, and they want to farm out the hit?"

Gwynn stood erect. "That's what I thought too, but they say they can't find this guy Carmichael. It's a test drive."

White frowned. "Test drive? What does that mean?"

"It means they want to find out if we're full of shit. If we find Carmichael and bring back his thumbs, it'll buy us a ton of credibility, and we'll be in."

"His thumbs?"

Gwynn said, "Yeah, Tony said he wants Carmichael's thumbs on Popsicle sticks for his dogs to chew on. It's pretty nasty, but that's what he said."

"Okay, that's good work. I'll find Carmichael, if he exists, and we can go from there. But there's something bigger—a lot bigger—going on than a drug agent on the take." White scanned the area again. "You need to know that your guy Tony, for the record, might be Escobar back from the grave. He grew up in Medellín, Colombia, the same as Pablo. Word on the street is that he's twice as ruthless and well on his way to becoming at least as powerful. When we popped Escobar, he was worth about thirty billion. Intel says Tony isn't in double digits yet, but he's already in the billions. Where did you meet him?"

Anya leaned against the railing. "We were on Leo's yacht last night while you were breaking into apartment. Tony was there."

White said, "Nice trick with the blonde hair, by the way. I almost didn't see it."

"This is why I use blonde hair and not brown. Is almost invisible."

White eyed Gwynn. "Is any of this tradecraft rubbing off, Davis?"

"I'm taking notes. And oh, by the way, the fighting we learn at the Academy is worthless."

White broke a branch from a low-hanging tree and pointed it toward Anya. "Don't get my agent hurt."

Anya grinned with pride. "She is excellent student. I will not hurt her, but she will hurt a great many people before we are finished."

"Okay, so back to Tony. I can't believe I'm about to say this out loud. It sounds preposterous, but we think he's trying to buy a Russian submarine to run cocaine from South America to the States. It's not solid intel yet, but there's a lot of chatter about it."

Anya showed no reaction, so White asked, "Does this not surprise you?"

Anya shook her head. "Soviet Union had many submarines before end of Cold War. Now these many submarines are in hands of countries who are no

longer under control of Moscow. Buying submarine would not be too difficult if you can find right person with submarine and enough greed."

White considered her ideas. "It's not like you can just hop in a sub and
take it across the ocean, though. It takes a large, well-trained crew to run a
sub, especially a nuclear boat."

Anya stared into the trees. "I do not think they will buy submarine with
nuclear reactor. Is too difficult to repair and too expensive to throw away if
it breaks. I think they will buy diesel submarine. Is easy to operate with
small crew, and diesel mechanic for truck can also repair submarine. This
makes sense to me."

White rubbed his forehead. "That's not what I wanted to hear. I wanted
you to say it's impossible."

Anya shook her head. "Is not impossible. With enough money, everything is for sale in former Soviet Union."

White moved from rubbing his forehead to grinding the heels of his
hands into his temples. "This is not what I needed this week." He paused,
deciding how much he should and would tell his assets in the field. "It's
like this. Operation Avenging Angel isn't exactly public knowledge in D.C.
We've not been what you might call 'forthcoming' with our sister agencies
about this one. At some point, I'll have to come clean and brief them up,
but for now, here's what I want you to do."

White held up a finger as his thoughts came together. "I've got it. I'm
going to find this Jerry Carmichael character, even if I have to turn Drug
Enforcement upside down, and we're going to deliver a pair of thumbs to
your new best friend. That's going to unlock some doors and give both of
you insider access we've never had. As far as I know, we've got nobody inside the organization besides you two."

Anya motioned toward the water. "Look closely just behind log with
limb. Sticking up is alligator."

"Yeah, we're in the Everglades. That's kind of where alligators live."

Anya ignored the jab and kept her eyes on the predator. "Momma says alligators mean 'cause they got all them teeth and no toothbrush."

White broke his stick and threw both pieces at the Russian. "Is that what we're doing now? Stupid movie quotes?"

Anya batted away the incoming sticks. "This is not stupid movie. This is movie with Adam Sandler, who is Waterboy. Do you want us to kill Leo?"

"Nice try, spy girl, but I've been to the psychological warfare school, too. I'm not ready to divulge how we'll culminate the mission. For now, look, listen, and keep digging your way deeper inside at every opportunity. When the time is right, we'll spring the trap, but so far, we've not even started building the trap."

"So, does this mean you do not want us to kill Leo?"

"That's exactly what it means . . . at least for now."

Anya tossed a stick toward the gator and watched him disappear beneath the black water. "Predators are most dangerous when their prey cannot see them coming."

White waved his hand. "Cut the Confucius crap, and get out of here. Meeting adjourned."

Gwynn burst from the platform in a sprint, and Anya checked her watch.

White pointed down the boardwalk. "Aren't you going to chase her?"

Anya said, "I will give to her twenty-second start ahead, and I will still win. Goodbye, Agent White. We should have tea again soon."

20

POLITICHESKAYA VOLOKITA
(POLITICAL RED TAPE)

Back in Washington D.C., Supervisory Special Agent Ray White's day was spent convincing his boss's boss, the principal deputy assistant attorney general, to let him talk with the assistant attorney general over the Criminal Division about Operation Avenging Angel going international. When he finally gained permission to explain the situation to the AAG, he spent nearly two hours waiting his turn.

The assistant attorney general listened, asked all the right questions, and in typical D.C. fashion, kicked the buck even further up the bureaucratic chain to the deputy attorney general, whose reins held the bit and bridle of the FBI, Bureau of Prisons, DEA, U.S. Marshals Service, BATF, and Interpol Washington, among others. The DAG reported directly to the U.S. attorney general, who reported only to the president.

White understood well that he had departed the realm of those who solved crimes and caught the bad guys and stepped into an arena where the gladiators carried briefcases instead of Glocks. He understood handcuffs and gunfights, but life on the upper floors of DOJ Headquarters was a battlefield entirely foreign to him. He wasn't certain his common access card would make the elevator door open on those upper floors, but he'd placed a cooperating civilian and a federal agent undercover inside an organization whose players were kicking the tires of a Cold War–era Soviet submarine and negotiating a cash price with no trade-in.

According to her executive assistant—a woman Ray White called a *secretary*—the deputy attorney general didn't have a vacancy on her schedule for eleven days, so White's "little issue" would just have to wait.

Ray said, "The Russian mafia is about to broker a deal between the biggest drug cartel in the world and a former Soviet admiral to buy a submarine capable of importing thousands of tons of cocaine into the U.S. over and over again. Tell your boss I've got two operatives inside the organization, and I can stop the deal in its tracks, but if she'd like to wait eleven days to talk to me, I'm sure your 'little job' is perfectly safe."

The executive assistant had little experience dealing with actual gunslingers, and the fastest draw in D.C. earned himself the ire of one secretary, as well as a 6:00 a.m. meeting with the deputy attorney general of the United States.

Ray White sat in his favorite chair, sipping a cup of equal parts hot tea and Jack Daniels. His hand rested on the Bible he hadn't opened in weeks, and his mind rested on the former Russian spy playing the deadliest game of cat and mouse that had ever been played on the streets of South Beach. Between sips and flashes of Anya in his head, he practiced the sales pitch he'd make in the DAG's office in less than seven hours.

The ringing of his home phone shook him from the stupor. The unfamiliar ring of the landline left him uncertain if it was actually his phone at all.

Who would call this late and on that line?

Uncertain why he'd done so, he rose from the chair, placed his tea on a folded napkin pretending to be a coaster, and lifted the receiver. "Hello."

"Raymond White?"

Ray held the receiver away from his face and stared into the black plastic. He couldn't remember the last time he'd used the phone or the last time anyone had called him Raymond. Finally, he pressed it back to his ear. "Who's calling?"

"Mr. White, my name is Donna Burgess. I'm a trauma nurse at New Smyrna Beach Hospital. Is Charles White your father?"

Ray thought he must be dreaming. No one except the Justice Department and maybe his bookie had his home number. "What's this about?"

"Mr. White, I need you to confirm that Charles White is your father."

Ray changed hands with the receiver and raked through the junk drawer for a pen. "Is he all right? Has there been an accident?"

The nurse ground her teeth. "Mr. White. Is Charles White your father or not?"

"Yeah . . . yes. I'm his . . . I mean, yeah, he's my dad. What's happened? Is he all right?"

"Mr. White—"

"It's Agent White. I'm a special agent with Justice."

"Okay, Special Agent White, your father was the apparent victim of an attack this evening. Apparently, some kids tried to break into his bookstore, and he surprised them. He's in surgery now, but the doctors say he'll likely fully recover. X-rays indicate he may have three fractured ribs, and there was at least some internal bleeding."

"Can I talk to him?"

Nurse Burgess groaned. "I told you he's in surgery. Aren't you listening to me, Agent White? We found your number in his wallet, and we sent a black-and-white to your father's house to notify anyone there. Is your mother . . ."

"No, my mother's dead. I'll be there in . . . Wait a minute. Did you say you found my number in dad's wallet?"

"Yes, sir, that's right. It was tucked behind his driver's license."

"Why didn't the perps take his wallet?"

"I don't know. I wasn't there. And I'm just a nurse."

"I'm sorry," he muttered. "I wasn't really talking to you. I was just thinking out loud. If it was a robbery, they would've taken his wallet, but that doesn't really matter right now. I'll pack a bag and be there as soon as possible. When he wakes up, tell him I'm on my way. Oh, and here's my cell number in case you need to call while I'm en route."

Nurse Burgess took the number, and they hung up with Ray running his hand through his hair and scanning his kitchen for nothing in particular.

Special Agent Ray White had never borne the burden of indecision. That's exactly what made him one of the Justice Department's finest agents. Throughout his career, when he'd come to a fork in the road, he'd never hesitated. The high road hadn't always been his choice, but he'd never been accused of wasting time at the intersection. Something about the decision to pack a bag and hail a cab for Reagan National left him motionless.

Seeing his father was nonnegotiable. He'd be on a plane to Orlando and in a rental car to New Smyrna Beach before he saw another sunset, but would that flight leave D.C. before or after 6:00 a.m.?

American Airlines made the non-stop flight twice a day at 3:30 p.m. and 8:30 a.m, and a one-stop redeye at midnight. The 8:30 flight would get him there earlier than the red-eye, even if he could make it to the airport in time to make the midnight flight.

The decision was made. He'd catch the metro outside DOJ Headquarters after his meeting with the DAG and be at Reagan to board the 8:30 flight with plenty of time to spare. All that remained was one sleepless night and the most important meeting of his career. And maybe his life.

* * *

As the mercury in D.C. fell into the teens, the temperature on South Beach rose when the sun fell across the western horizon. The new girls in town—the fearless Russian and her protégé—were undisputed contributors to the nightly heat wave, at least in the club owned by the Lion of Leningrad.

When the convertible Porsche slid to a stop in front of the valet stand, every head turned, waiting to see what the leggy blonde and flawless brunette would be wearing when their stilettos hit the sidewalk.

The valet in his purple silk vest caught the key fob a second after Anya launched it into the air, and the bouncer on the front door dropped the velvet rope.

"*Spasibo*," Gwynn hissed as she brushed past the musclebound Ukrainian on the door.

"You are welcome. Leo made clear the two of you are not to wait outside club, ever, and you are to never pay for drink inside. You are special guest, and club is yours."

"That's very nice of him," Gwynn said. "I'll be sure to tell him what a great job you're doing. Just out of curiosity, what might happen if you made us wait on the sidewalk?"

The man shot a horrified look inside the club and back at Gwynn. "He would cut my throat."

Gwynn giggled, and Anya squeezed her hand and said, "He is not making joke."

Agent Davis suddenly understood the difference between American loyalty and Russian *vernost'*.

The bouncer hadn't overstated the new policy of the club. Anya and Gwynn only had to *think* they wanted a drink, and one would appear in their hand. The courtesy of the staff wasn't the only change. The men who'd routinely approached and even pressed themselves between the two women now stood with drinks in hand and only stared. The one man who dared approach and laid a hand against Anya's hip as she ground her body in time with the thudding music, landed face-first in the filthy alley behind the club at the hands of a pair of bouncers who materialized out of thin air. The rules had changed, and these rules were enforced gulag style.

When Gwynn felt a hand press against the small of her back, she turned in amusement to see who the next victim of enforcement would be. To her surprise, she looked up into Tony's brilliant smile. She rewarded him with a smile of her own and a kiss on each cheek.

She let him lead, and they danced until they were drenched with sweat. Anya met Leo's eye across the crowded club and motioned for him to join her on the dance floor. The Lion slowly shook his head and held up a bottle of Krug Clos d'Ambonnay.

The Russian parted the ocean of gyrating bodies as she made her way to his table. He rose, and she kissed his cheeks. In Russian, she said, "This is too much. It's a two-thousand-dollar bottle of champagne."

He made a show of uncaging and releasing the cork without the pop and overflow the uninitiated believe are hallmarks of correctly opening champagne.

As he poured, she slithered onto the couch, giving him an uninterrupted view of her thigh through the slit of her dress. He poured a second flute, barely managing to keep his eyes on the wine before it overflowed the glass. Tony and Gwynn arrived just in time to raise their glasses in a salute —vodka for Leo and tequila for Tony.

Leo bellowed, "To mutually beneficial friendship!"

Tony yelled, "Salud!" while Anya and Gwynn gave the traditional Russian, "*Za druzhbe!*"

Anya let the champagne pour from the flute across her lips and savored the feeling of the effervescence as the minuscule bubbles danced across her tongue. "This is wonderful champagne. You are beautiful host. We are going to be spoiled women very soon."

Leo emptied his glass. "As you should be."

Leo refilled glasses every time they approached empty, and Anya almost felt bad about pouring the three-hundred-dollar glasses of champagne onto the floor while no one was watching. Gwynn couldn't bring herself to follow Anya's lead, instead drinking slowly and falling in love with every sip.

Leo polished off his bottle of vodka and stood. "Come inside my office where we can talk without yelling over this music."

With the door closed, the thudding beat of the techno music was still evident but no longer deafening.

"So, you have found our drug enforcement agent, no?"

Anya licked her lips. "Finding man like this who does not want to be found is not so easy. Sometimes, it takes many days, especially when he is skilled in—"

Gwynn laid her hand on Anya's arm. "What my friend is trying to say is, Tony can tell his dogs to get ready for Jerry Carmichael's thumbs on Popsicle sticks."

21
VTOROY V KOMANDE
(SECOND-IN-COMMAND)

At precisely five minutes to six, the executive assistant to the deputy attorney general of the United States ushered Special Agent Ray White into the elegant office and installed him in a red wingback chair that reminded him of a particular house of ill repute in the French Quarter of New Orleans, where he'd spent most of his spring break and all of his cash during his sophomore year in college. The thought of that week a quarter century before made it impossible to be nervous sitting across the enormous mahogany desk from the second-highest-ranking official in the U.S. Department of Justice.

"Good morning, Special Agent White. I don't believe we've been formally introduced. I'm Deputy AG Marcia McLeish. It's a pleasure to finally meet you."

White rose from his chair and shook the offered hand. "The pleasure is mine, ma'am, and I appreciate you making time for me this morning."

She waved a dismissive hand. "Not at all, Agent. I understand we have some issues of some weight to discuss. I'm in the office by five-thirty every morning anyway. I usually don't take appointments until seven, so we've got an hour."

White cleared his throat and slid an innocuous-looking manila file across the desk. "I don't think we'll need an hour, ma'am. If you'll take a look inside that folder, you'll find four pictures."

DAG McLeish opened the folder and pulled out the stack of photos.

"The man you see in the first picture, ma'am, is Antonio Alvarez. His friends call him Tony."

McLeish shook the photo. "Oh, yes. I'm quite familiar with Mr. Alvarez. He fancies himself the new Pablo Escobar, if I'm not mistaken."

"You are not, ma'am. That's exactly how he thinks of himself, and as you might imagine, his ego is almost as big as your desk."

She slid her hands across the blotter. "Yes, well, this wasn't my idea, I'm afraid. I inherited it from my predecessor, who, I guess, used it as a ping-pong table, or perhaps a place to land airplanes when they ran out of room at BWI."

"Yes, ma'am, well, be that as it may, Mr. Alvarez has befriended a man who calls himself Leo, the king of the jungle. You'll find his picture next in the stack."

She slid Alvarez's picture to the side and studied the second. "He looks like a sleazy nightclub owner."

White crossed his legs. "You're not far off in your assessment of good ol' Leo. He's the kingpin of the Russian mafia in Miami, and he does in fact own three nightclubs. One of them even appears to be a legitimate, money-making endeavor. The other two . . . well, let's just say neither is a place for a lady."

She lifted her glasses from the desk and slid them onto her face. "I see. So, may I assume the only ladies in these clubs are a little short on clothing?"

"Yes, ma'am. You may assume such, and you would be quite correct. The legitimate club, however, is the most popular techno club in the city, but we're getting a little off track. We're uncertain what Leo's real name is, but we believe he may be Ukrainian."

McLeish slid her glasses down her nose and looked across the frames. "A Ukrainian in charge of the Russian mafia in Miami?"

"Yes, well, you see, the term *Russian mafia* is a bit of a misnomer. It's more correctly the former Soviet Union mafia, but that's a mouthful. Before the wall came down, these guys all thought of themselves as country-men. When the Soviet Union crumbled into a bunch of individual countries with their own politics and politicians, they forgot to tell the prisoners they weren't exactly brothers any longer. So, as a result, the Russian mafia isn't very particular about which Eastern Bloc country you hail from as long as you've done time in the right prison. Most of these guys are ex-convicts."

She laid Leo's picture aside and raised her chin, examining the two remaining pictures carefully. "And who might these two be?"

"The first is Special Agent Guinevere Davis. She's one of the best and brightest of the young agents we're lucky to have, ma'am. She reports directly to me."

"And the blonde? I must say she looks decidedly Eastern Bloc, herself."

"Right again, ma'am. Her name is Anastasia Burinkova, but she prefers to be called Anya. She's a confidential cooperating participant."

The glasses came off. "Is that the term you use down in Organized Crime and Gang Section?"

Ray scratched his chin. "Well, yes, ma'am, but it's not my term. It simply means—"

"I know what it means, Agent White. It means you caught her doing something for which she should be in prison, but instead, she's working off her sentence doing your dirty work."

"That's not exactly . . ."

"I get the picture. Please continue, Agent."

"Yes, of course. Well, you see, Agent Davis and Ms. Burinkova are working their way inside Leo's organization in Miami. Anastasia—Anya—has a quite specialized skill set that makes her, shall we say, attractive to the Bratva. That's the Russian word for *brotherhood*."

The DAG checked her watch, and White noticed.

"So, to get to the point.. .."

"Tell me about this skill set the Russian has . . . other than the obvious."

"She is a KGB-trained assassin who prefers edged weapons. Knives."

McLeish rolled her eyes. "Yes, I know what an edged weapon is. What I want to know now is whether or not this Anya of yours is an American citizen."

"She is. She defected four years ago and has been legally living in the U.S. since then."

The DAG picked up her glasses and stuck the stem into the corner of her mouth. "I want to make sure I have the picture here. You have an American citizen who's practically an indentured servant working alongside one of your agents, and these two women are horning their way into the Russian mafia in Miami."

"Yes, ma'am. That pretty much covers it."

"What did she do?"

Ray shook his head. "I'm sorry, what?"

"Her crime, Agent White. What did the Russian do to get picked up?"

"She killed two guys we sprang from jail in Florida."

"Why did you spring two guys from jail in Florida, Agent White?"

Ray looked at the desk and imagined a regional jet touching down near the lamp and taxiing to parking near the inbox. "Uh, well, ma'am. We, um . . . We sprang them from jail so Anya would kill them."

The deputy attorney general of the United States closed her eyes and shook her head like a metronome badly needing to be rewound. "I appreciate your candor, Agent, but if it's all right with you, let's never use that particular phrase again. Deal?"

"Yes, ma'am, but it's important that you know I'm here in the interest of full disclosure. We want Leo, at least, and the line behind him is nearly as long as your desk. But we're starting with him. The two primary things I came here to discuss this morning—"

She held up a hand. "You can't have two primary things, Agent White. You can only have one primary thing. That's what primary means. So, let's hear the primary thing first, and I'll let you know if I care to hear the sec-ondary thing."

"The problem is that the two things are inextricably connected, making both things primary."

She rolled her hand through the air. "Keep talking, Agent, but I need you to stop telling me about the conception and just deliver the baby."

"Yes, ma'am. It turns out that one of your DEA agents may have been on the take. His name is Jerry Carmichael, and he allegedly took a hundred thousand dollars in cash from Tony Alvarez and vanished."

"That's a serious accusation."

"Yes, I know, but the accusation just happens to be the key to getting my operatives firmly ensconced inside Leo's organization. Alvarez wants to feed Carmichael's thumbs to his dogs, and he expects my operatives to fa-cilitate that feeding."

McLeish held up one finger and turned to her computer. A few rapid keystrokes preceded the glasses sliding back up her nose as she read the screen. Her eyes traced the lines, and the glasses came off again. "Well, it seems Agent Carmichael has taken an extended leave of absence, citing some personal family issues overseas."

"Where overseas?"

The DAG flipped off the computer monitor. "The personnel file doesn't specify, but I'd like to know what your KGB-trained assassin plans to do if she finds former Special Agent Carmichael."

Ray locked eyes with the second-highest-ranking official in the DOJ. "Former?"

She swallowed hard and examined her nails. "I may have misspoken."

"I don't think you did, ma'am. What aren't you telling me about Carmichael?"

She pushed away from her desk, building eighteen inches of additional distance between herself and Ray. "Tell me, Agent White, what is the second part of the primary element of your operation?"

Ray wanted to explore the discomfort Marcia McLeish was experiencing after reading Carmichael's file, but he didn't want to get thrown out of her office for probing too hard. "Madam Deputy, forgive me, but I'm a trained interrogator, and a good one thanks to twenty years of chasing—and catching—some of the nastiest organized crime figures in modern times. You saw something in Jerry Carmichael's file that caused you to turn off the monitor and refer to him as a former agent. If Jerry Carmichael is a player in this thing, I need to know. My operatives on the inside need to know."

McLeish checked her watch again. "What is the second part, Agent White?"

Ray hesitated momentarily as he considered pressing the issue but decided on discretion for the sake of preserving what little rapport he had with the DAG. "The second part is that Alvarez wants to buy a Russian submarine to run thousands of tons of cocaine out of Columbia, and Leo is brokering the deal."

McLeish didn't flinch, but there was a barely perceptible narrowing of her eyes.

Ray could see her wheels turning as she asked, "Who authorized you to dispatch a confidential cooperating participant and a rookie agent to infiltrate the Russian mob?"

White didn't mind throwing his boss's boss under the proverbial bus, especially if it got him what he wanted from well up the ladder. "The principal deputy assistant attorney general over the Criminal Division handed me the assignment, ma'am. I know the FBI is involved on a logistical level, as is Central Intelligence. The Technical Services Branch provided the equipment, and the FBI played wardrobe."

McLeish squeezed the tip of her tongue between her lips and stared past Ray. "A Russian nuclear submarine?"

"No, ma'am. I doubt Alvarez wants a nuke. A diesel boat is much easier to operate and maintain. It's more likely he's in the market for a much cheaper old diesel."

McLeish continued her distant stare. "Does DHS know?"

Ray shrugged. "I haven't told anybody over at Homeland Security, but that's well above my paygrade. I'm under orders to keep this close to the vest, so nobody outside my department, aside from you, knows anything about the mission."

"That's good," she said. "Let's keep it that way. The fewer people who know about this, the better. So, land the plane, Agent White. What is it you want from me?"

"I'm not a politician. I'm a street fighter, Madam Deputy. I want to find Carmichael, take some pictures with my Russian's knife sticking out of his throat, and hand his thumbs to Tony Alvarez. I know the boys over in tech services can make anything look real. If Carmichael is in the stable, we're one photo shoot away from giving my operatives a seat at the adult's table down in Miami. And if I can get them deep enough inside, I can stop the purchase of the sub and maybe even bring you Antonio Alvarez's head on a silver platter."

McLeish leaned back in her chair and examined the chandelier. "You really are a cowboy, aren't you, Agent White?"

"No, ma'am. Cowboys mend fences. I'm a gunslinger. I stand in the middle of the street at high noon and shoot it out with the bad guys."

She leaned forward, placed her elbows on the desk, and took a long, deep breath. "Well, you listen to me, gunslinger. Carmichael isn't on a leave of absence. He's on the lam with a dead partner and burned-down house in his wake. If you and your Russian can find him, you can have his thumbs. I just want his badge back. It doesn't belong to him anymore."

22

SLISHKOM MALO, SLISHKOM POZDNO
(TOO LITTLE TOO LATE)

Supervisory Special Agent Ray White's DOJ credentials got him on the plane two minutes after they'd closed the door and began retracting the Jetway. The groans of the other passengers were muffled as word that an air marshal had joined the flight made its way down the aisles in whispered tones. Ray wasn't an air marshal, but he made no effort to cure the case of mistaken identity.

The plane touched down just under two hours later at Orlando International, and Ray headed for the rental car counter. With his government employee discount, he paid a hundred bucks for a Ford F-150 pickup and headed up Interstate 4, his badge and credentials displayed on the dash just above the speedometer indicating 105 mph.

New Smyrna Beach Hospital is a nine-story structure of reinforced concrete that has endured eleven hurricanes in its existence. With the exception of a few air conditioning units from the roof, Mother Nature had been held at bay by the medical fortress.

"He's in room six seventeen," the bright-eyed young nurse said.

"Thank you. Is it all right if I go in?"

She smiled. "Of course. He's your father. He'll be happy to see you."

I don't know about that. If I had intervened with the local police, he wouldn't be in this hospital, and I wouldn't be dreading seeing him lying in a hospital bed, beaten and battered.

"Hey, Dad. It's me. How you doin'?"

Charles White pressed the button on the controller to raise the head of his bed. "Oh, hey, son. Come on in. You shouldn't have come all this way."

Ray pulled the door closed behind him and walked to the edge of the bed. "Don't be ridiculous, Dad. Of course I'd come. How are you feeling?"

Charles squirmed uncomfortably, trying to find a position in the bed that didn't hurt. "Oh, you know me. I'm too cantankerous to die, so I'll be fine. Doc says it's just a couple of broken ribs. I'll be back on my feet in a few days, good as new. How are you doing, son? You look tired."

Ray ran his hand through his hair. "I just didn't get much sleep last night. You know . . . I was worried about my old man."

Charles coughed and grabbed at his ribs. When he caught his breath, he said, "You've got enough to worry about with your big important job in D.C. You don't need to be worrying about me."

Ray looked down at the white-haired, frail old man who'd taught him to play catch and ride a bike and drive a 1956 Chevy. The man who'd worked three jobs to put him through college and law school.

He bounced his palm on the bed rail. "Look, Dad, I'm sorry I didn't come down and take care of those kids at the store. I was. . . ."

Charles laid his weathered hand on Ray's. "Son, stop it. It isn't your responsibility. I should've listened to you and called the cops, but I didn't think there was anything they could do."

"Yeah, it is my responsibility. You're my father, and I need to look out for you. Describe the kids who did this to you."

Another coughing spell and more squeezing of ribs. "It's in the cops' hands now, son. They'll handle it."

"I'm sure they will, but just humor me. How many of them were there?"

Charles focused on the ceiling above his bed. "I'm not sure, but there were at least four, maybe five."

"Try to describe them for me . . . age, height, weight, race, hair color. Anything you can remember."

"I don't know. It was dark, and it all happened so fast. I had one of those fancy new alarm systems that called my number if anybody set it off.

I had it set for silent at the store, but when the phone rang, I knew something was going on."

"Why didn't you have it monitored by the security company? They would've called the police."

"Yeah, yeah. Too little too late. It's done now. So, anyway, I took the old shotgun—you know, the one that knocked you down the first time you shot it. Anyhow, I snuck up on 'em. I was going to rack the slide and scare the bejesus out of 'em, but I stumbled on the metal water bowl I keep out back for the cats. That made just enough racket to get their attention. I guess they were old enough to drive, but not much older than that. I really can't remember much more."

"Why do you think they wanted to get into the bookstore?"

Charles directed his attention back to the ceiling. "I don't know. I never keep more than a hundred dollars in the cash register at night, and there's nothing there to steal except a few thousand books. There's not much of a black market for used books, so I can't imagine what they wanted."

Ray was in full-blown cop mode. "What happened to the shotgun?"

"I don't remember. When I came to, I was in the hospital. I guess those kids probably got it, but it might still be behind the store."

"I'll talk to the cops and find out. If they took it and it turns up in a pawn shop, we'll be able to follow the money."

"That old gun isn't worth anything," Charles said. "After you threw it on the ground when you were twelve, it never has been the same. I wouldn't think a pawn shop would want the old thing."

Ray patted his father's hand. "You'd be surprised, Dad. Some people will do anything for a little cash—besides getting a real job. I'm going to step outside and make a couple of calls. I'll be right back. Do you want me to have the nurses bring you anything?"

"No, go on and make your calls. I'm not going anywhere."

Ray found a quiet waiting room with a few tattered chairs arranged mostly in a line with a television playing CNN. He muted the TV and pulled his phone from his pocket. Agent Gwynn Davis answered on the fourth ring, just before going to voice mail.

"I can't believe you're calling me. Is everything all right?"

Ray checked the area again. No one was within earshot. "I'm sorry for calling. I know it's against protocol, but I couldn't wait. Can you talk?"

"I can listen," she said, barely above a whisper.

"That's good enough. I'm in the hospital at New Smyrna. My dad tried to surprise some kids breaking into his bookstore, but they got the jump on him. Broke a couple of ribs, but he's going to be okay."

"Oh, Agent White, I'm so sorry."

"It's okay. He'll be fine. It'll just take some time, but that's not the reason I'm calling. I've got some news on Jerry Carmichael."

"I'm listening."

"I met with the deputy attorney general this morning, and she pulled his personnel file. He's on the lam. She said he left a dead partner and a burnt house behind. Apparently, there's no active manhunt, so that leads me to believe the DOJ thinks he's already dead, but I couldn't get any more out of her."

Gwynn said, "So, does that mean Anya and I are starting the manhunt for Carmichael?"

"No, not yet. For the time being, I want you two to stay where Leo can see you. We may pull you out in a couple of days under the guise of hunting Carmichael, but for now, stay where you are and keep doing what you're doing. I've got Johnny Mac sniffing around for crumbs. He'll pick up a scent sooner or later that points to Carmichael."

"Whatever you say, boss. I'll brief Anya."

White checked for prying ears again and saw none. "Is she okay?"

"Anya? Yeah. She's in her element, and I'm learning something new every ten minutes."

"Okay, good. I may be out of pocket for the rest of the day, but leave me a voicemail if anything comes up. If anything critical arises, Johnny Mac is on call."

"We're good down here. I'll check in tomorrow."

Ray's next call was to the New Smyrna Beach Police Department. "This is Supervisory Special Agent Ray White. I need to speak with the chief of detectives."

"Stand by, Special Agent White."

Seconds passed with slightly out of tune hold music playing.

"Captain Reese."

"Reese, this is Supervisory Special Agent Ray White with DOJ Criminal Division Organized Crime and Gang Section. Are you the chief of detectives?"

"We're a small department, Agent White. I'm second-in-command under the chief of police, so I suppose that makes me chief of the four detectives we have. What can I do for you?"

"I'm following up on the assault of Mr. Charles White last night at his bookstore. What can you tell me about the investigation so far?"

Captain Reese cleared his throat. "Did you say you're with Organized Crime and Gangs Section?"

"That's right."

"Section of what, Agent White?"

"I'm with Justice out of D.C., Reese. Do you want the number to the attorney general so you can vet me?"

"No, White, I don't want the AG's number. Nobody would be dumb enough to call here pretending to be whatever the hell you are. I just want to know why the feds are poking around in my investigation of some teenaged hoodlums roughing up a local bookstore owner."

"As I said, Captain, I'm from Organized Crime and Gangs Section, and—"

"Yeah, yeah, I got that. Did you say your name is White?"

"Yes, that's right, Supervisory Special Agent Ray White."

Ray could hear Captain Reese reposition himself in his worn-out office chair.

"Are you any relation to the victim, Mr. Charles White?"

Ray sighed. "He's my father."

"Thought so. Look, Special Agent White, you would've gotten a lot farther with me if you'd started with that information instead of flashing your fancy D.C. credentials around. We're pretty sure we know who at least one of the kids are. I'll have him picked up this afternoon, and we'll put the fear of God in him. He'll roll over on the others in the gang."

"Thanks, Captain Reese. I'm sorry. I feel bad for not getting involved when my dad first told me about the kids trying to break into his store. I really appreciate your understanding. Can I give you my cell number?"

"Sure, you can give it to me, but I can't promise that calling you will be high on the list of priorities. Even if we find these little bastards and they talk, it's simple assault, and the local DA will likely plead them out."

"I think it's probably a little more than that, Captain. My father had an antique twelve-gauge pump shotgun. It's likely that the kids who assaulted him took the shotgun. I'm not a member of the Florida Bar, but aggravated assault during the commission of a felony is not simple assault."

"Breaking and entering isn't a felony in Florida, Agent White."

"No, but theft of a firearm is, Captain Reese. I'll give you a call back after I get off the phone with the district attorney."

Reese mumbled, "And you wonder why the whole world hates lawyers."

* * *

Anya and Gwynn had been in a boutique when White called, so Gwynn waited until they were behind the closed door of the apartment before beginning the briefing.

Gwynn began the conversation. "Remember when Agent White got the call from his father in the car in D.C.?"

"Yes, I remember," Anya said.

"Well, those kids tried to break into his dad's bookstore. Apparently, Mr. White surprised them, and they beat him up pretty badly. They put him in the hospital with some broken ribs."

Anya frowned. "The police arrested these people, yes?"

"Not yet, but that's not the only reason he called. He found some news on Jerry Carmichael. Apparently, he's in the wind. He said something about a dead partner and burning down a house. Johnny Mac is working on it, but it may take a while to find him."

"I was afraid of this. One hundred thousand dollars is not enough money to run for long. Carmichael will run out of money and turn up somewhere soon."

Gwynn bounced a pencil against her thigh. "I think you're right, but we have to put out a wide net. Johnny Mac is really good at finding people who don't want to be found. It's sort of his specialty."

Anya snatched the pencil from Gwynn. "What is *your* specialty?"

"Learning from you."

Anya rolled her eyes. "You will call chief of police in New Smyrna Beach and get names of boys who hurt Agent White's father, and we will take care of them."

"No, Anya, that's not how this works. We're staying right here, just like Agent White ordered us to do."

Anya pulled her hair into a bun at the top of her head and stuck the pencil through it. "Agent White does not give to me orders. You will call police, and I will go to New Smyrna Beach."

23

DYMOVYYE SIGNALY
(SMOKE SIGNALS)

The following morning, Special Agent Gwynn Davis—whose name on the streets of South Beach was quickly becoming Gabrielle—sat on the living room floor stretching like a ballerina before *Swan Lake*. "That thing you did where you threw the knife into the back of that guy's hand . . . Can you teach me to do that?"

Anya, who always seemed to be ready to dance her solo without a minute's stretching, pulled a pair of butter knives from a kitchen drawer. "Throwing is like making love. I cannot teach to you how to do it. I can only demonstrate for you how I do it. It is up to you to find how your body does it."

Gwynn tilted her head in the confused puppy look, and Anya tossed her one of the butter knives, handle first.

Gwynn caught the knife, and her confusion continued. "What are we going to do with these? You can't throw a butter knife and expect it to stick in anything."

Anya pulled a cardboard box from the closet that contained some of the gear the FBI delivered the day they arrived in South Beach. She collapsed the box and folded it into a target two feet square and several inches thick and propped it against the front of the couch Gwynn had already pushed aside.

She offered a hand to Gwynn and pulled her to her feet. "Stand in front of me, and point your toes from your right foot toward my body." She adjusted Gwynn's stance, aligning her shoulders with her hips. "Good. Now, hold knife in right hand with butt resting in crease in palm."

Gwynn followed her instructions and situated the dull blade with the handle resting comfortably in her palm.

Anya took two steps back and assumed a fighting stance. "Now, do not move feet, but pretend you are slicing from my left shoulder to my right hip with long, slow motion."

Gwynn did as she instructed, pulling the blade slowly through the air between them, her knuckles white from squeezing the handle. Anya took her hand in hers. "Relax. Do not squeeze. Only hold enough so knife does not fall out of hand."

They continued the exercise until Gwynn was slashing at almost full speed while keeping her feet firmly planted.

Anya stepped aside and motioned toward the flattened box. "Now, slice box instead of me."

Gwynn raised the knife high above her shoulder and slashed downward as if trying to slice the box in half.

Anya nodded. "This is very good. Now, make grip on knife even looser, and try again."

Davis did as she was told, and the dull, round-point knife flew from her hand and buried itself into the cardboard. Her face exploded in excitement and disbelief, but before she could celebrate too much, Anya placed the second butter knife in her palm.

"Do not think. Only do this again."

Gwynn almost did what she was told but intentionally released the knife rather than letting it glide from her grasp. The blade sailed across the couch, down the hall, and came to rest beneath her bed.

Anya shook her head. "Your brain made thoughts, no?"

Gwynn nodded. "Yes, my brain made thoughts even though you told me not to."

"Is okay. You have thrown two knives in all of your life, and you made half of them stick into target. That is much better than my record."

"What's your record?"

Anya shrugged. "I do not know, but I have thrown many thousands of knives. I do not miss now, but while I was learning, I was terrible student. Like you, my brain got in the way. Do not think. Just let it happen."

Gwynn continued her practice from five feet away from the target until she was consistently sticking the blade greater than fifty percent of the time. Anya watched her student and occasionally made small corrections to her technique. After half an hour, Gwynn began to make corrections without Anya's input, and a style began to emerge.

"Tomorrow, we will try with sharp knives, but we will need much stronger target."

The doorbell rang, followed immediately by a sharp knock. Anya yanked one of the butter knives from the impaled cardboard target and stepped toward the door. "Who is there?"

A muffled voice came from the other side. "It's Michael from downstairs. I have a package for Gwynn."

She pulled open the door, and the tall, handsome man stood with a nondescript package in one hand.

"Hello, Anya. This came for Gwynn a few minutes ago. Can you see that she gets it?"

Anya reached for the box the size of a small book and let her fingertips graze Michael's hand. "Yes, of course. Thank you."

Men are such simple creatures, she thought as she spun on her heel, giving Michael a glimpse of her backside before closing the door.

"What is it?"

Anya tossed the box toward Gwynn. "I do not know. It is for you."

Gwynn made the catch and used the remaining knife to cut away the tape. Inside the unlabeled box was a black cell phone with a slip of yellow paper stuck to the keypad. On the paper, someone had typed "Dial *22 and program your personal access code." She pulled the phone from the box and followed the prompts to program her six-digit code.

"Who would send phone to you?"

Gwynn looked up. "It's got all the hallmarks of an FBI gadget, but I can't be sure. I don't even know the number on it. Maybe I'm supposed to set it on fire and send smoke signals to somebody."

"You could call my phone, and we would then have number."

Gwynn shook the phone at her. "You spies are a sneaky bunch. I'll give you that."

She dialed Anya's number and waited for the ring.

It came, and Anya held up the phone. "It says unknown number. I think maybe you are now spy."

To Gwynn's surprise, the phone vibrated, and she peered at the small screen. "It's a D.C. number."

"Hello?"

"Is this Special Agent Guinevere Davis?"

"It is, and who's calling?"

The mousy voice on the other end said, "This is the Central Intelligence communications center. It's crucial that you phone Special Agent Johnathon McIntyre immediately."

Gwynn heard a click and stared down at the phone. The caller had hung up.

"That was somebody claiming to be the CIA comms center. They said I need to call Johnny Mac."

Anya showed her palms. "Is not for me."

Gwynn dialed Johnny's number from memory and listened for him to answer.

"Davis. I was hoping it would be you. Listen, I think I've found your missing DEA agent."

Gwynn scowled. "What's with all the cloak and dagger? Why didn't you just call my cell?"

"Because if it hasn't already been compromised, it will be soon. You can't use your personal phone for any official comms. Somebody is probably listening."

"You're paranoid, Johnny Mac, but you're a heck of a hound dog when it comes to sniffing out trails. Tell me where Carmichael is."

"You'll never believe it, but I think he's working private security for a couple of guys from L.A. They're on the side of a mountain in Big Sky, Montana. It's a resort town south of Bozeman."

"How on earth did you track him down there?"

Johnny said, "It was the craziest thing. A partial fingerprint match came back when somebody did a cursory background check on him in Los Angeles. It looks like he was wearing some sort of prosthetic fingerprint devices when he gave up his prints, and one of the prosthetics must've slipped off. It was a left thumbprint. Because of the shape of the thumb, it's tough to get those prosthetics to stick."

"That's great work, Johnny. I don't know how you do it."

"What can I say? I'm a good cop."

She chuckled. "Yes, you are . . . most of the time."

"Yeah, whatever. I couldn't get the boss to answer, so I figured you'd want to know."

"His phone probably doesn't work in the hospital, but don't worry. I'll make sure you get all the credit for finding Carmichael."

"I can send the marshals after him," Johnny said, "but I hate to make a move without the boss authorizing it."

"Yeah, I don't think we need the marshals on this one. I've got an idea. Don't do anything until you hear from me. I'll call you before the sun comes up, so keep your phone by the bed."

"Hey, Gwynn. . . ."

"Yeah, what is it?"

Johnny stammered for a moment. "You're being safe down there, right?"

"Cut the big-brother routine, Johnny Mac. I'm fine. Anya's teaching me to fight and throw knives. I'm probably safer here than you are back in D.C."

"It's just that, I mean . . . I just don't want anything to happen to you. I'd hate to have to break in someone new. You know how it is."

"Yeah, Johnny Mac, I know how it is. And I appreciate you worrying about me, but I'm in good hands. I'll call you sometime in the early morning."

Johnny hung up without another word, but the thought of his junior partner—and the lowest ranking member of the team—basking in the sun on South Beach almost made him wish he'd been born a girl.

* * *

Anya checked her watch. "We can get inside club and wait for Leo there. I think this is better plan than going through front door again."

"I'm game," Gwynn said, "but I think this one calls for blue jeans and boots instead of slutty dresses and stilettos, don't you?"

An hour later, Gwynn got to try out the new lock-picking skills Anya had taught her, and to her surprise, the back door of the club practically popped open in her hand. "That was easier than I expected."

Anya said, "Do not get cocky. Is only doorknob. Dead bolt is much harder."

They slipped inside, thankful no one was in the hallway leading to Leo's office. Some of the staff were stocking the bars, and a worker was doing something on a ladder with the lights over the dance floor."

In the interest of time, Anya did the lock-picking and had Leo's office door open in seconds. "Now we make ourselves comfortable and wait. I believe Leo will be here in two hours."

Gwynn eyed the room. "Patience isn't my strong suit, so you're not going to enjoy waiting with me. I get bored way too easily."

"You will learn patience. This is one of the things that life always teaches us. Sometimes it takes longer than it should, but it will come."

Gwynn laughed.

Anya pressed the door closed behind them. "What is funny?"

"I just realized you're like my own personal Master Yoda."

The Russian furrowed her brow. "I do not know what this means."

"You mean you've never seen Star Wars?"

Anya continued the look. "No."

"Okay, it's on." Gwynn pointed to the floor and made a circular sweep with her finger. "When all this is over, we're having a for-real slumber party, just the two of us, and we're watching Star Wars. I'm definitely introducing you to Yoda. That's what you are. You're my very own Russian Yoda."

Before Gwynn could lead Anya any farther down the sci-fi trail, the sound of a key sliding into the door lock caught their attention.

Anya shoved Gwynn away from the door and whispered, "Get into closet."

She obeyed and disappeared into Leo's coat closet the same instant Anya dived beneath the desk.

Two pairs of footsteps entered the office, and the door closed and locked behind them. The footfalls were far too light to be Leo's, but who else would have a key to his office?

Anya listened intently as the two intruders crossed the room. The two-inch gap at the bottom edge of the desk gave Anya a somewhat-obstructed view of the bottom of the barely ajar closet door. A pair of brown leather loafers made to look more expensive than they were shuffled across the floor beside a pair of red high-heels.

The man was the first to speak. "If we get busted, he's going to kill both of us. You know that, right?"

"We're not getting busted. Relax. Besides, he doesn't know I've got a key. He'll never know we were in here."

"And you're sure he doesn't count the till every night?" the man asked.

"Yes, I'm sure. He counts it before we open every night. How many times have you been in here with him after close, huh?"

No response.

"That's what I thought. If you knew the things I had to do to that disgusting pig, you'd understand why I deserve the cash in that box. Now get the drawer open. It's the bottom left."

Anya listened as the man rounded the corner of the desk and began pulling on the handle of the drawer. "It's locked."

"No, it isn't, you moron. Pull the lap drawer open a little. That's how fancy desks work."

"Like you'd know anything about fancy desks."

"I know this much," the woman argued. "I've done things on that desk you've only seen in pornos."

Anya watched a manicured hand grip the bottom of the lap drawer above her head and yank it open a few inches. Next came the larger drawer, and the hand disappeared. A heavy metal box landed on the desk, and the man said, "It's locked."

A sound of exasperation left the woman's mouth. "Can't you do anything? It's a stupid little cashbox lock. Pick it."

"What are you talking about? I don't know how to pick a lock. You're the one who said you had the keys . . . plural."

The woman pulled a paperclip from a cup on the edge of the desk and sent the straightened metal into the simple, flimsy lock. "There . . . see? How hard was that?"

"Look at that!" the man said. "There must be a hundred grand in there. How much are we taking?"

"We're taking all we can carry without it looking obvious. That's how much."

It occurred to Anya that Leo would suspect Gwynn and her for the theft when he arrived and found them camped out in his office, so she made the only play on the table and leapt from beneath the desk with her knife in hand.

The woman saw her first and bolted for the door, but Gwynn burst from the closet and clotheslined the woman before she made it halfway across the floor.

The man froze in shock with his left hand full of cash and his right pressed against the top of the desk. Anya brought the knife down hard into the back of his hand. The blow pierced both the back of his hand as well as his palm and pinned him to the desk. He opened his mouth to scream in agony, but Anya shoved his mouth full of cash and wrapped her left arm beneath his chin, locking it in place with her right. In seconds, the man melted in her arms as his brain lost touch with reality.

The woman kicked against Gwynn, but when the muzzle of the Glock landed beneath her nose, pressing her lips against her teeth, she lost the will to fight.

Anya eased the man's limp body across the desk, leaving his hand pinned to the blotter with the blade of her knife. She looked up at Gwynn. "Tie her into chair, but leave one hand free."

"Get up," Gwynn ordered, and the woman trembled in fear as she climbed to her feet.

In a last-ditch effort and moment of desperation, the woman lashed out, clawing at Gwynn's face and throwing misaimed kicks into thin air.

That was the moment Special Agent Davis had been waiting for. It was time to put her newfound fighting skills to use. She brushed away the clawing attack of the woman's left hand and stepped into her space—far too close for the woman to land anything worse than a flailing slap. With the speed of a wild animal, Gwynn spun on the ball of her right foot, sending a punishing elbow strike to the hysterical woman's right temple. The blow sent the woman crashing to the floor and left her brain reeling as it saun-tered toward the spirit world for the next several minutes.

When she came to, the woman found herself tied to Leo's plush office chair and the crazy blonde woman with the knife slapping her face. "Wake up, or your boyfriend is going to bleed to death."

The fog of partial consciousness made the scene in front of her a waving oasis of a knife protruding from a hand with a pool of blood forming around it. The woman gagged at the sight of the ever-expanding crimson puddle.

Anya threw a shirt from the closet across the man's brutalized hand. "Hold shirt tight against his hand, or he will die, and this will be your fault."

Through trembling lips, the woman managed to say, "Look, I don't know who you are, but if you'll just let me go, you can have the money. I don't want it."

Gwynn shoved the muzzle of the Glock against the woman's forehead. "You wanted it badly enough to break into Leo's office with a stolen key and your stupid boyfriend, so now you get to answer directly to the Lion himself."

A look of recognition flooded the woman's terrified face. "Hey, you're those two girls who've been coming in here and drinking free champagne."

The realization of the moment overtook her, and she started sobbing. "Oh, Bobby, we're dead. He's going to kill us. We're dead."

Anya sent a hammer fist to the mastoid bone behind the woman's ear, rendering her unconscious again.

The Russian looked at Gwynn across the two limp bodies piled on the desk in front of her. "Is this enough to keep you from being bored?"

24

NUZHNO UBIT'
(ONE MUST KILL)

Special Agent Guinevere Davis surveyed the scene in front of her: at least fifty grand in cash, two unconscious would-be thieves, one with a tanto fighting knife driven through his hand and pinning him to the top of a Russian mafia kingpin's desk, and her new mentor, a former Russian spy turned American government operative. "I don't think it's possible to get bored around you, but what do we do now?"

Anastasia Burinkova took in the scene as well, but from her perspective, the situation couldn't be better. "Now we wait, but this time, we have appetizer and main dish for the Lion."

Gwynn watched the blood continue to ooze from the man's hand. "He's going to bleed out if we don't do something."

"Find for me necktie inside closet, and I will make tourniquet."

The tie slowed the blood, but if Leo let the man live, he would be in dire need of medical attention and a transfusion. KGB-trained assassins rarely deliver less-than-lethal affection, and Anya was no exception, regardless of the tiny plastic American flag tucked into the front pocket of her jeans.

The wait was far shorter than either woman believed.

Leo stuck his key in the door less than thirty minutes later. "What in the hell is happening here?"

Alexi stepped around his boss and into the office-turned-bloody-crime scene. Instinctually, he drew his pistol as he tried to make sense of what he saw before him, but there were too many unanswered questions to piece it together.

Anya pulled her knife from the wound, wiped the blade on the unconscious man's shirt, and slid the cutlass back into its sheath. "We have for you very nice gift. We came to tell to you news you will like, and we found these two stealing money from inside lockbox."

Leo took another stride into the office and hastily closed and locked the door. He motioned between the two unconscious thieves. "These two were stealing from the club? From me?"

Anya nodded. "Yes, this is truth."

Leo wiped his mouth on his sleeve. "Are they alive?"

Gwynn fielded that one. "For now, but stealing from a man like you is surely a death penalty, right?"

Leo ignored her and turned to Alexi. "Get these two out of here, and make sure they understand how badly they have chosen to die."

Minutes later, the man and woman were carried out the back, and the only remaining evidence of their existence was the blood-covered desk and piles of cash scattered about the floor.

Leo stood, mouth agape, staring at the desk. "What were you two doing in my office, and how did you get in here?"

Anya said, "We came to tell you very good news. We have found DEA Agent Jerry Carmichael for Tony."

Leo continued surveying the scene in disbelief. "That's great news, but it doesn't tell me how you got inside my office."

Anya shrugged. "I picked lock. Is very easy. We did this because we did not want anyone to see us here. We wanted only to see you before we go to take care of DEA agent."

Leo glared at the office door. "You picked that lock?"

"Yes, was easy, but the woman had key, and she said she has been inside office many times with you."

He almost smiled as the memory of what he had done with the woman who'd try to steal the previous day's cash. He lifted the desktop phone from its cradle and spoke into the receiver in a language Gwynn thought she should understand but couldn't.

He hung up and turned back to Anya. "Where is Jerry Carmichael, and how did you find him so quickly? We have been looking for him for weeks."

Anya glanced at Gwynn and then back to Leo. "We have skills and resources your people do not have. I will not tell you where he is, but I will bring to you his thumbs and also his heart if this is what you want."

"What I want is to look into his eyes and watch him soil himself in fear before I put a bullet through his skull. This is what I want."

Anya stepped against the Lion and let her breath waft across his skin. "Then I will give to you what you want. It will take maybe three or four days."

Leo swallowed hard. "You do that. You bring that bastard back here and stand him in front of me, and you will have my gratitude. This is not a thing I give away lightly."

She placed her lips just beneath his ear. "Four days, and we will both have what we want."

* * *

Gwynn pulled the apartment door closed behind her. "What did Leo say on the phone? I thought he was speaking Russian at first, but I couldn't understand any of it."

"He was speaking Romanian, and he told Alexi, 'Do not kill the girl.'"

"What about the guy?"

Anya shrugged. "I do not know, but is time for you to call police department in New Smyrna Beach."

Gwynn shook her head. "I still don't know if that's such a good idea. I mean, what are you going to do when you get the information?"

"I am going to find people who hurt Agent White's father and make them sorry. This is the thing people like that understand. They are not afraid of police. They only know intimidation and bully."

"That's not what we do, Anya. We're not vigilantes."

"Yes, we are. You will come to know this in time, but there are sometimes when police cannot do what is needed."

"Is that what you were doing when we caught you in Saint Augustine?"

Anya's thoughts flashed back to that night. "Those men were very bad, and they would have hurt my friends. I do not like that I was careless and was caught, but I am glad those men are dead."

Gwynn relished the rare moment of tenderness from the Russian. "You really care about your friends, don't you?"

"*Friend* means very different thing in Russian. Is more than person you know. Russian word is *drug* and means there is nothing I would not do for you. I think you will be my *podrooga*. This is feminine form of *drug*."

Gwynn let her gaze fall to the floor, and Anya noticed.

"Why does this make you unhappy?"

The young agent gathered her composure and looked up. "Everyone warned me that you would do that, and they were right."

Anya scowled. "They warned you I would become your friend? This does not make sense."

"They warned me you would seduce me. Not sexually, of course, but they told me you'd been trained to lure people in and make them trust you."

"This is true. I have been trained to do this, but I do this only for reasons when necessary. I do not do this to you. I will teach to you how to stay alive, and I will keep you alive until you learn these things, but friendship will come, or it will not. I have nothing to gain by misleading you."

Gwynn cocked her head. "Why do you roll your towels after you shower?"

Anya recoiled in confusion. "This is changing of subject."

"No, not really," Gwynn said. "I just want to know why you do it. I think it's cute, but I've never seen anyone do that. You did it back in D.C. after the—"

Anya said, "After the interrogation."

"Yeah, after the interrogation. And you do it here. I'm just curious."

Anya subconsciously glanced down the hall toward the bathroom. "I wanted to be gymnast like Svetlana Boginskaya. She was great Russian gymnast. I tried to do everything she does so I can also be great gymnast, but I grew too tall for this. Svetlana did this with her towel, and so I did also. It is silly thing, but sometimes it makes me think of being a little girl and learning to tumble."

Gwynn stood with a look of fascination on her face, and Anya said, "What is wrong?"

"Nothing is wrong. It's just hard for me to believe you ever wanted to be anybody other than who you are. You're beautiful and deadly. Every woman I know, including me, would kill to be like you."

"To be like me," Anya whispered, "one must kill, and this is not something that is good."

"I get it," Gwynn said, "but I need you to promise me you aren't going to play games with me. I have a lot to learn from you, and we're spending all our time together, but I have a job to do, and you're not going to get in the way of that job. I've watched you seduce Leo and every other man you come in contact with. Just don't do it to me, okay?"

Anya's irresistible smile made its appearance. "You are now to call police and find for us a flight to Montana."

* * *

Claude drove them to the airport for their early morning flight to Dallas, where they'd catch a connecting flight to Bozeman. The previous evening was spent shopping for suitable clothes for the harsh winter conditions that made Montana the dream of serious skiers, but shopping for winter wear in South Beach is like trying to buy a surfboard in Oklahoma. Their money would have to be spent in Bozeman if they were going to dress like snow bunnies.

"What did the police department in New Smyrna tell you?"

Gwynn rolled her eyes. "Really? That again?"

"Yes. It is important."

"Stopping Leo and Tony from buying a submarine is important. Those punks in New Smyrna are not."

Anya lowered her voice. "Imagine if four of your father's students attacked him and broke his ribs. Would those students be important to you?"

Gwynn huffed and pulled out her cell phone. "This is Special Agent Guinevere Davis with the DOJ Organized Crime and Gangs branch."

The call lasted six minutes, and Gwynn did a lot of listening. When she hung up, she turned to Anya. "Okay, I've got four names and descriptions, but I'm not turning you loose to chop up four teenagers in Florida. We'll go together, and we'll put the fear of God in them, but you're not going alone."

Anya said, "I do not have to wait for you. You are not the boss of me."

Gwynn grinned. "Yeah, I kinda am, but we can deal with that when we get back. What are you planning to do when we find Carmichael?"

"I am not planning to do anything except stand beside you while you arrest him. You are the only one with a badge and handcuffs. Oh, there is one thing I plan to do. . . ."

"What's that?"

"I plan to cut off thumbs and find Popsicle sticks."

25

SLISHKOM POKHOZHE NA MOSKVU
(TOO MUCH LIKE MOSCOW)

They landed in Bozeman and headed for the rental car counter. Gwynn slid her license and credit card to the clerk.

The woman glanced down at the cards. "Oh, good. You're from D.C. You've driven in snow before."

"Yeah, you could say that."

The clerk scanned the screen in front of her. "I have some bad news. You reserved a sedan, but we had two accidents last night, so all we have left is a Toyota Sequoia and two Ford pickup trucks. Since it was our fault, I'll give you either for the same price as the sedan."

"We'll take the Sequoia. It is four-wheel-drive, right?"

"Yes, it is. Just sign here and check the appropriate box for the insurance."

The clerk slid the keys across the counter. "It's waiting just outside the doors all the way at the end. Enjoy your stay."

Gwynn snatched the keys, and they walked out of the terminal into the crisp Rocky Mountain, twenty-six-degree air. Anya shivered and pulled the collar of her sweater up in a wasted effort to fend off the cold. A plow patrolled the airport parking lot, piling walls of snow well over their heads.

Gwynn made a show of inhaling the crisp afternoon air and scanning the horizon. "Isn't this place beautiful?"

Anya pulled her arms tight against her chest. "This place is cold. Is too much like Moscow."

Gwynn couldn't resist chuckling. "You really are a terrible Russian."

The miniature flag came out of her pocket. "I am Russian only because I was born there. I am American because I choose."

"I think you made a good choice. There's the Sequoia. Let's get you inside before you freeze to death, comrade."

The drive to Big Sky beside the Gallatin River down Highway 191 was breathtaking. The river's frozen edges were glistening shelves of ice reflecting the brilliant sunlight from the cloudless winter sky. Every car they passed had skis attached to the top.

The Glacier Club was the newest and most posh of the ski resorts in Big Sky, Montana. The lodge itself was a piece of alpine architectural perfection. The massive columns and beams of local timber towered over the guests. A wildlife display of a grizzly staring into a mountain stream made up the centerpiece of the lobby. The grizzly's appetite for a trout gleamed in the black, glass eyes of the stuffed predator.

"Good afternoon, ladies. Welcome to the Glacier Club. What name is your reservation under?"

Anya tried to make eye contact with the gentleman behind the counter, but he couldn't take his eyes off Gwynn.

Gwynn checked his name tag. "Thanks, Garret. I'm Guinevere Davis. It should be under my name."

A few keystrokes later, the young man looked up. "Ah, here it is, Ms. Davis. It looks like a last-minute reservation. You got lucky. We're usually booked solid all winter."

Gwynn smiled. "Yeah, we get lucky a lot."

Garret looked up, trying not to laugh. "I bet you do."

Gwynn blushed. "That's not what I meant. I mean . . ."

It was Garret's turn to blush. "I'm sorry, that was inappropriate. I shouldn't have . . ."

Gwynn leaned on the counter and whispered. "It's okay, Garret. I'm not going to tell."

The man was left temporarily incapable of creating a coherent sentence, so he focused back on his computer. "I think I can get you a little better rate. You're staying four nights, right?"

"We may not stay all four nights, but that's our plan for now."

"Okay, here we go. Yep, I can get you the four nights, including tax and resort fees, for twenty-two-eighty-five. That's about twenty percent off."

"I guess we really did get lucky." Gwynn motioned toward Garret's name tag. "We got to meet the manager and got a great rate."

Garret glanced down at his name tag. "Oh, I'm not the resort manager. I just run the front desk."

Gwynn offered a flirtatious smile. "Well, I'm still impressed."

Garret dropped the keycards he'd pulled from the box and then cracked his head on the edge of the counter when he bent down to pick them up.

Gwynn stifled her laughter, but Anya could not. While the Russian turned away to keep Garret from seeing her laugh, Gwynn gasped. "Are you okay?"

Embarrassed, Garret's face turned almost as red as the knot on his forehead, but Gwynn reached across the counter and slid her fingers across the back of his left hand. "Since you're not married, maybe we could have a drink when you get off. I could make you forget about the bump on your head, and you could tell me about Big Sky."

He slid the keycards through the magnetic slider, programming them to open the appropriate door. "Uh, yeah. No, I mean, I'm not married or anything. I don't even have a girlfriend. That'd be great. I get off at ten, though. Is that too late?"

"It's not too late for me. What time does the bar close?"

Garret glanced across the lobby to the bar. "That one closes at midnight, but there are four other bars on the property. We could—"

Gwynn winked. "Relax, Garret with no girlfriend. I'm pretty sure you know which room I'm in. Why don't you give me a call when you get off, and we'll go from there?"

Garret glanced at Anya. "What about your friend?"

"Oh, she's an early-to-bed kind of girl. Don't worry about her."

Garret slid a map across the counter. "Okay, then. I'll call at ten, and here's a map of the property. Your room key is your lift ticket."

Gwynn kissed the tip of her finger and pressed it against the rising knot on Garret's forehead. "I'll see you at ten."

They made their way through the enormous resort and finally found their room. Once the door was closed, Gwynn gave Anya a playful shove. "Did you see that? Now I know how you feel everywhere you go."

"What are you talking about?"

Gwynn did a little pirouette. "Front desk manager Garret prefers brunettes. He didn't even notice the Russian blonde."

Anya huffed. "He is clumsy fool."

"Yeah, but he's *my* clumsy fool tonight. How else are we going to find out where our favorite former DEA agent is staying in a resort this big?"

"You are learning, Special Agent Davis."

Anya headed for a warm shower while Gwynn made a call back to D.C.

"Hey, Johnny Mac. We just checked into the Glacier Club. This place is gorgeous and huge."

"Good. How was the flight?"

"It was long, but not bad. Have you heard from Agent White?"

"I talked to him a couple hours ago. He'll be back in D.C. in forty-eight hours. He said they're letting his dad go home tomorrow morning."

"That's good news. I hope he's going to be all right."

Johnny cleared his throat. "Yeah, me too, but I guess you're calling for more info on Carmichael, huh?"

"That's right. I need some names and descriptions."

The sound of shuffling papers came through the earpiece. "Okay, here's the goods. It's a one-man security detail for a couple of guys who don't really need security. They call themselves movie producers, but they're actually trust-fund babies with no real jobs at all. The first one is Maxwell Stuart.

186 · CAP DANIELS

He's thirty-six, and the other one is Trey Bishop, thirty-four. His old man is the head of Bishop Productions. Have you heard of them?"

Gwynn let the names pour through her head. "Maxwell and Trey . . . that sounds like a pair of rich kids, but no, I'm not familiar with Bishop Productions."

"I'm not surprised," Johnny said. "They don't exactly make the kind of movies you usually watch. They're best known for *Good Girls Gone Bad One, Two,* and *Three.*"

"Oh, those kinds of movies. Yeah, that's not my thing, but I'm impressed they could find enough good girls to make three movies."

"Something tells me they weren't really good girls to start with, but anyway," Johnny continued, "Max and Trey fancy themselves real ladies' men and like to throw their money around. Your guy, Carmichael, is likely there just for show. Nobody's trying to kill a pair of L.A. douchebags at a ski resort in Montana."

"That should make them pretty easy to pick out of the crowd, but what I can't figure out is why a guy with a hundred grand in cash would be working security for porn producers."

"A hundred grand isn't really all that much money, Gwynn. My bet is he's running some kind of scam on these rich kids. If he's got the cojones to steal from a Colombian drug lord, a pair of trust-fund babies should be a piece of cake."

"That's great work, Johnny. Email me their pictures and dossiers if you can, please. I'd like to have a picture of Carmichael, too."

"You got it. I'll send them as soon as we hang up."

Anya returned from the shower wrapped in a thick, terrycloth robe. "The shower is great, and I am finally warm again."

Gwynn shoved her phone into her pocket. "That was Johnny Mac. He's sending us pictures and dossiers. He says Carmichael is playing security guard for a couple of rich kids who call themselves movie producers."

Anya curled herself onto one end of the couch. "Why would movie pro-ducers need a bodyguard?"

"Johnny thinks it's just for show. He says they like for people to know their net worth."

Gwynn's phone vibrated, and she pulled it from her pocket. "There's the email from Johnny Mac."

She repositioned to sit beside Anya and opened the pictures in the email. "Those are our boys, Maxwell Stuart and Trey Bishop."

Anya leaned toward the phone for a better look. "I do not like them already."

"Same," said Gwynn, "but here's our real target, former DEA Agent Jerry Carmichael."

Anya lifted the phone from Gwynn's hand and studied the picture. "He looks like a cop."

Gwynn took back her phone and zoomed in. "I agree. He's got that look."

They read through the short dossiers, and Gwynn put her phone away. "I guess all that's left is to get ready for my date and find out where the rich kids and their babysitter are staying."

"I'm hungry, and we have shopping to do."

Gwynn raised her eyebrows. "You just said 'I'm.' I think that's the first time I've ever heard you use a contraction."

Anya rolled the flag between her fingertips and didn't say a word.

* * *

Although everything was twice the price it should've been, the pair bought enough cold-weather gear to keep them alive on the edge of Yellow-stone National Park for four days.

Dinner was at The Mountain Pot, a fondue restaurant tucked away in the only quiet corner of the main lodge.

Gwynn dunked a cube of French bread into the pot and carefully maneuvered it to her mouth. "This cheese is amazing."

Anya tried her first-ever bite of fondue and made a sound so sensual it solicited stares from the next table. "This is the best thing I have ever tasted."

"If you think this is good, just wait 'til dessert gets here."

Anya caught a stream of dripping cheese with her tongue. "If it is better than this, I won't be able to stand it."

Gwynn pointed her fondue fork at the Russian. "You did it again."

"I did what again?"

"Used a contraction. I'm liking this new, more-American Anya."

They devoured the cheese, and the server returned with a new pot of broth and placed it on the burner in the center of the table. On her heels was a second server with plates of marinated chicken, steak, and shrimp, as well as a bowl of vegetables. "Okay, ladies. Is this your first time?"

Gwynn said, "Not for me, but it is for her."

The server went through the cooking times for each meat and vegetable.

Anya devoured the meal without a word, and Gwynn watched in amusement. "I can't believe you've never had fondue."

Anya wiped her mouth. "I do not think they have this in Russia."

"It's from Switzerland," Gwynn said. "That's pretty close."

"Is close in only geography. Nothing else."

The server reappeared and cleared the table.

Gwynn licked her lips. "Here comes the part that will make you fall in love."

The server placed a fresh pot of chocolate, peanut butter, chopped peanuts, and rum on the burner. Next, a pair of plates loaded with cake, sliced bananas, strawberries, brownies, and Rice Krispies squares landed on the table.

The server gave the pot a stir. "Enjoy, ladies, and if you want more of anything, just let me know."

Anya's fork found a strawberry and submerged it into the chocolate. The sensual sound she made after the first bite of cheese was practically wholesome compared to the noise that escaped her lips after the chocolate.

The Russian rubbed her stomach. "I will have to run one hundred miles because of this meal, but I did not want it to end."

Gwynn checked her watch. "Oh, I have to hurry. One of us has a date, and the other one, well, I guess the other one is just getting fat on cheese and chocolate."

Anya lifted one of the long, slender fondue forks, gave it a flip, and stuck it in the surface of the wooden table. "If you ever call me fat again, I will kill you while you sleep."

* * *

Back in the room, the phone rang just after ten, and Gwynn lifted the receiver. "Hello?"

"Hello, uh, is this Guinevere?"

"Yes, but you should call me Gwynn."

"Okay, um, Gwynn, do you still want to have a drink. I'm mean, if you don't, I understand. It's just that . . ."

"Garret, stop talking. Yes, of course, I still want to have a drink with you. Where shall we meet?"

"How about the Black Diamond? The bartender there is a friend of mine, and he's really good. Also, it's quieter than the other bars, so we can talk without yelling."

"I'll be there in fifteen minutes," Gwynn said. "If you get there before me, I'd like a cosmopolitan. No, wait. I changed my mind. I think I'll have a White Russian."

26

POVEZLO
(GETTING LUCKY)

The Black Diamond was, as Garret had described, a relatively quiet lounge with an enormous stone fireplace in the center of the bar. Had there not been a roaring fire, Gwynn believed she could walk through the massive fireplace without ducking. Low tables and equally squatty furniture ringed the fireplace. Garret had changed out of his work attire and actually looked presentable.

Gwynn spotted Garret sitting alone on an oversized loveseat with a pair of cocktails resting on the table in front of him. "Hey, there. How was the rest of your shift?"

He looked up and then stood. "Oh, hey, you showed up. That's great."

"Of course I showed up. Why wouldn't I?"

He shrugged. "Oh, I don't know. That just seems to be the thing lately, but I'm really glad you came."

He motioned toward the table. "I ordered your drink. I've never had a White Russian. I'm more of a red-blooded American guy. I like bourbon."

"Is that what you're having?"

"Yeah, it's an old-fashioned with Buffalo Trace."

They took their seats and made small talk while enjoying their cocktails.

"So, the woman you're with . . .is she just a friend or what?"

"She and I sort of work together."

Garret looked confused. "How do people *sort of* work together?"

Gwynn took a long swallow of the White Russian and licked her lips. "It's really boring. We work for the government in international trade negotiations, and she's kind of like my trainer. She has a lot more overseas experience than I do. I've still got a lot to learn."

Garret took a sip. "That does sound boring, but it's got to be better than working the front desk at a ski resort."

"I don't know," Gwynn said. "You probably get to meet lots of famous people."

"Yeah, some, I guess, but most of them are assholes. They have this air of entitlement or something. They think the whole world is supposed to get out of their way and give them whatever they want. Do you know what I mean?"

"Sure I do. I hate people like that."

Garret played with the oversized ball of ice in his old-fashioned. "So, what brings you to Big Sky? When the bellman took your luggage up, there weren't any skis. That's about all there is to do up here unless you're into snow machines."

"What do you mean?"

Garret pointed toward a picture hanging near the fireplace. "See that? That's Old Faithful, the geyser up in Yellowstone. The resort offers a day trip on snow machines to see it."

"That sounds fascinating!"

Garret took another sip. "Oh, it is. You're from D.C., so it probably wouldn't bother you, but the only complaint we ever get is that it's too cold."

"Do you do these trips every day?"

"Yeah, pretty much. Tomorrow is weird, though. We usually do one big group of about twenty people. You can ride on your own, or sometimes couples ride together on one machine."

"Why do you say tomorrow is weird?"

Garret surveyed the room as if he didn't want anyone to hear what he was about to say. "There's these two guys from L.A. I think they're some big shots in the movies or something. They're doing the trip up to Old Faithful tomorrow, but they insisted on a private tour with just their guide, the two of them, and their bodyguard. We get a lot of crazy requests from guests, but that one was way out there. Nobody's ever asked for that before."

"So, are you going to do it for them?"

"Oh, yeah. As long as it's possible, we never say no, regardless of how weird the request is. The problem is, we already had twelve people booked for the trip tomorrow."

"Did you have to cancel the trip for the twelve people who'd already signed up?"

"No, we just brought in another guide, and we'll run two trips. We're letting those guys from L.A. go first, and then we'll run the regular trip on time. They'll never know."

"Smart. I bet you came up with that idea, huh?"

Garret stared at his shoes. "No, but I wish I did."

Gwynn laced her hand through his arm. "You would've come up with the idea if they would've asked. I think this place would suffer without you."

He looked down at her hand resting on his forearm. "Oh, I don't know about that."

"That snowmobile ride sounds like a lot of fun. Are there any slots left for the regular trip tomorrow? I think my friend and I would enjoy it."

Garret lit up. "There are. In fact, tomorrow's my day off. I could go with you."

Gwynn's mind reeled, but her response came as naturally as if it had been the truth. "I'd love that, but my friend just went through a really nasty breakup. That's sort of why we're here. She needed a girl's trip to get her mind off of the whole thing. You know how it is."

His eyes fell back to his scuffed loafers. "Yeah, I know how it is. Well, I'll book the two of you for the trip tomorrow. It's on me, okay?"

"Oh, no. You don't have to do that."

"No, I want to. I really do. It's part of the perks of being the desk manager. We have some latitude to make sure our guests stay happy, but maybe while you're here . . . I mean, if you want to and all . . . Maybe we could have another drink together, or maybe even dinner. That is, if you think your friend would be okay with it."

Gwynn leaned in and kissed Garret on the cheek. "I'd love to have dinner with you before we leave, so it's a date. Oh, and one more thing. . . ." She took his face in her hands and inspected his forehead. "I think I promised to make you forget all about that bump."

She pulled his face to hers and softly kissed his forehead. Then, she relaxed her grip and lowered her lips to his, rewarding him with a soft kiss with just enough of something more to make him believe it wasn't a sympathy kiss.

* * *

Back upstairs, Anya was waiting by the window with a mug of hot tea steaming in her hands. "How was your date?"

"I got lucky!"

Anya grinned. "Your hair and makeup do not look like you got lucky, and you've only been gone an hour. I used contraction again, just for you."

"No, silly, not that kind of lucky. There's a snowmobile trip up to see Old Faithful tomorrow. I found out Jerry Carmichael and his"—she made air quotes—"*protectees* insisted on a private trip with just the three of them. They'll be leaving about twenty minutes before our group."

"Our group? What does this mean?"

"We're booked on the regular trip. We won't see them on the ride up, but seeing Old Faithful will give us the perfect opportunity to cut Carmichael out of the herd and get him alone."

Anya frowned. "I do not know what this thing Old Faithful is."

"It's a world-famous geyser that goes off every ninety minutes and blows water and steam into the air like two hundred feet or something."

Anya considered the description and wrinkled her forehead. "And we are going to ride snowmobiles to see this geyser?"

"Yes, exactly. Garret set it up for us. He said he gets to do things like that to keep the guests happy, and we're the guests."

Anya closed her eyes. "Please tell me you did not kill him."

"No, I didn't kill him. Why would I kill him?"

Anya opened her eyes. "For same reason I roll towel."

* * *

When the sun finally arrived the following morning, it did little to warm the frigid air. The snowmobile guide stepped onto the seat of his machine and held his helmet in the air. "Good morning! My name is Terry, and I'm the only person in the group who can keep you from getting lost today. Keep that in mind. Is there anyone who does not have a helmet that fits?"

No one answered, so he continued. "That's a good start because we're out of helmets."

His joke got a little laughter, but not what he expected. Anya stood as close to Gwynn as possible without climbing inside her insulated coveralls with her.

"Okay, listen up. I promise you will not see any bears today, other than the stuffed one in the lobby. They're all having a nice little winter's nap. If I break my promise and we do see a bear, it's because he didn't pack on enough pounds to sleep through the winter. He's going to be skinny, hungry, and angry. You don't want a skinny, hungry, pissed-off bear for a new friend. The good news is, skinny bears can't run very fast, so you'll probably be safe. If you look particularly tasty, and some of you do . . ." He shot a look toward Anya and Gwynn. "If you look like a juicy morsel, you better remember where the throttle is, and I encourage you to use it. That's the only time it's permissible for you to pass me. Unless there's a bear breathing down your neck, stay behind me and keep me in sight. If you can't keep me in sight for some reason, at least keep the snow machine in front of you in sight. Are there any questions about that?"

None came, so Terry continued. "We'll be outside enjoying this beautiful, balmy winter day for six to seven hours. If you've never ridden a snow machine before, raise your hand and we'll have a little introduction class for you."

No hands went up.

"Excellent. The only thing left to mention is this. Do not leave the group for any reason. Stay with the group. If you get lost up there, well, I'll put it this way. You do not want to get lost up there. Is everybody ready to have some fun?"

A roar of cheers went up from everyone except the terrible Russian, and the engines came to life. Anya and Gwynn intentionally let the rest of the group follow closely behind Terry. Neither wanted to be memorable when the story about a bodyguard missing in Yellowstone hit the evening news.

The suits the company provided, along with the engine between her knees, did a nice job of keeping Anya acceptably warm. The face shield of the helmet fogged up a little more than she liked, but it was worth it to keep the wind off her face.

As civilization disappeared behind them, the majesty of one of America's most beautiful national parks opened up in front of them. No more than fifteen minutes into the ride, a pair of bald eagles made a low pass over the line of riders, and Anya wished her gloves and coveralls would permit her to withdraw her American flag.

The first stop for the group was near an overlook that afforded breathtaking views of one of the many waterfalls in the park. Anya stood in mesmerized wonder at the unforgettable sight.

Gwynn nuzzled up beside her. "Isn't it gorgeous?"

"It is the most beautiful thing I have ever seen. I would like to come back to this place."

Gwynn raised her face shield. "You will. All of this will be over soon, and you can go wherever you want."

Anya flipped the agent's shield back down. "Oh, you silly girl. You know this is not true."

"Okay, let's go! If we're going to see Old Faithful blow, we need to make up a little time. Otherwise, we'll have to wait another hour and a half for the next show."

The line of snowmobiles laced its way through the blinding white snow that covered everything. As the sun made its way across the frozen sky, the glare would've been unbearable without the shields.

An hour later, the rectangular lines of manmade rooflines at the Old Faithful Inn appeared. Other herds of snow machines dotted the landscape, and perhaps a hundred people stood on benches and in small groups awaiting the predictable return of the most famous geyser on Earth.

Puffs of steam and streams of scalding water occasionally gushed from the geyser, teasing the crowd for the coming show. Every eye except Anya's and Gwynn's was focused on the steaming hole in the ground. Theirs searched the crowd for their prey.

Finally, after a dozen minutes examining every face, Gwynn said, "I think I've got him. He's in the yellow snowsuit holding the black helmet."

Anya replayed the pictures in her mind. "That is him."

Almost before she could get the words out of her mouth, Old Faithful reminded the gathered crowd how it got its name. A massive plume of steam preceded a column of water a hundred feet tall into the perfect blue sky. The women took the opportunity of the natural distraction to approach Carmichael. Anya ambled up on his left while Gwynn moved close enough to his right to smell his breath.

Anya leaned close to the man. "Hello, Jerry. Tony Alvarez sends his regards."

Terror consumed Carmichael's face, and he swung his helmet wildly toward the Russian's head. She ducked the blow and sent an uppercut to his chin, momentarily staggering him. Gwynn peeled off her gloves and went for her Glock beneath the layers of gear, but it was too late. Carmichael used the momentum of his fall to continue into a roll and come up on his feet in a sprint. No one noticed the commotion as Old Faithful continued her astonishing performance.

Carmichael hit his snowmobile at full speed and yanked the rope.

Relieved the machine started on the first pull, he hit the throttle and sent a rooster tail of white powder into the air behind him.

Anya's machine faltered when she pulled the rope, but Gwynn's did not. The determined agent pinned the throttle to its stops and gave chase. Almost a hundred pounds lighter than her prey, Gwynn was closing on him with every tick of the clock. A glance over her shoulder revealed no one behind her. She was on her own and chasing the only creature in the park that was likely more dangerous than the grizzly.

Carmichael slalomed through lodgepole pines and aspens across virgin snow feet deep in some places. Gwynn kept the throttle full open as the distance between them lessened by the minute.

Thoughts poured through her mind. *What will I do when I catch him? Does he have a gun? Can I get to my gun? Where's Anya?*

One of her questions was answered as a bullet struck the nose of her snowmobile, sending fiberglass in every direction. She glanced down, studying the instruments. Oil pressure was still good, and the temperature was in the green, so she continued the chase. The shot made it clear she was in for the fight of her life when she finally caught the man, but she had to stay alive long enough to bring the fight to him. She dodged the same trees as Carmichael, but she remained behind the cover of every tree possible, making her almost impossible to hit, especially while shooting backward from a racing snowmobile.

A second shot sent a bullet tearing through the material of her snowsuit at the shoulder. Self-assessment under such conditions was impossible. If the bullet had torn through the flesh, she would bleed out, growing weaker by the minute. She didn't feel the burning sensation she'd heard described by gunshot victims, but her adrenaline could be keeping the pain at bay. His fresh tracks in the untouched snow would make Carmichael impossible to lose, so she rolled off the throttle and let her machine come to rest behind a snowbank.

Pulling off her right glove, she stuck a pair of fingers into the torn material of the shoulder. What she felt was warm and maybe wet, but when she withdrew her fingers, she was relieved to see there was no trace of crimson. Perhaps Garret was right after all. Maybe she was having a streak of luck.

Gwynn pulled her glove back onto her hand and hit the throttle hard. As the drive belt of the snowmobile tore at the powder beneath her, she began to accelerate. To her astonishment, a black streak roared past her in the direction Carmichael had gone. Reenergized by Anya's appearance, she kept the throttle full open and rejoined the chase.

The time she'd spent checking for a wound had given Carmichael at least a sixty-second lead, but covering his tracks would be impossible. No matter how hard she pushed the machine, she couldn't seem to gain any ground on Anya.

How is her snowmobile so much faster than mine?

Forcing herself to keep her focus on the tracks ahead, she fumbled for her pistol as limbs sliced at her windshield. She finally felt the steel of her Glock through the heavy gloves and withdrew it from its holster. Shooting left-handed while wearing gloves and navigating a snowmobile at fifty miles per hour would be a new experience, but she was up for the challenge.

The trails of Carmichael's and Anya's machines parted at the base of a steep embankment. One set of tracks led up and over the bank while the second set disappeared down the slope. Believing Anya would not have given up the high ground in a potential fight, she shoved her machine to the left and accelerated down the slope toward what she hoped was Jerry Carmichael.

Rounding a ninety-degree turn to the right, Gwynn was rewarded with the first sight of Carmichael in over five minutes. She'd made the right decision, but where was Anya? She scanned the ridgeline to her right, hoping to see the Russian bearing down on the former DEA agent.

The ride along the base of the hill was smooth and fast, making it perfect for getting off a shot or two, so Gwynn raised her pistol above the windshield and squeezed the trigger twice. Her prey never flinched, and the gap between them grew smaller.

With her left hand, she reached for the right handlebar grip and throttle. Shooting with her strong hand, she could easily stop the chase. Leaning to the right and sighting around the windshield instead of over it, she saw the white of the front sight fall on the drive belt of the snowmobile ahead. She took up the trigger slack and continued squeezing, expecting the report, muzzle flash, and recoil any second, but what she saw froze her trigger finger in place.

Gwynn watched the scene unfold in slow motion, but from Jerry Carmichael's perspective, it had to appear instantaneous.

Anya's snowmobile was airborne from the hill on their right and flying directly for Carmichael. He looked up to see the bottom of the tracks an instant before the five-hundred-pound machine impacted his helmet, sending him careening off of his snowmobile and suffering the crushing energy of Anya's machine.

The Russian brought her snowmobile to a stop and turned around to see Gwynn standing over Carmichael with her pistol pointed at his chest.

Anya knelt and pulled the man's helmet off, revealing bleeding from his nose and mouth. His eyes were open, and his chest rose and fell in rhythmic cycles, but the massive internal injuries would soon bring his breathing to a halt.

Anya pulled off her helmet and leaned to within inches of his face. "Do not die yet. First, you will tell me where is one hundred thousand dollars, and second, you will give back to me your badge. Neither of these things are yours."

Carmichael let out a breathy, gurgling sound just before his last breath left his body. As ominous as the man's final sound was, it couldn't compare to the guttural growl descending the slope to their right.

Both women looked up to see the thinnest, hungriest, most angry bear either had ever seen. He lacked the energy to descend the slope in a run, but he ambled toward them with every ounce of strength he still possessed.

Anya yanked Carmichael's gloves from his hands and withdrew her knife. "You have phone, yes?"

Gwynn eyed the approaching grizzly. "Yeah, I've got my phone, but I'm sure there's no service. We've got to get out of here."

Anya pressed Carmichael's hands together and drew her blade into the joint of each thumb, separating the digits from the hands that were only minutes away from becoming bear food. "I do not want you to make telephone call. I want you to take picture."

Gwynn snapped half a dozen shots and yanked the rope to restart her snowmobile. Anya did the same, and they pulled a hundred yards away before stopping to look back.

"Make video of this," Anya demanded, and Gwynn held up her phone, recording the gruesome scene of the bear finding exactly what he'd hoped for when he crawled from his cave.

27

MSTITEL'
(VIGILANTE)

When they walked out of the Miami International Airport, Anya pulled off her sweater and breathed in the warm, salty air. "Is much better here."

Gwynn tugged at her arm. "Come on, silly. I know you hated the cold, but you have to admit, it was beautiful out there."

"A bear eating a man is not beautiful."

"Okay," Gwynn admitted, "maybe that part wasn't beautiful, but you did get to see Old Faithful."

"No, I did not. I was too busy finding Jerry Carmichael, but I will go back with you to see it in summer."

"It's a date," Gwynn said. "Now, let's go see if that hair is still in the door."

Back at the apartment, Gwynn eyed the top of the door jamb. "There it is, right where we left it."

Anya held up one finger and pointed toward the hinge side of the door frame. "Also, this one is still in place."

"You put two hairs in the door?"

"Yes, if someone is looking, first one is easy to see and replace, but second one is never expected."

"I guess that's one more entry in the tradecraft journal."

Anya froze. "You are not writing down the things I teach you."

"No, even I'm not that dumb." Gwynn touched her temple. "But I'm tucking them away up here."

They rolled their bags to their bedrooms and unpacked.

Gwynn called down the hall. "We don't really have to go out tonight, do we?"

"I don't think we *have* to, but we probably should. I have thumbs of dead man in my bag."

Gwynn, exhausted, staggered from the bedroom and planted herself on the couch. "I knew I should've gotten a job in a law firm someplace. This secret agent stuff is a lot of work."

Anya handed her a cup of tea. "This will make you feel better, but I have something else that will not."

Gwynn let out a long sigh. "What is it now?"

Anya handed over another yellow scrap of paper. "This was inside teapot."

Gwynn stared down at the paper.

Next time, don't make the second hair so obvious. Meet me on deck at nine a.m.

"Why does he do that? He could just call."

"It is game for him, and he enjoys this game. I will change the rules, and we will see if he still likes to play. Since we have to go to meeting in early morning, I think we should not go out tonight. I think we should sleep."

Gwynn finished her tea. "That's the best idea I've heard so far."

She was asleep within minutes of her head hitting the pillow, but the Russian, reinvigorated by the tea, was wide awake. The six-hour round-trip drive to New Smyrna Beach and back would eat up most of the night, leaving her less than two hours to complete her task.

The boy's house was two blocks off the beach, but his Mustang wasn't in the driveway. A glance at the clock on the dash of the Porsche reminded Anya of the limited window to accomplish what she'd come to do. After circling the block for the third time, she turned north on Atlantic Avenue and headed for the downtown district. A left onto Flagler Avenue put her in the heart of the late-night action.

The scene reminded her of Duval Street in Key West, with restaurants, shops, bars, and tourists escaping the reality of home. If her targets weren't somewhere in the melee of Flagler, she'd likely have to make a second late-night foray in hopes of finding them and correcting their poor decisions.

Waiting for the light to change at Pine, the black convertible Mustang she hoped to find in the boy's driveway was three cars back from the light and heading the opposite direction.

The top was down, and Taylor Anderson was behind the wheel. Of the remaining occupants of the car, two were sitting on top of the rear seats, and the third was smoking a cigarette in the passenger seat.

Four targets, probably unarmed, but young, strong, and fast, would be a challenge. For the first time, Anya wished she'd brought Gwynn. Two on four were much better odds.

The light turned green, and the lines of cars started their slow procession.

As she passed the front bumper of the oncoming Mustang, Anya smiled and waved flirtatiously. "Hey, boys. Wanna play?"

Testosterone makes teenage boys the most predictable creatures on the planet. Anya didn't have to check her mirrors to know Taylor was turning around before the end of the block. Anya found an empty parking space and whipped the Porsche into the spot, giving the boys time to catch up. The Mustang passed, and she accelerated out of the space, positioning herself directly behind the boys. Honks of protest from the driver behind her were ignored. Her focus was on the black Mustang and its collection of miscreants inside.

The light at Peninsula Avenue turned red, and Anya pressed the accelerator to the floor, swerving into the oncoming lane. She offered another playful wave as she flew past the Mustang and yanked the car onto Peninsula. More horns blared, but she wasn't fazed. Her eyes darted between the road and the rearview mirror, hoping to see the Mustang pull the same aggressive maneuver beneath the traffic light. Hormones defeated logic, and the lights of the Mustang came into view.

Anya let them almost catch her before she ignored the red light at South Causeway and accelerated westbound on the four-lane. The Mustang had more horsepower, but it also weighed more than the Porsche, so Anya was forced to intentionally keep the chase at speeds the boys could handle. Perhaps for the moment, she was the mouse, but the arrogance of the cat would be its downfall.

Traffic on South Causeway in the middle of the night was light, but policemen would be on patrol. Anya had no fear of the cops, but they would throw an enormous monkey wrench into her plan if they gave chase.

The pursuit continued westward, and Anya led them beneath the interstate and into the undeveloped darkness beyond. When no other headlights were visible in either direction, she braked hard and spun the wheel to the left, sending the car down a narrow road through an ocean of southern pines on either side.

The view in the mirror confirmed her prediction that Taylor Anderson wouldn't negotiate the turn with the same precision she'd demonstrated. She downshifted to give him time to get his car back on the narrow road. When the headlights were in sight again, she started her search for the perfect playground.

She didn't have to wait long. The road took a gentle turn to the right and opened onto a clearing in the pines. Anya hit the brakes and slid the car sideways across the gravel road, then leapt from the car and waited for the Mustang to appear. When Taylor's headlights hit the Porsche sitting sideways across the road and the blonde driver now leaning against the hood, he hammered his foot onto the brake and slid to a stop only feet from her.

She gave them a smile as she appraised each of them. From what she could see, Taylor was muscular and fit. The two boys in the back were tall and lean but likely had no idea how to fight. The passenger was the problem. He was thick-chested and brawny. Anya believed she could manage

Taylor and the two from the back without using a blade, but the passenger would be a challenge.

"Hey, boys. Nice car. I hope I did not embarrass you in front of your friends, but I think I won."

She leaned against the front door of the Mustang and peered inside. No weapons were visible, but that didn't mean they weren't present. It was time to have a little fun.

"Have you boys read any good books lately?"

Confusion replaced intrigue on their faces.

"I heard you boys like to break into bookstores and beat up old men. Is that what you do for fun?"

Taylor reached for the shifter and released the brake. Whoever the woman with the crazy accent was, he didn't want to play her game any longer. His hands were fast, but Anya's were faster. She caught his chin with her right hand and shoved his head to the right. Planting her knees against the door, she leaned back and pulled Taylor Anderson from the seat. He landed shoulders-first on the gravel with his legs over his head. The presented target was irresistible, so Anya sent an elbow strike no man would enjoy. When he rolled over while grabbing his crotch, she sent a heel kick to his temple, rendering him instantly unconscious.

One of the boys from the back seat lunged forward, trying to claim the driver's seat, but Anya caught him and drove his face into the top of the windshield, sending blood and spittle in every direction. She shoved the unconscious boy into the passenger's lap to build a delay in his efforts to join the fight.

The second boy from the back made the best decision of the night and turned to jump from the back seat and away from her. She admired his decision-making skills, but not his execution. His long legs flew into the air behind him, giving her the perfect opportunity to make him pay. She locked an arm around his left ankle as his body went airborne. The force of his leap pulled Anya from her feet and into the cramped back seat. She hadn't counted on that inconvenience, but she was still in the fight. Her hold on the boy's ankle stopped his forward motion through the air and landed his kneecap on the upper edge of the door. As his body fell to the gravel road, his left knee bent backward with a horrific crack. His escape attempt was over, and he writhed in agony beside the Mustang.

The passenger was the only remaining threat, and Anya didn't want to give him a chance to get to his feet. He tossed his unconscious friend from his lap and onto the ground, and Anya's unlucky break of getting pulled into the back seat suddenly turned into a winning lotto ticket. She drew a throwing knife with her left hand and the tanto fighting blade with her right. Positioning herself directly behind the passenger, she pressed the small throwing knife against the inside of his left elbow and the fighting knife beneath his chin. The boy's strength, his only advantage, dissolved in an instant. Any forceful move he made would either open the veins of his left arm or his neck. Neither option appealed to him.

Anya felt his big body relax beneath her blades, and he said, "What do you want?"

Anya whispered, "I want you to stay away from bookstore. I am watching, and I am everywhere. If I see any of these boys near the store, you are responsible, and I will kill you in your sleep. Do you understand?"

The boy swallowed hard and nodded.

Anya pressed her blade against his flesh. "You will say it to me!"

"Okay, okay, I understand. If we go near the bookstore, you'll kill me in my sleep."

With blinding speed, Anya sliced the seatbelt webbing and bound the boy's wrists. She wrapped the excess webbing around his neck and tied his hands pressed against his face. With her right hand, she opened the door. "Step out. If you run, I will put knife in your back."

The muscular boy did as she ordered and stepped from the car, stumbling over his friend with the broken leg. He came to rest on his knees beside the car. Anya slid behind the wheel, pressed the brake, and pulled the car into gear. She snapped the mirror from the windshield and shoved it between the accelerator and the console. The engine roared, and the Mustang lunged forward. She dived from the car and rolled to a stop in the sandy soil beside the road, watching as the car careened into the irrigation pond.

Anya climbed back to her feet and stepped in front of the boy with his hands tied around his neck. She bounced the blade of her fighting knife against his nose. "You will remember what I told you, yes?"

He nodded. "Yeah, I remember. If we go—"

She never let him finish. Instead, she drove the pommel of her knife into his temple, and he melted, unconscious beside his friends.

28

YA TEBYA PODVEL
(I HAVE FAILED YOU)

Gwynn found Anya in the kitchen making tea. "Where did you go last night?"

Anya poured the boiling water over a tea bag in her mug. "What do you mean?"

Gwynn walked to the door and picked up a brown hair from the floor. "I told you I'm learning. This was tucked above the door last night, and this morning, it's on the floor. Someone opened this door overnight. It wasn't me, and you would've killed anyone trying to sneak in, so it wasn't an intruder. That leaves you, Anya. Where did you go?"

The Russian placed the kettle back on its base and stirred her tea. "I could not sleep, so I went for a drive."

Gwynn pressed her lips into a thin horizontal line. "A drive to where?"

"I do not answer to you."

Gwynn nodded in slow, measured motions. "No, you don't, but if you did something to put this operation in jeopardy, it affects my life, and this mission is already dangerous enough without adding the potential of you doing something stupid and getting us both killed."

"I did nothing to put you in danger. This I promise to you."

"Tell me what you did, or I walk away. And if I walk away, it's likely you'll be in federal prison by the end of the week. I don't want that, Anya. I want to see you complete this mission. I want to see *us* complete this mission. Then, I want to see you walk away and live the life you want. I know we're not exactly partners, but we *are* in this together."

Anya stared into her mug as the thin white bubbles on the surface of the dark tea swirled and danced together. "I went to have talk with boys in New Smyrna Beach."

"You did *what*?"

"I found them, and we had long talk. They will not be problem for Agent White's father again."

Gwynn pressed her palm to her forehead. "Oh, my God, Anya. Did you kill them?"

"I did not. All of them were alive when I left them."

She spent the next ten minutes recapping the experience by the irrigation pond, and Gwynn took in every detail.

"Listen to me, Anya. You can't do things like that. What if you'd gotten caught? What if one of the boys had pulled a gun?"

Anya sipped her tea and sat in silence until Gwynn let out a tiny chuckle and then shook her head.

"I can't believe you did that, but why didn't you take me with you?"

Anya smiled. "I wished for you at one point in time. There were four of them and only me. I handled them, but an extra pair of hands would have been nice."

"Just don't do anything like that again, please. If something has to be done, we'll do it together."

"I am sorry for trying to deceive you. I will not do it again unless it is absolutely necessary."

"It's never going to be necessary to deceive me."

The drive across the Tamiami Trail was becoming routine and boring, but Gwynn made the best of it by passing every car they encountered, including one unmarked Florida Highway Patrol sedan. Perhaps it was the wave from Anya, but for some reason, the trooper made no effort to pursue the Porsche.

They made the meeting on time, and they were surprised to see Johnny Mac leaning against the railing beside Agent White when they arrived on the platform.

"Well, if it isn't the Wild West duo. You two made quite the mess up in Yellowstone. We're having one hell of a time keeping that one under wraps."

Anya winked. "Good morning to you, too, Agent White."

"No pleasantries this morning, I'm afraid. The plan has changed, and we're running out of time. We're hearing chatter about a meeting in Vladivostok between Leo and a Russian admiral named Komonov."

"I know this man," Anya said. "He was commander of Pacific Fleet, and he is very powerful. If anyone can get old Russian submarine for sale, it is this man, Komonov."

White rubbed his neck as if he felt a migraine coming on. "That's what I'm afraid of. Here's what I need you to do. Go see Leo, and if possible, Tony Alvarez. Give them the thumbs and show them the pictures and video. I need you to make yourselves absolutely indispensable—part of the inner circle—and I need you to do it as quickly as possible." He pointed at Anya. "I need you on that airplane and at that meeting with Komonov. No matter what you have to do to make it happen, you have to be at that meeting. Got it?"

"I can do this," Anya said, "but what about Gwynn?"

Johnny Mac had been uncharacteristically quiet, but the mention of Gwynn getting on the plane brought him to life. "I'm not sure that's a good idea."

White eyed the young agent. "What Johnny means is that having a non-Russian-speaking agent at the meeting serves no productive purpose. Leave Gwynn out of it if you can, but if Leo insists on all or nothing, be prepared to go as a team."

Gwynn said, "I'm not exactly a non-Russian speaker. I do have some of the language."

Agent White turned to Anya. "*Dostatochno li sil'ny yeye yazykovyye navyki, chtoby sokhranit' yey zhizn'?*"

Anya shook her head. "No, her language skills are not good enough to keep her alive."

Gwynn sighed. "Okay, you made your point. So, maybe I need a little more time to master the language."

White asked, "Do you need anything from me?" No one spoke, so he said, "Johnny Mac, why don't you and Agent Davis take a walk while I speak with Anya?"

Johnny knew it was not a request. He motioned for Gwynn to follow, and they headed down the boardwalk.

When they were out of sight, Ray said, "I got a call from the chief of police in New Smyrna Beach this morning."

Anya showed no reaction.

"He said somebody roughed up the teenagers who hit my dad's bookstore. He said whoever it was left them in pretty bad shape and ran Taylor Anderson's car into a pond. You wouldn't know anything about that, would you?"

"It sounds like perhaps Johnny Mac had some fun with four boys last night."

White nodded. "I never said there were four boys, Anya."

"Hmm. Lucky guess. I hope your father is okay."

He motioned down the boardwalk with his chin. "Get out of here, and go stop Tony Alvarez from buying a Russian sub."

* * *

"So, what did Agent White have to say?"

Anya pulled from the parking lot and accelerated through eighty miles per hour on the trail. "He said someone beat up some boys in New Smyrna Beach, and he wanted to know if I knew anything about it."

Gwynn said, "What did you tell him?"

"I told him it sounds like Johnny Mac's work to me."

The two shared a laugh, and both waved at the state trooper sitting behind a bush as they passed at just over ninety.

"I guess we are going to club again tonight to find Leo, yes?"

"I've got a better idea. I may not be an international woman of mystery *yet*, but I did manage to score Leo's cell number. Now we don't have to go in search of the Lion. We can just call him up."

Anya slammed the brakes and slid into a gravel parking lot for an airboat charter operation. "Give me the number."

Gwynn recited the ten digits from memory, and Anya climbed from the car and picked up the receiver on one of the few remaining phone booths in Florida. She dialed the number and waited. After three rings, Leo roared, "Who is this?"

"This is person with thumbs of Jerry Carmichael."

"Ah, my little Russian Avenging Angel. Where are you?"

"This does not matter right now. What matters is where I will be when sun goes down. I would like for that to be on your yacht with friend Tony and a good bottle of champagne."

"Sunset is too early, but my driver will pick you up at seven."

The line went dead, and Anya slid behind the wheel. "His driver is picking us up at seven."

* * *

Anya and Gwynn met the driver on the curb ten minutes before seven. They expected the same ride as the first time they'd been taken to Leo's yacht, but instead, the driver took MacArthur Causeway to Watson Island and the Island Gardens Marina. They were met dockside by an elaborate luxury golf cart with Alexi behind the wheel.

Alexi reached for Anya's hand as she stepped from the limousine. "I trust you've not stuck anyone's hand to any desks today."

"Not yet," she said, "but the night isn't over."

He installed them into the luxury cart and headed down the boardwalk between rows of mega yachts on both sides. Alexi brought the cart to a stop beside *L'vinaya Gordost'*. "Welcome back to *The Lion's Pride*, ladies."

A deckhand helped them aboard, despite the fact that neither woman needed any help to climb aboard a boat of any size.

Gwynn accepted the offered hand. "*Spasibo.*"

"You are welcome, ma'am. I will take you up to the lounge."

They followed the deckhand to the upper deck, where they'd landed on their first visit to the yacht. The space had been rearranged into yet another sitting configuration with a firepit in the middle of a ring of luxurious deck chairs.

Leo and Tony rose.

"Ah, you've arrived," Leo said. "Come join us. What would you like to drink?"

Anya lowered her chin.

"Of course. Champagne for the ladies. The best we have on board."

The deckhand bowed and disappeared.

The champagne arrived, and a waiter poured two flutes. Anya lifted her glass with her right hand and reached into her small purse with her left. She cupped her fingers around the contents of the purse and said in Russian, "I am sorry, but I have failed you."

The joviality of the moment was instantly quenched, and Leo glared. "What do you mean, you've failed me?"

Anya took a sip of the champagne. "I promised I would bring to you drug enforcement agent who took Tony's money, but I could not do this. I have failed."

"But you said you found him. What happened?"

Anya withdrew her left hand from the purse and rolled the bloody thumbs across the table. Leo and Tony recoiled at the sight.

"I could only bring to you his thumbs for Tony's dogs. What is phrase American children use? The dog ate my homework, yes?"

Leo leaned back, away from the severed thumbs. "Yeah, I've heard it."

"Well," Anya said, "a bear ate my homework. Maybe he was a Russian bear, but I do not know." Anya waved her fingers towards Gwynn's phone. "Show to him video."

Gwynn opened her purse and produced her cell phone with the pictures and video of Jerry Carmichael in the torturous final minutes of his life. Tony lifted the phone from the table and watched the video several times, laughing more maniacally every time he watched the grizzly tear into Carmichael's flesh.

When he'd finally watched until he was satisfied, Tony pulled the napkin from beneath his cocktail and wrapped the thumbs inside the paper. He slid the napkin into his pocket as he stood and reached for Anya. "You are an angel from Heaven, sent just for me. I wanted to look into that man's eyes one final time and tear him apart piece by piece, but watching the bear do it for me was just as good . . . Maybe better! I'm now in your debt, and I am a man who always pays his debts."

Glasses and toasts rose from the table. When the excitement waned, Tony demanded to know every detail of how they found Carmichael. Gwynn and Anya told the story over and over in every gory detail until a waiter appeared and announced dinner.

It wasn't fondue, but grilled lobster was almost as good.

When dessert arrived, Tony said, "Name your price. Anything you want is yours for making that bastard pay for his sins."

Gwynn and Anya shared a look, and then Anya said, "I wish to see Mother Russia again, if only for a short while. I will be immediately arrested if I step one foot back in my country, but I want so badly to see my home one last time."

Tony and Leo exchanged knowing glances before Tony said, "It is yours! I promised you anything, and as I said, I am a man of my word. Leo and I are flying to Vladivostok, and you are coming with us. There will be no customs and no immigration officials. You are my guest, and I swear to you no one will touch a hair on your head. This is my gift to you."

29

MGNOVENNOYE UDOVLETVORENIYE
(INSTANT GRATIFICATION)

"What you did on the boat tonight . . . that was genius. Do you plan things like that, or do you improvise as you go along?"

Anya looked up from the open book on her lap. "What thing?"

"When Tony said you could name your price, I immediately thought about money, but you told him you wanted to see Russia again."

Anya closed the book. "How much money do you think he would have given to us?"

Gwynn said, "I don't know, but at least a hundred grand, I think."

"Agent White said I should be on the plane to Russia no matter what the cost. I guess the cost is one hundred thousand dollars."

Gwynn frowned. "Not everything people say is literal, you know."

"I know this, but sometimes literal is best."

"You're not taking me with you, are you?"

Anya drummed her fingers against the book. "I don't know yet. I think it depends on what happens before we leave."

"I want to go."

Anya reopened the book and slid her finger down the page until she found where she'd stopped. "You only think you want to go because you do not know what will happen over there. It sounds exciting, but it is not. If you do not speak Russian, you will be terrified at every moment."

"Then, teach me."

"Russian is one of the most difficult languages in the world. If you truly want to learn, we will speak only Russian inside apartment. This is called immersion and is best way to learn language. Is this truly what you want?"

Gwynn stared at the Russian. "*Da eto to chto ya khochu.*"

Anya returned to her book, and Gwynn practiced throwing everything in the apartment with a sharp point.

A knock at the door caught both of them off guard. Gwynn drew her pistol, and Anya yanked a knife from the dartboard.

"Who is there?"

"It's me, Alexi. I have an invitation for you."

Gwynn stepped into the alcove near the kitchen with her pistol still at the ready, and Anya slid the knife into her back pocket.

She opened the door an inch and peered into the hallway. "Come in, Alexi. Is good to see you." She pulled the door all the way open as he stepped through.

"Where is Gabrielle?"

"She is making tea inside kitchen. Would you like some?"

"Yes, thank you."

Gwynn holstered her Glock and slipped into the kitchen as Anya led Alexi to the living room. He picked up Anya's book and inspected the binding. "You're reading Tolstoy?" He thumbed through the pages. "And in Russian. I'm impressed."

Anya took the book from him. "Anna Karenina is the greatest novel ever written . . . in any language."

"I wouldn't know," Alexi said. "I only read about the dogs at the track."

Gwynn came from the kitchen and handed out mugs of steaming black tea.

Alexi smiled and let his fingertips linger on her hands as he took the mug. "Thank you. It's nice to see you again."

"Thanks, Alexi. It's good to see you again, too. I'm sorry the place is a mess. I've been . . ."

He glanced up at the dartboard. "It's fine. I wish I had the discipline to learn to throw knives. I am more of an instant gratification person."

"What is this invitation you speak of?" Anya asked.

"Leo wants you two to come to Bimini with him. He's got a place over there, and it's really nice."

Anya continued finding her place in the book. "When does he want this?"

Alexi shrugged. "Leo is like me. He also likes instant gratification, so he wants you to come now."

Anya drank half of the tea in her mug and savored the rich taste. "We will pack bag for overnight and meet you downstairs. This is okay with you, yes?"

Alexi finished his tea and left the mug in the sink. "I will see you downstairs. I'm in the Black Escalade on the curb."

Gwynn stuck her head into Anya's room. "What do you think this is all about?"

Anya looked up. "*Russkiy.*"

Gwynn switched to Russian. "Sorry, I forgot. Why does Leo want us to go to Bimini?"

"If Tony is coming, he invited us so he could see you in a bikini. If Tony is not coming, Leo is planning to kill us."

"What?"

Anya nodded. "Tony believes we are what we say, but Leo is doubtful."

Gwynn dug her nails into the doorframe. "Do you really think Leo would kill us?"

"He would try, but we are not so easy to kill."

* * *

The Escalade was comfortable and still had the new-car smell.

"I like your car," Gwynn offered in passable Russian.

Alexi checked the mirror. "*Spasibo.*"

Five minutes into the ride, Alexi's phone rang. He picked up and listened. When he hung up, he looked up into the mirror. "I'm sorry, but we've got a little problem. The chopper pilot is sick, so Leo wants me to bring you to the boat instead. It'll be slower than the chopper, but you already know it's a really nice boat."

Anya said, "I can fly helicopter."

Alexi slid his sunglasses down his nose and turned around. "You know how to fly a chopper?"

"Yes."

He stuck the phone back to his ear and shared the news with the boss.

"Okay, looks like we're headed for the heliport."

Gwynn leaned in. "Can you really fly a helicopter?"

Anya nodded. "*Da.*"

Alexi pulled into the Miami Heliport next to the seaplane base and opened the back door for Gwynn. Anya tossed her bag across her shoulder and headed for the Sikorsky S-76. The auxiliary power unit was plugged in, so Anya began the preflight inspection. Everything about the helicopter was in pristine condition.

She opened the right front hatch and climbed inside to familiarize herself with the instrumentation and controls. She found a copy of the pilot's operating handbook and went over the checklist items. Although it was a far cry from the Russian helicopters in which she'd learned to fly, the S-76 wouldn't be a challenge.

Leo's limousine pulled up and deposited him and Tony on the tarmac beside the helicopter.

Before his feet hit the ground, Leo said, "Are you sure you can fly this thing?"

"Yes, I am sure, but you should ride up front with me so you can show me which house is yours."

Tony and Gwynn climbed into the luxurious cabin while Anya and Leo strapped on their seatbelts up front. Anya spun up the engines and introduced fuel. The fires lit, and the rotor blades started their acceleration overhead. A lineman disconnected the APU and gave the all-clear signal. Anya set the throttle, pulled pitch, and lifted off. She lowered the nose and accelerated over the water beside the line of cruise ships waiting to take on five thousand more passengers for six days and seven nights in the Caribbean.

They soared past the jetties and out over the open North Atlantic. Anya handled the three-and-a-half-ton helicopter as if it were a sports car.

Leo pulled the microphone to his lips. "You are just full of surprises. What else can you do that I don't know about?"

She set a direct course for Bimini and activated the autopilot. "I have many skills you will find useful. You wish to stay below radar, yes?"

"Yes, and don't turn the transponder on."

Anya pointed to the black screen where the four-digit squawk code would appear if the transponder were on. "No one can see us except Navy and Coast Guard."

Twenty-two minutes into the flight, Leo pointed out the window. "Do you see the house on the point with the red roof?"

"I see it."

"You can land on the grass."

Anya turned the Sikorsky into the wind, lowered the landing gear, and touched down as gently as if she'd landed the chopper a thousand times.

As she ran through the shutdown checklist, Leo watched her every move with admiration. "Are you sure you're not a cop?"

Anya pulled off her headset. "When was last time cop delivered thumbs of dead DEA agent?"

The rotors spun to a stop overhead, and Leo said, "You know, I checked out your story, and my sources say it happened just like you said it did, but the authorities are keeping it under wraps. Why do you think that is?"

"I do not know how the authorities think, but it is probably bad for reputation of agency if the truth is in morning newspaper."

"Truth is what you make it, right?" Leo waved a hand. "Let's have a drink."

Tony and Gwynn climbed down from the back and walked arm-in-arm toward Leo's oceanfront villa. Leo pressed his thumb to the biometric reader and then tapped in the six-digit code to open the front door. A second panel inside required an additional code to prevent the alarm from sounding.

The green light flashed, and Leo pointed toward the panel. "You can never be too careful. There are crooks all over the world."

The house was massive and extravagant, but there didn't appear to be anyone inside.

"Welcome to my home. Make yourself comfortable. There's no staff here, so help yourself to whatever you'd like. I have to make a call, then I'll join you by the pool out back."

It was tequila for Tony and strawberry daiquiris for the girls. By the time the three of them were settled by the pool, Leo emerged from the house with a tumbler of bourbon and a Speedo.

Tony shielded his eyes. "My God, Leo. Put on some clothes. Have some decency."

Leo held up his glass and spun on one foot. "It's my house. You're lucky I'm wearing anything at all."

Drink, cigars, small talk, and excessive flirting between Gwynn and Tony consumed the next hour.

Anya pushed herself from her chair. "More drinks, anyone?"

She took the orders and headed for the kitchen. Two virgin daiquiris, a mojito for Tony, and the bottle of bourbon for Leo made their way onto the tray.

Tony took his drink from the tray. "Assassin, helicopter pilot, and cocktail waitress. You're the original triple-threat."

Anya said, "I thought brains, beauty, and talent were the triple-threat."

Leo puffed his Cuban and pointed the tip toward Anya. "You've got those three covered, too!"

As the sun moved ever closer to the western horizon, the evening temperature dropped, forcing them inside.

Leo said, "Follow me up to the gallery."

He staggered up the spiral staircase and deposited himself in an overstuffed pillow on a wicker chair. They watched the sun disappear in silence, and Anya let her eyes wander to the north toward Honeymoon Harbor.

Her mind drifted back to a time when it was just her and the man who'd fallen in love with her—the man she'd been dispatched to flip or kill. She couldn't do either, so she dreamed of how a life with that man would have been. Would there have been children, a house, and quiet nights alone? Would that ever be a life she could call her own? Would every sunset remind her of Chase Fulton, the man who'd risked his own life, time after time, to save hers and to offer her the freedom he was born into? Was the gentle giant, Marvin "Mongo" Malloy, watching the same sunset and feeling his enormous heart break into a thousand tiny pieces? Chase had found the love he so desperately longed for, and she was now his wife. As a man of such physical stature, society shunned Mongo Malloy and branded him as nothing more than a Goliath. Anya knew the truth about the big man, though. She'd seen his kindness and gentle nature. He loved her not for her beauty, but because they carried the same cross. The world saw the beautiful Russian as near physical perfection and the giant warrior as a beast. They were opposite sides of the same coin. She couldn't love him, but she could understand him. He would never understand her, but he loved her as if she carried his soul.

Anya felt a hand take hers. "Are you okay?"

She pulled herself from the stupor. "Yes, I am fine. I was just thinking of some people I once knew in another world and another lifetime."

Leo nodded slowly. "I know what you mean. I have those, too. It's the life we choose, or maybe the life that has chosen us. It builds walls between us, and that's our greatest loss in this life."

She hadn't expected sincerity from the man who gave human life little regard and gave the lives of his enemies nothing less than contempt.

Leo stumbled to his feet. "There's something we need to discuss, but first, we must eat. Follow me."

He led the way back down the spiral stairs, the bourbon making the descent more perilous than necessary. The doorbell rang on their way down, and Leo shuffled across the floor to answer it. When he opened the door, a team of caterers poured through the opening. They laid out a spread fit for a king . . . a king of the jungle.

Dinner ended without the discussion Leo mentioned, so Anya took the initiative. "Thank you for wonderful dinner, but what is this thing we must discuss?"

Leo slapped the table. "Oh, yes. I almost forgot. We're leaving tomorrow night, and the two of you are coming with us."

Anya gave Gwynn a look and then refocused on Leo. "Where are you taking us tomorrow night?"

Leo pulled a Cohiba from a tableside humidor and toasted the end. He took a long draw and held the dark cigar in the air in front of him. "We are taking you to the same place this beautiful cigar was rolled on the thighs of virgins in Old Havana."

30

POYEKHALI V ROSSIYU
(LET'S GO TO RUSSIA)

Anya woke with the sun the following morning, with Leo still snoring like an animal on the other side of the enormous bed. She pulled on a robe from the closet and made her way downstairs, where she discovered Gwynn by the pool sipping a cup of coffee.

She slid the door open and stepped onto the pool deck. "Good morning."

Gwynn turned, a look of doubt on her face. "Good morning. How did you sleep?"

Anya stepped beside Gwynn and took her hand. "You do not have to go. I have to do this thing, or you will put me into prison."

"No, Anya, I'm not the one who will put you in prison."

Anya sighed. "Maybe not you, but the people you work for."

"What's going to happen in Cuba?"

Anya pondered the question. "It could be many things. Perhaps it is pleasure trip. Maybe Tony is importing cocaine to Havana and he wants to show off for new girlfriend. Or there is one other possibility."

She had Gwynn's attention.

"Maybe airplane flight to Russia begins in Havana."

Gwynn slapped her forehead. "Of course, that's it. That's how they can get around customs and immigration. They'll fly from Cuba, but we don't know where they'll take us in Russia."

"I know where we will go. Komonov was commander of Pacific Fleet, so he will be in Vladivostok. This is where submarines are."

"I may be a long way from mastering the language, but I'm going with you."

Arguing with Special Agent Guinevere Davis would've been an utter waste of time, so Anya nodded and turned for the house. There was no tea in the kitchen, so she brewed coffee and watered it down. It would have to do.

By nine o'clock, everyone was awake and stirring. Gwynn and Anya practiced hand-to-hand combat by the pool until Tony stepped through the sliding door. "Who is winning?"

Anya held up both hands, signaling Gwynn to stop. They turned to the Colombian, and Anya said, "You are winning. If we are strong and deadly, we are valuable to you. Finding beautiful women is easy for you, but finding beautiful women who can kill is something else."

Tony raised a glass of orange juice. "Come, come. Sit with me. I have something to discuss."

Anya and Gwynn joined Tony at the poolside table, and he checked over his shoulder. "When we are in Cuba, I have the language, and I will know everything that is happening, but in Moscow, I do not. I want to know I can trust you to tell me when negotiations aren't going so well."

Anya raised her eyebrows. "Moscow?"

"Yes, well, maybe not Moscow, but somewhere in Russia."

Anya feigned confusion. "We are going from Cuba to Russia?"

"Yes, I promised I would take you to Russia, so I am keeping my promise, but I need you to listen for me and keep me informed when the negotiations turn angry."

The Russian smiled like a little girl on Christmas morning, then flung herself out of the chair and hugged Tony as if he were Santa Claus. "Of course I will listen and tell you if something is wrong, but what is negotiation about?"

Tony shot another look toward Leo's house. "I want to buy a piece of hardware, and I want to make a deal to do a little bit of importing of my product into Mother Russia. I trust Leo, sometimes, but I want to make sure he is telling me the truth when he translates for me."

"I will do this for you, but we must go back to Miami first. We have only clothes for tropical weather. All of Russia is frozen."

Tony said, "I don't know about that. I heard Leo tell his captain to bring the yacht here so we can go straight to Havana today."

"This will not work. We must have clothes."

Tony chewed on his cheek as he considered the situation. Finally, he said, "Take the helicopter and get the clothes you need. If you are not back before we leave, you will fly the helicopter to Havana and meet us there."

Gwynn stood. "That's a perfect plan."

Tony grabbed her arm. "Don't tell Leo. Just go. I will tell him where you are. Call me when you leave Miami, and I will tell you if we are here or on our way to Havana."

Gwynn kissed the reincarnated Pablo Escobar, and they headed for the helicopter.

Anya pushed the Sikorsky to its limit and made the flight in just under twenty minutes. Twenty minutes after that, they were unlocking their apartment door without looking for the hairs.

Gwynn pulled out the batphone and called Johnny Mac. She briefed him on the accelerated schedule, and he came unglued.

"What do you mean you're going to Russia? We're not prepared. This isn't how it's supposed to go down."

"Listen to me, Johnny. Find Agent White and brief him up. Call me when you've done so, but make it quick. We're under the gun here, and we don't have any time to spare."

The line went dead without another word, and Gwynn shoved the cold-weather gear she'd bought in Montana into the biggest bag she could find. Anya did the same and included a nice collection of blades.

Packed and committed to go, Anya stepped into Gwynn's room. "This is your last chance to get out. I do not know what will happen after we return, but it will be too late for you to run. Changing your mind would be smart choice. I will protect you as much as possible, but you will be in foreign country with no support."

Gwynn sat on the corner of the bed. "I won't be without support. I'll have you. I'll admit I'm scared, but if Tony buys that submarine and gets it back to Colombia, it'll be all but impossible to stop him from pouring thousands of tons of cocaine into this country. I'm not DEA, but I can't let that happen. What should I take with me other than all the cold-weather gear I have?"

"Take with you everything you want to keep. We will never see this apartment again."

Gwynn let out a long sigh. "I hadn't thought of that, but this is likely the beginning of the end. If we break up the sale, our cover is blown. Do you have an egress plan if this thing blows up in Russia?"

"Yes, but if I use plan, Agent White will send me to prison. When I was prisoner in Russia at Black Dolphin Prison, Chase brought a team through the Kazakh mountains and rescued me. If we are captured, this is our only possibility of rescue. The government will not sanction official mission to save a DOJ agent and former Russian spy."

Gwynn took Anya's hand. "In that case, we'll make sure we don't get caught. Let's go to Russia."

The elevator ride to the ground floor was silent, but when the doors opened, Anya's heart sank. Standing in the lobby were four men in cheap suits, silk ties, and over-polished shoes. Each wore a bulge beneath his left arm and sported aviator sunglasses.

She turned to Gwynn. "Do you know these guys?"

"I know they're feds. Nobody else dresses like that, but they're not mine."

Two of the bulky men blocked the elevator, preventing Gwynn and Anya from exiting, while a third man stepped inside and pushed a button. "I think you ladies forgot something upstairs. I'll go with you to help you carry it."

Neither woman knew what was happening, but one of them feared she'd broken an unspoken rule and was headed for federal prison. The other feared she'd overstepped the scope of her mission and would be banished back to a cold, gray desk in D.C.

"My name is FBI Special Agent Donnelly, and these are for you." He held out his palms, displaying four tiny electronic gadgets in each. "These are GPS tracking devices. They turn themselves on four times a day for six minutes each time. They're good for maybe ten days. Attach them to everything you think is important, including yourselves. They're undetectable except when they're transmitting during those twenty-four minutes every day. To activate them, press the black corner. Once activated, there is no off switch. Got it?"

Both women nodded.

Donnelly continued. "You've got twenty seconds to tell me where you're going. Go!"

Anya said, "We are flying the helicopter to Bimini then taking the yacht to Havana. From there, we will fly to Russia, but I do not know where. Moscow or Vladivostok, most likely."

"That only took ten seconds. What else do you need?"

Gwynn said, "The smallest sat-phone you've got."

Donnelly withdrew a black plastic phone from his pocket and shoved it into Gwynn's bag. "It's fully charged, but there's no charger, so keep it turned off until it is absolutely necessary. It has about two hours of talk time before it becomes a rock. Use it wisely. Anything else?"

Anya said, "A camera would be good choice."

Donnelly showed them his empty palms. "Sorry, you'll have to use your cell phones. What else do you need?"

They shook their heads as the doors opened on their floor. Agent Donnelly pressed the lobby button and stepped off the elevator. "Keep your heads down and your powder dry."

The doors closed, and the elevator started its slow descent to the street. When they reached the lobby, the other feds had vanished, and Claude stood by the door. "Good afternoon, ladies. I heard a rumor that you need a lift to the heliport."

Neither woman spoke, but each wore the smile of a woman overjoyed to see their favorite driver.

They slid into the back of the waiting Town Car and headed across the causeway.

Claude checked the mirror. "Did Donnelly give you the old standard head-down-powder-dry speech?"

Gwynn chuckled. "Yes, he did."

"Did he give you everything you need?"

Gwynn deferred to Anya, who said, "I would like to have a battleship and plan of egress, but I think Donnelly does not have either."

Claude nodded. "I'm just an old spook, so I'm no help, but from what I've seen of you two, there's not much you can't do. It's been a real pleasure, but I guess this is goodbye."

"Thank you for everything, Claude."

The old man turned and threw his arm across the back of the seat. "When you get home, give my son Michael a call and let him know you're all right. He's the doorman you've been flirting with for a couple of weeks."

Anya said, "I think this is what you mean in America when you say world is small."

"Something like that," Claude said, "but I suspect it's not going to feel so small for the two of you. Take Donnelly's advice, okay?"

They stepped from the car and climbed into the cockpit of the Sikorsky. Anya ran through the preflight and engine start checklist while Gwynn dialed Tony's number.

"That was faster than I expected. Are you on your way?"

Gwynn covered the mouthpiece as the twin jet engines whistled to life. "Yeah, we'll be airborne in ten minutes."

Tony said, "That's good. We're fifteen miles southwest of Bimini. I hope that Russian is good enough to land on the deck of a yacht."

31

VSE BYVAET V PERVYI RAZ
(FIRST TIME FOR EVERYTHING)

With the take-off checklist complete, turbines spinning, and rotor blades turning, Anya glanced at Gwynn and pulled the microphone to her lips. "Is everything a go?"

For the first time since they met, Special Agent Guinevere Davis made the conscious decision to withhold a vital piece of information from the former Russian spy. Instead of mentioning the deck landing, she flashed the thumbs-up. "Good to go!"

Anya set the throttle, eased the collective upward, pulling pitch in the main rotor blades, and added enough left pedal to keep the nose of the six-million-dollar helicopter pointed into the wind blowing off the Atlantic. Seconds later, she retracted the landing gear, pushed the cyclic forward, and watched the airspeed build as they climbed out, leaving Miami and America astern.

Anya configured the helicopter for cruise flight at 120 knots and set the autopilot. "We will be in Bimini in twenty minutes. Have you ever heard of Honeymoon Harbor?"

Gwynn bit her lip and chose to ignore the ETA. "No, what's Honeymoon Harbor?"

"It is a place where I once told a lie. The worst kind of lie. It was lie of omission like you are making now. I will make deal with you. You tell me yours, and I will tell you mine."

Gwynn stared between her feet at the cobalt-blue North Atlantic only feet below. "Tony and Leo aren't in Bimini anymore. They're on the yacht and headed for Havana. We have to land on the yacht. Have you ever done that?"

Anya didn't flinch. "I told to Chase Fulton I wanted to have real honeymoon with him, but I did not tell him he was first man I have ever loved."

Gwynn lost all interest in the ocean between her feet and gawked at Anya. "Why didn't you tell him?"

"Is better for him. He has now wife who loves him because he is strong and brave. These are not reasons why I loved him. I loved him because he was kind to me. He is a good man, and yes, brave and also strong. But mostly, he is kind."

Gwynn had watched the Russian press razor-sharp blades through men's flesh as if she were slicing bread. She'd seen her crush a man with a snowmobile. She'd even seen her wrap men around her finger with a smile and a shake of her hips, but seeing the look on her face when she talked of loving a man purely for his kindness, somehow left Gwynn mesmerized by the dichotomy.

"You still love him, don't you?"

Anya folded her arms over her stomach. "How long ago did they leave Bimini?"

"What?"

Anya disconnected the autopilot and took the controls in her hands. "How long have they been underway from Bimini? I need to know this so I can find yacht."

"An hour. Maybe a little more."

Anya programmed the GPS for a flight from Bimini to Havana, and a magenta line appeared across the map running southwest from Bimini. "I will fly near Leo's house and turn for Havana. We will find yacht on this line."

Gwynn watched the symbol for the helicopter join the line on the GPS. "How hard can it be to find a three-hundred-foot yacht?"

Anya set the autopilot again. "Is impossible if they are not sailing directly to Havana. One more thing is also important."

"What's that?"

"You did not use correct pronoun."

Gwynn frowned. "What are you talking about?"

"You said '*We* will have to land on yacht.' This is not true. *I* will have to land on yacht. You are only passenger."

"Touché. Can you do it?"

"Yes, I can."

"How many times have you landed on a ship?"

"I have never landed on ship, but there is first time for everything."

Suddenly, the Catholic schoolgirl turned special agent returned to her roots and crossed herself while having a little chat with the saints.

Before Gwynn finished the exercise, Anya pointed ahead. "There they are."

With no marine VHF on board the helicopter, and being well outside cell phone coverage, there was no way to communicate with the yacht's captain except nonverbally. Anya approached the yacht from her starboard aft quarter, flew the length of the ship, and then crossed the bow, making herself impossible to miss. With the crew now fully aware of her intention to land, she completed the circuit of the vessel and lined up a thousand feet astern. The helmsman began a slow turn to port and rolled out of the turn heading southeast.

Gwynn watched the maneuver. "What's he doing? Doesn't he know we want to land?"

"He is turning boat into wind and slowing down to make landing easier."

Gwynn wrung her hands and curled her feet beneath her seat as they drew nearer to the yacht that felt enormous from standing on deck but looked like a dinghy through the windshield of the helicopter. Anya lowered the landing gear and continued the approach, manipulating the controls like a master aviator until they were only feet above the deck. The rotor wash struck the deck, changing the handling performance of the aircraft. Anya's hands and feet moved in small, rapid motions as she tried to remain in control, until the oscillation became too much and she pulled away from the deck in a climbing left turn.

"What happened?" Gwynn cried out.

"Is okay. I will get it this time. I was not expecting so much wind on deck. Is harder than landing on ground. Please do not scream."

Gwynn nodded sharply without a sound as Anya began the second approach. She managed the controls with more deliberate and aggressive movements and stuck the wheels to the deck, immediately standing on the brakes and lowering the collective to eliminate any possibility of taking the machine back into the air. She set the throttle to flight idle and turned to Gwynn. "I told you I could do it."

A pair of deckhands secured the landing gear to the deck with heavy cables and gave the all-secure signal. Anya shut down the turbines and breathed a sigh of relief.

Gwynn breathed for the first time in minutes. "That was incredible! Now I *really* want to be you when I grow up."

They stepped from the cockpit, thankful to be on deck, and pulled their bags from the back seats. The deckhands relieved them of their luggage, and they stepped through the glass doors and into the luxurious main salon, where Tony and Leo stood, both slow-clapping.

Anya took a small bow. "This is how I make grand entrance."

Leo called for champagne. "I have fired the sick pilot, and you are now the chief pilot."

Anya accepted the glass. "Perhaps you should bring back real pilot. I am never trying that again."

The captain brought the yacht about, returning to his original course, and Leo checked his watch. "We will wake up in Havana, where the women are almost as beautiful as the two of you, and the rum and cigars are the best in the world."

Anya took a sip, and for the first time, actually enjoyed the taste of the fine champagne. "What are we going to do in Havana?"

Leo turned to Tony as if asking permission, and the Colombian nodded, even though he was only granting permission to offer information both women already knew.

Leo raised his glass. "We will enjoy Cuban breakfast and board Tony's jet for Vladivostok."

Anya beamed as if it were the first time she'd heard the news. "I cannot believe I am going home, if only for short time."

Tony flashed his best used-car-salesman smile. "I am a man of my word. I tell you that you can have anything, and you chose to see Russia again. This is my way of thanking you for Jerry Carmichael's thumbs. My dogs loved them."

* * *

The sun cracked the eastern Caribbean sky over the old city of Havana as the clock struck seven a.m., and Anya watched it happen from the upper deck. Theirs was the finest vessel in Havana Harbor, by far, and no officials made any effort to demand passports, docking fees, or inspections. Anya wouldn't have been surprised if Castro himself came aboard to pay homage to the Lion and his Colombian partner.

Just before eight, the deck crew launched the rigid hull inflatable boat that served as the tender for *The Lion's Pride*. The tender could easily accommodate twelve in absolute comfort, so four passengers plus the helmsman barely touched the surface of the RHIB's capability. They cut across the murky, polluted water of the harbor and docked alongside a pair of patrol boats with machine guns mounted on their bows.

Four uniformed soldiers with AK-47s slung across their shoulders offered hands to climb from the tender onto the dock. Gwynn took her first step onto communist soil and felt her stomach turn.

Tony scratched at a white stain on the shoulder of one of the soldiers and sniffed his fingernail. In rapid-fire Spanish, he said, "This man is a disgrace. How dare you embarrass me in front of my guests by sending me a guard with bird shit on his uniform?"

The ranking man in the squad grabbed the soldier by his collar and dragged him off the dock, yelling at every step.

Tony pulled a handkerchief from his pocket and wiped his fingertip. "Forgive me for being this way, but I can't let myself be disrespected like that. I'm sure you understand."

Leo laughed his raucous belly laugh and turned to Anya. "I wish for you to go kill that man and throw him into the sea for disrespecting my friend."

She stepped around him and jogged toward the soldier who was still being berated by his superior.

Leo called out. "No, don't do it. I was only making a point. Come back here. We are on holiday. No killing on holiday, unless, of course, someone is trying to kill us."

As if she'd been called back from some menial task, Anya fell back into step with Tony, Leo, and Gwynn as they continued from the dock.

A 1941 black Packard Formal Sedan waited for them at the edge of the port, and they climbed inside. They were deposited outside a tiny restaurant with six tables lining the decrepit sidewalk.

As they stepped from the car, Tony said, "I know this place looks like a *basurero*, but it is the best restaurant in all of Havana."

A man in a filthy apron and LA Dodgers cap poured through the propped-open door and shook Tony's hand with both of his. His Spanish was fast and impossible for Anya or Gwynn to understand, but the tone was one of sincere respect and maybe even fear.

Tony threw his arm around the man's shoulders and turned to face the others. "This is Fernando, my oldest friend in all of Cuba. That doesn't mean he's been my amigo the longest, just that he is perhaps the oldest man on the whole island."

Everyone laughed, and Fernando grinned, showing off the six teeth he had left in his mouth. "This is true . . . so true. Come, come sit wherever you like."

They planted themselves in black wrought-iron chairs around a wooden table with postcards of Fidel Castro sealed beneath yellowing lacquer. Soon, a Cuban feast covered the table, concealing Castro's face, and they ate as if they were famished.

Tony looked up to see his old friend standing in the doorway, peering nervously toward the table. "¡Perfecto! ¡Magnífico, mi amigo!" Fernando showed his teeth again and retreated to the kitchen. When they finished the spread, Tony stacked more money on the table than most Cubans earned in a year, and they headed for the Packard.

The driver pulled away from Fernando's *basurero* but did not head for the port.

Anya noticed the discrepancy. "Where are we going now?"

Tony said, "We're going to the airport. My jet is waiting to take you home."

"But what about our bags? We left everything on boat."

Gwynn thought of the miniature sat-phone and GPS trackers. If they were forced to leave everything behind, they would certainly be discovered, and she and Anya would have a lot of explaining to do . . . if they lived long enough.

Tony gave Leo an elbow. "They don't know how these things work, do they?"

Leo offered a sly grin. "Not yet, but they will soon learn."

Gwynn's heart pounded so hard she could hear the blood rushing through her veins, and Anya began her search for anything she could use as a weapon. The Russian ran her fingertips along the wood trim at the edge of her door. The custom woodwork flexed almost imperceptibly as she applied enough pressure to test the strength. The grain patterns in the wood gave her the confidence the trim would splinter in long, thin strips, leading to a naturally sharp tip. It would only require an elbow strike to split the wood. The results wouldn't be a custom fighting knife, but a makeshift wooden dagger wasn't a bad substitute. Killing the two men in Havana, where they seemed to be revered as godlike, wasn't the best option, but it certainly qualified as better than catching bullets to the brain if their mission was discovered.

32

NEPRIKOSNOVENNYY
(UNTOUCHABLE)

Anya concealed her concern behind the eyes of a seasoned operative, but Gwynn's face telegraphed her fear boiling inside.

Tony took her hands in his. "What's wrong? You suddenly look terrified."

She squeaked. "I really need my bag from the yacht."

Leo stomped his foot onto the carpeted floorboard. "Tell her, Tony. Don't torture the poor girl anymore."

He squeezed her hands and laughed. "We do not carry our bags, my beauty. We have people for that. Your things have already been taken to the jet. When you are with me, you are royalty. With us, my pet, you are untouchable, especially . . ."—he turned to Anya—"if you are becoming what she already is."

Gwynn leaned back in the seat and let her nearly panicked heart return to normal sinus rhythm. "Untouchable royalty. I think I like that."

When they arrived at San Antonio De Los Baños, an Artemisa military airfield, the driver rolled to a stop outside the gate of a high fence with concertina wire coiled ominously along its top. The driver spoke to the guard and pointed a thumb toward the back seat. The guard immediately popped to attention, delivered a sharp salute, and ordered the gate to be opened immediately.

Someone had literally rolled out the red carpet at the base of the stairs leading onto the largest private jet Gwynn had ever seen. She committed the tail number to memory and climbed the steps. The opulence inside the jet was even more impressive than its size. The furnishing rivaled that of Leo's yacht, and she tried to pretend that she'd been aboard a hundred-million-dollar private jet before.

Anya showed little interest and absolutely no indication of being impressed with the extravagance. She chose a captain's chair beside Gwynn and made herself comfortable. As if triggered by the closing of the cabin door, the pilots began taxiing before Leo and Tony had chosen their seats.

Tony caught Anya's attention and motioned around the luxurious cabin. "Can you also fly this thing?"

Anya let her eyes roam the space. "Probably."

"Good. It is a long flight, and I'm sure the pilots would enjoy having a break."

She caught herself allowing a look of concern to creep onto her face, but he let her off the hook. "I'm only joking. We have two flight crews on board. Thirteen hours is too long for anyone."

Anya projected a globe onto her mind's eye and imagined the six-thousand-mile route from Havana to Vladivostok. If her calculations were correct, they'd fly directly over the heart of the United States, western Canada, Alaska and the Aleutian Islands, then down the Pacific coast of Siberia to the port city of Vladivostok, where the Russian Pacific Fleet called home.

For the first several hours of the flight, Tony made phone calls in Spanish, Portuguese, and English. Leo drank, napped, and played touchy-feely with the flight attendants. The more he drank, the more he played. Gwynn finally relaxed enough after her fourth glass of champagne to drift off to restless sleep.

Anya planned the coming days in as much detail as possible, having no information to go on. She had no doubt Tony would spare no expense to keep himself in the most opulent surroundings possible. That would make the stay more pleasant, but the time would come when they would meet with Admiral Komonov, as well as someone with the clout to receive, process, and distribute massive amounts of cocaine. She had no fear of the drug dealers. It was the high-and-mighty military leaders who were unpredictable and most dangerous. The criminals had no interest in bringing attention to themselves, but the admiral was likely a man of enormous ego, perhaps even to rival the Lion's.

The tell-tale mechanical thud of the landing gear deploying was the only indication the flight was nearing its end. The pilots greased the enormous jet onto the runway with hardly a bump. One of the pilots came over the intercom and announced in Russian, "Welcome to Vladivostok. The local time is twelve ten p.m., and the temperature is minus three degrees centigrade."

Tony looked immediately to Anya.

She said, "It is noon time and cold . . . twenty-six degrees."

The cabin door opened, and they descended into the painful slicing of the Siberian winter.

Gwynn took in the surroundings like a tourist on vacation, but Anya turned up her collar. "Is too much like Montana."

A pair of Russian military staff cars waited just behind the left wing, with uniformed officers holding the rear doors of each.

Gwynn laced her hand through Tony's arm and headed for the first car, but he dropped her arm and reached for the Russian. "I will take Anya with me because I don't speak the language. You will ride with Leo."

The Lion took Gwynn's hand and led her into the rear seat of the second car. "It is only a short ride to the hotel. I promise to return you to your Colombian king soon."

The thought of being separated from Anya in Russia didn't give Gwynn a warm and fuzzy feeling, but she believed she'd be safe on Leo's arm. The likelihood of anyone intercepting the military cars was extremely low, but she still feared a checkpoint like she'd seen in the movies.

Vladivostok was nothing like the movies. It was a booming, moderate-sized metropolis that could've been a Western city if the street signs had been in English.

The cars stopped under the portico of the Lotte Hotel, and a jacketed bell captain led the reunited foursome to their two-bedroom suite on the top floor of the city's most luxurious hotel. By the time they reached their rooms, their bags had been delivered and unpacked. Chilled champagne waited in stainless-steel buckets of ice, alongside bottles of the finest vodka and American bourbon.

Leo stood by the window with his arms spread like wings. "Here it is, Angel . . . your country. And you were afraid you would be immediately arrested and thrown in the gulag."

Anya took in the city and felt no familiarity, no sense of home, and no desire to stay longer than absolutely necessary, but playing a role is what she'd been forged and hardened to do. As if he'd given her the moon, Anya threw her arms around Leo and kissed his cheeks more affectionately with every peck. "I thought it was not possible, but I know everything is possible with you. You are the true lion."

Leo reveled in the affection of the deadly and stunning blonde practically throwing herself at him. "Tell me something, Angel. Did Tony ask you to be his interpreter?"

The former spy had only seconds to wrestle with the question before saying, "He did not ask me to be interpreter, but he wants me to let him know when negotiations are not good. He said you will be too busy making deal to talk him through every sentence."

She took his hand and placed it on her hip, then laced her arms around his neck. She was almost as tall as Leo, so they stood nearly eye-to-eye. She slid off her shoes to give the Lion another inch of superior height and gazed up at him. "I am loyal to only you. I am not drug dealer. I am *ubiytsa* . . . your assassin."

He let his hands roam, exploring her body through her clothes, and she feigned pleasure beneath his touch. "We have advantage here. We are Russian in Russia. Like lion in jungle, this is where we are most dangerous, especially together."

Leo's eyes turned to narrow slits, and he tightened his grip, pulling Anya against his body. "No one can stop us!"

Tony tapped on the door and walked into the room without an invitation. "You arranged to meet the admiral today, right?"

Leo eased his grip off Anya and glanced at his watch. "Of course. We are to meet him at four o'clock. The cars will be waiting when we're ready."

Just before 3:30, they pulled away from the Lotte Hotel for the twenty-minute drive to the Russian naval yard. The low clouds spat flakes of snow the size of golf balls into the frozen sky, making the whole world feel like the inside of a maniacal snow globe. The two military cars had been replaced by one armored van with two soldiers in the front seat and one kneeling inside the back doors, each armed to the teeth with sidearms, grenades, and Kalashnikov automatic rifles.

The driver never slowed down as he approached the gate to one of the most secure military sites in the former Soviet Union. The posted guards raised the barricades and saluted as the van roared past through the blowing snow.

They came to rest beneath a white tent next to a massive black submarine that was tied alongside one of the dozens of piers on the waterfront.

Tony made love to the ominous machine of war with his eyes as they walked toward the gangway.

A young naval officer offered a crisp salute. "Welcome aboard, sir."

Leo led the way down the ladder to a room inside the sub the size of a modern suburbia kitchen. Standing in the center of the room was a bearded man, perhaps in his mid-fifties, wearing a black overcoat over a black turtleneck and cargo pants. His boots were like mirrors despite the terrible conditions outside.

Leo nonchalantly took in the space and let his eyes fall on the man. In formal Russian, he said, "Admiral Komonov, I presume."

The man appraised Leo. "And you are Leonid, yes?"

244 · CAP DANIELS

"That's right, but my friends and those who fear me call me Leo. And that pretty much covers everyone."

The admiral huffed. "And why have you brought these women?"

Leo glanced back at Gwynn and Anya. Gwynn, to his surprise, appeared even more stoic than Anya. "They are trusted advisors in matters financial."

Admiral Komonov studied the two women. "I agreed to meet with you and Mr. Alvarez. As you can see, I am alone, but you are not."

Leo shrugged. "Okay, I'm sorry to hear our money has no value because we brought advisors. Forgive me for interrupting your glorious career. We'll be leaving now."

Anya's heart stopped. Leo was playing games with one of Russia's most powerful military commanders, and that was never a good plan.

Leo turned and motioned toward the ladder. "Let's go home. Our money isn't green enough for the admiral."

Without hesitation, Tony, Gwynn, and Anya headed for the ladder but froze when Komonov barked, "How dare you turn your back on me?"

Leo turned back to the senior officer. "How dare you turn your back on millions of U.S. dollars, Admiral. I'm wearing shoes that cost more than your annual salary, so you can save your orders for little boy sailors who would starve without you. I can be inside China or North Korea before the sun goes down tonight, and either would happily take my money, and they wouldn't care if I brought a team of cheerleaders with me. Now, are we going to negotiate a price, or shall I have my pilots start the engines?"

Komonov motioned toward the table. "Sit."

Leo pulled out metal chairs for everyone and seated himself opposite the admiral.

Tony was the last to sit. He stared around the space, nodding. "This is my submarine?"

The admiral glared at him. "You do not have enough money to buy this submarine."

Tony leaned back in the chair and propped his feet on the table. "I don't think you know who I am, Admiral. You don't have enough submarines to run me out of money, so let's stop measuring boy parts and talk about price."

Komonov turned back to Leo and switched to Russian. "Your friend is arrogant and dangerous."

Leo shook his head. "No, my friend is wealthy and dangerous."

Komonov smiled for the first time. "*Vosem'sot millionov.*"

Tony shot a look toward Anya, but Gwynn leaned in. "He said eight hundred million."

Tony snapped his fingers. "I could have eight hundred million dollars in your account that fast and still have more money than your whole country, but I don't want an eight-hundred-million-dollar boat that I might have to scuttle and send to the bottom of the ocean. Talk to me about one of your old diesel boats that is worthless to you but valuable to me."

"*S raketami ili bez?*"

Leo turned to Tony. "With or without intercontinental ballistic missiles?"

Tony's smile returned. "Now we're negotiating. But I have no need for missiles. I want cargo space."

Leo and Komonov spat heated exchanges until the admiral said, "*Dvadtsat' millionov.*"

"He says twenty million for a fully operational diesel sub."

Tony glared at the admiral. "Tell him three million."

Leo wiped the sweat from his brow. "He may shoot us all if I tell him three million."

Tony didn't change expression or position.

The heated exchange continued until Komonov said in Russian, "Ten million dollars and fifty kilos of cocaine."

Leo turned and presented the offer.

Tony laughed and slammed his palm on the table. "Tell him I have fifty kilos in my bedroom. That is nothing. If he wants to be a player, the game starts at one hundred kilos. That's worth two point five million U.S. He gets that, plus three million cash or gold."

The yelling stopped, and Leo and Komonov spoke in rational tones for ten minutes while the others feigned boredom.

Finally, the admiral stood, pushed in his chair, and left the room.

Leo inhaled a long, tortured breath and slowly let it out, staring down at the table and covertly pressing his fingertips into Anya's leg. Barely above a whisper, he said, "This is his final offer. Seven million and one hundred kilos."

Anya bit her lip to avoid gasping at the lie Leo had just told his friend. Komonov had said five million and one hundred kilos. Leo was trying to skim two million dollars from a man who was supposed to be his friend and partner.

Gwynn's eyes darted wildly back and forth between Leo and Tony.

The Colombian finally said, "What happens if I say no?"

Leo sighed. "There are a lot of men outside with a lot of machine guns, and we are a long way from Colombia."

"I don't like it," Tony said, "but I came prepared to pay twelve million, so tell the comrade admiral he's got a deal."

Leo nodded, slid back in his chair, and removed his shoes. He placed the Italian loafers on the table. "Let's go have a look at your new submarine."

Tony pointed at the loafers. "What's that all about?"

Leo couldn't look his friend in the eye. "He demanded my shoes on top of the money and coke."

Back outside, Leo discovered a pair of boots polished to a mirror-finish waiting for him at the gangway. He slipped his feet into the boots and continued to the van.

The driver moved around the perimeter of the harbor to a pier, where four Cold War–era diesel subs rested moored alongside.

The admiral appeared on the dock wearing a five-thousand-dollar pair of Italian loafers. "Choose."

Tony pointed toward the nearest submarine. "That one. And I insist on having my photograph taken with my new boat."

"This is not possible," demanded Komonov. "No pictures."

Leo stepped toward the admiral. "How about a thousand dollars cash right now for one picture?"

Komonov said, "One thousand American cash, right now?"

Leo pulled out a roll, peeled off ten bills, and slapped them into the admiral's hand.

He stared down at the money and slid it into his pocket. "You should take pictures quickly. Sun is going down."

Anya and Gwynn became the official photographers and snapped at least a hundred shots each. The admiral appeared in at least half of them.

As soon as they were back in the hotel, every picture was uploaded via satellite directly to the email box of Supervisory Special Agent Ray White.

33

YEKATERINA VELIKAYA
(CATHERINE THE GREAT)

Gwynn found Tony standing alone on the snow-covered balcony overlooking the city of Vladivostok. Unlike most cities in the Western world, the easternmost Russian metropolis turned dark when the sun fell across the horizon. Nightlife, lighted skyscrapers, and the ever-present night owls who roamed the streets in hedonistic pursuits were all but extinct in the Russian port city.

Gwynn pressed her body against Antonio Alvarez's back and wrapped her arms around him. He smelled of cigar smoke and alcohol, but to her, he felt like a gladiator beneath her touch. Antonio wore his strength and reputation as if it were armor. She was playing a role, but even for a woman who'd chosen to devote her life to preserving law and order at the highest levels of her beloved country, holding the wealthiest, most feared criminal on the planet made her believe, if only for a moment, she might truly be, ultimately, untouchable.

He laced his ungloved fingers through hers, lifted her hands to his lips, and kissed her knuckles. Breathing in the scent of the woman he could never imagine being his enemy left him longing for a life of simplicity, uncomplicated by the demands of his endeavors in devotion to polluting the world with the poison he produced and distributed across the globe—a pursuit with the newfound capability of prowling the depths of the sea, hidden from the prying eyes of the law-abiding world.

As if talking to no one, he asked. "Do you know what it means?"

Gwynn drew even closer to him. "It means you are now even more powerful than you were when you woke up this morning."

He took two long breaths, exhaling the mist into the night sky as each breath escaped his lips. "No, the name of this city, Vladivostok. Do you know what it means?"

"No. I assume it was named after someone named Vladimir."

"It means Lord of the East. The Russians fought for a Pacific port since Catherine the Great ruled the Empire. They finally got one in eighteen sixty when the Treaty of Aigun took this place from the Chinese and gave it to the Russians as a military outpost."

"That's fascinating. Why would the Chinese give up a port city?"

He seemed to ignore the question. "Have you heard of *The Manifesto on Freedom of the Nobility*?"

Gwynn shook her head.

"It was an edict issued under Peter III and confirmed under Catherine the Great. It released Russian nobles from mandatory military service. When Russia no longer expected men of enormous power to put themselves on the battlefield, it began a decline from which they would never recover. Look what I did today. They allowed the son of a poor Colombian farmer to buy one of their machines of war, and by doing so, they enslaved thousands of their own people under the dependence on the product I will pour into this country like rain. They are fools. Desperate, arrogant fools."

"How do you know that kind of stuff?"

He lifted her hands from his chest and turned to face the enemy in his own camp. "These are the things I must know so I don't repeat the mistakes others made before me. By studying the past, I learn who to trust and who to fear."

He pushed a strand of hair from her face and tucked it behind her ear. "I believe I've allowed myself to be lured into a trap because I've trusted the wrong person."

Gwynn's heart stopped, and her hands trembled in terror. The fall to the frozen sidewalk below wouldn't hurt. She'd never feel the impact that would end both her career and her life.

How could he have learned my true identity? I would be easy to kill, but Anastasia Burinkova would avenge my death, even if it cost her her own life.

He took her trembling hands into his and cradled them against the cold. "You're freezing. We should get you inside. But first, I have a question for you."

Her stomach tied itself into a knot, and she tried to savor one of the last breaths she believed she'd ever draw. Her voice came in terrified jerks and gasps. "What is it?"

Rage burned in Tony's eyes, and his grip turned vicelike. "Do not lie to me. That would be the worst mistake you could make. Do you understand?"

She couldn't force words to come, so she nodded in utter horror at the thought of what lay ahead.

He shot a glance into the suite and growled. "When Komonov agreed on a price today, Leo said the price was seven million dollars. Look in my eyes and tell me the number you heard from Komonov's mouth."

Her next words could become the blade of a guillotine she would hold over Leo's neck, or they could write his death warrant to be served by the reincarnation of Pablo Escobar.

She laid her hand against his face with indecision in her touch. "My Russian isn't good. *Pyat'* means five, and *sem'* means seven. They were talking so quickly I couldn't tell exactly what Komonov said, but it sounded like *pyat'* to me."

He pulled a pack of cigarettes from his pocket, stuck one between his lips, and lit up. It was impossible to tell the difference between the smoke and the condensation in his breath.

Uncertain if she truly wanted to know the answer, she asked, "What are you going to do?"

He took one last draw from the cigarette and flipped it over the railing. The red ember floated on the frigid wind, sparking and glowing as it fell.

"I am a businessman. I understand I must rely on people like Leo to broker deals like this one for me, and I understand that comes at a price. I can throw two million dollars over that rail, and it would be just like the cigarette. It wouldn't change my life in the least, but trust is something very different. Trust should never be tossed to the wind."

Gwynn pulled away, but Tony took her arm, preventing her from returning inside the room, where more than just the air was warmer.

"You will ask Anya what she heard."

It was clear that Tony's instructions were *not* a request.

She pulled her arm from his grasp and laid her hand over his heart. "Anything for you."

Back inside the suite, Gwynn found Anya making tea and whispered, "We need to talk."

Anya scanned the adjoining room. "We are alone. Leo is sleeping, and Tony is, I think, on balcony. What is wrong?"

Gwynn hissed. "He knows."

Anya leaned in. "Who knows what?"

"Tony knows Leo said seven million and Komonov said five."

Anya froze.

"What do we do?" Gwynn said.

"*We* do nothing. *You* go downstairs and make report to Agent White on satellite phone. I will have talk with Tony."

Anya met Tony as he stepped from the balcony back into the room. She pressed her finger to her lips, telling him to be quiet. She then held up five fingers, nodded, and motioned back through the door toward the balcony.

Tony backtracked and held the door for the Russian. When they were alone on the frozen balcony and the door was secure, Tony started to speak, but Anya pressed her finger to his lips.

"Do not speak. Only listen. Komonov said *pyat'*, not *sem'*, but I cannot kill Leo in Russia."

Tony ignored her demand to only listen. "I don't need you to kill him. I can—"

Again, her finger flew to his lips. "Trust means more than air we breathe. I will kill him. Is for you only to watch and enjoy. I am killer. You are man of business."

He studied the eyes of the soulless assassin and slowly nodded his unspoken agreement.

* * *

Anya's promised visit to the Rodina ended less than twenty-four hours after landing, and once again, the cocaine lord, underworld Russian crime boss, DOJ agent, and assassin found themselves seven miles above the Pacific at five hundred miles per hour. This time, though, they were eastbound.

Leo believed Tony's silence was caused by his mind churning at the newfound massive income potential as the major provider to the Russian cocaine market, as well as the endless possibilities created by the silent, nearly invisible submarine now in his arsenal. The world of the Colombian had more than doubled in size and wealth directly because of Leo's connections and involvement. He would surely be rewarded beyond his wildest imagination for his service.

* * *

Four hours after landing in Havana, the foursome already felt the jetlag as their bodies and minds tried and failed to adjust to the massive blow the clock and thirteen time zones had dropped on them.

Leo's suggestion of "We will sleep on the yacht and celebrate on South Beach," found Tony taking Anya's hand. "Come with me. You must see the church where I was christened."

Anya had no interest in seeing the church where the world's foremost drug dealer was baptized before he could even hold up his own head, but the walk had nothing to do with the beginning of a life; it had everything to do with the end of one life in particular.

Leo led Gwynn to the waiting car. "We will meet you on the boat. I won't let the captain leave without you."

Tony didn't look back. He simply kept walking, and Anya easily kept pace with his long strides.

"There is no church. I was christened in Colombia the week after I was born. I only wanted to talk with you alone."

Anya said, "This is what I expected. I have made decision. I will kill him for you in Miami. Is too dangerous for you and for me here in Havana."

Tony glanced over his shoulder. "I've changed my mind."

Anya blinked and stared at him. "What? You no longer want him to die?"

"He is going to die, but he will do it in Medellín, where everyone can see what happens to men like him—men who try to hide deceit behind the veil of friendship."

She whispered, "When will you do this?"

"That is up to you." He gently brushed the back of his hand across her cheek. "I will do it when the new Catherine the Great is ready to assume the throne left vacant by the mighty Lion in Miami."

She hadn't anticipated his plan, but for the first time since her capture in the darkened streets of Saint Augustine, she realized and understood the necessity of her mission. The people she would defeat were the greatest threats to the America she wanted to champion, and they were the reason she carried the flag not only in her pocket, but also deep in her heart.

She searched for the words that should come from the lips of Catherine the Great. "So it shall be."

Despite their minds reeling with thoughts of what lay ahead, merciful sleep consumed the foursome aboard *The Lion's Pride*, but not before Gwynn pulled Anya aside in a passageway and whispered, "They're going to raid the club tomorrow night."

* * *

Gwynn and Tony awoke to the crashing sounds of breaking glass and Leo raging at the top of his lungs in the main salon, just as the captain maneuvered the enormous yacht for docking back in Miami. They wiped the sleep from their eyes and pulled on robes and shoes.

When they stepped into the salon, the scene laid out before them was impossible to reconcile with reality. Anya lay on her side, blood dripping from her mouth and nose. Leo stood over her with Gwynn's pistol in his hands, the muzzle trained on the Russian lying in a puddle of her own blood and broken glass.

"You betrayed me, you worthless bitch! I trusted you, and you betrayed me! Now, you will pay."

His rage was unlike anything Gwynn had ever seen, but instead of freezing in disbelief and shock, she knelt, lifted a long, curved shard of mirrored glass, and focused on Leo's index finger as it bore down on the trigger of her service pistol. In less than a second, a nine-millimeter hollow-point round would tear through Anya's body, expanding and ripping flesh from bone, turning life-giving organs into little more than bloody muck.

Gwynn saw the trigger move, and she raised the shard of glass above her head, leaned forward, and delivered the downswing that sent the improvised blade soaring through the air.

The room exploded with a cacophony of sounds: boots on the deck, weapons coming to bear, and the commanding voice amplified through a bullhorn. "FBI! Get down! Get down! Everybody on the ground, now!"

Gwynn threw herself into the prone position on the carpeted deck of the main salon while the FBI Hostage Rescue Team, DEA, and Homeland Security agents filled the boat with their weapons shouldered and handcuffs at the ready. Through the chaos of booted feet, agents yelling commands, and her heart pounding out of her chest, Special Agent Guinevere Davis watched Leonid "Leo" Petrovitch collapse with his life's blood gushing from the wound around the knife-shaped wedge of mirrored glass protruding from his neck. The pistol shot that was only an instant away never came, but the woman Gwynn had learned to respect and revere lay, still bleeding, only feet away from the vanquished Lion.

Antonio Alvarez was cuffed and dragged from the yacht by a pair of agents who could've been linebackers for the Dolphins. Two more agents roughly cuffed Gwynn and yanked her to her feet. Minutes later, she was forced into the back seat of a Homeland Security SUV with a cage separating the front seat from the rear and no door handles in the interior.

She knew the drill. An undercover agent would be treated identically, and often a little rougher, than the actual perpetrators during the raid and subsequent arrest. It would all be sorted out prior to the interrogation, when she would go home, and the perps would adjust to their new six-by-nine luxury suites, compliments of her favorite uncle.

Gwynn closed her eyes and relaxed against the headrest, breathing normally for the first time in days as the emotion of the operation poured over her. Savoring the safety of the darkness, she offered up a prayer of thanks to the same saints she'd called upon just prior to the landing on Leo's yacht.

The agent who committed Gwynn to the backseat of the SUV had pressed a handcuff key into her palm and lowered the tinted window a few inches before closing the door. Gwynn clumsily opened the cuffs, pocketed the key, and rubbed her wrists. Through the partially lowered window, she watched a duo of paramedics roll a gurney from the dock with a blood-stained sheet covering the occupant's corpse.

The Catholic schoolgirl turned federal agent made the sign of the cross and called once again on the saints to receive the soul of the woman who'd taught her how to stay alive while tearing the life from those around her—the woman who'd become her mentor and friend.

After kissing the knuckle of her right index finger and closing her prayer with a tearful "Amen," she opened her eyes to see the second gurney being rolled toward a waiting ambulance. Anya Burinkova was sitting up with an IV in each arm and scanning the scene around her like the warrior she was.

As the paramedics rolled past the SUV, Gwynn called through the slightly lowered window for them to stop, and Anya turned to face her protégé.

"You're alive," Gwynn breathed with relief.

Anya smiled in spite of the pain coursing through her body. "Yes, I am alive because my friend is now killer like me. We delivered Tony Alvarez to FBI, and you delivered Leo to Hell. This means my debt to government is now paid, and I will miss you. *Spasibo*, my friend."

Agent Ray White stepped from behind the SUV, rolling up his sleeves under the Miami sun. "You two can save the tearful goodbyes for later. Operation Avenging Angel has just begun."

ABOUT THE AUTHOR

CAP DANIELS

Cap Daniels is a former sailing charter captain, scuba and sailing instructor, pilot, Air Force combat veteran, and civil servant of the U.S. Department of Defense. Raised far from the ocean in rural East Tennessee, his early infatuation with salt water was sparked by the fascinating, and sometimes true, sea stories told by his father, a retired Navy Chief Petty Officer. Those stories of adventure on the high seas sent Cap in search of adventure of his own, which eventually landed him on Florida's Gulf Coast, where he spends as much time as possible on, in, and under the waters of the Emerald Coast.

With a headful of larger-than-life characters and their thrilling exploits, Cap pours his love of adventure onto the pages of his novels to captivate readers across the globe.

Visit www.CapDaniels.com to join the mailing list to receive newsletter and release updates.

Connect with Cap Daniels

Facebook: www.Facebook.com/WriterCapDaniels
Instagram: https://www.instagram.com/authorcapdaniels/
BookBub: https://www.bookbub.com/profile/cap-daniels

Made in United States
Orlando, FL
09 August 2023

35913428R00155